"Tangled Sheets"

Night after night, bar owner Cole Winston was seduced by prim and proper Sophie Sheridan's way with hot chocolate . . . until her sexy and outrageous twin, Shelly, walked into the bar . . .

"Tangled Dreams"

To uncover a family heirloom, two ghosts orchestrate a most passionate tryst between a demure lady and the sexy bartender she can't get out of her mind—Chase Winston . . .

"Tangled Images"

When Mack Winston agreed to model loungewear for a catalog, he had no idea he'd be working with the only woman who's ever intrigued him—serious, standoffish Jessica Wells . . .

Lori Foster's full-length novel Wild—
available now—
features Zane Winston.
Turn to the back of this book for a special sneak preview . . .

The Winston Brothers

Lori Foster

JOVE BOOKS, NEW YORK

THE BERKLEY PUBLISHING GROUP
Published by the Penguin Group
Penguin Group (USA) Inc.
375 Hudson Street, New York, New York 10014, USA
Penguin Group (Canada), 90 Eglinton Avenue East, Suite 700, Toronto, Ontario M4P 2Y3, Canada
(a division of Pearson Penguin Canada Inc.)
Penguin Books Ltd., 80 Strand, London WC2R 0RL, England
Penguin Group Ireland, 25 St. Stephen's Green, Dublin 2, Ireland (a division of Penguin Books Ltd.)
Penguin Group (Australia), 250 Camberwell Road, Camberwell, Victoria 3124, Australia
(a division of Pearson Australia Group Pty. Ltd.)
Penguin Books India Pvt. Ltd., 11 Community Centre, Panchsheel Park, New Delhi—110 017, India
Penguin Group (NZ), 67 Apollo Drive, Rosedale, North Shore 0745, Auckland, New Zealand
(a division of Pearson New Zealand Ltd.)
Penguin Books (South Africa) (Pty.) Ltd., 24 Sturdee Avenue, Rosebank, Johannesburg 2196, South Africa

Penguin Books Ltd., Registered Offices: 80 Strand, London WC2R 0RL, England

This is a work of fiction. Names, characters, places, and incidents either are the product of the author's imagination or are used fictitiously, and any resemblance to actual persons, living or dead, business establishments, events, or locales is entirely coincidental. The publisher does not have any control over and does not assume any responsibility for author or third-party websites or their content.

THE WINSTON BROTHERS

A Jove Book / published by arrangement with the author

PRINTING HISTORY
Jove mass-market edition / December 2001

ISBN: 978-0-515-13173-4

JOVE®
Jove Books are published by The Berkley Publishing Group,
a division of Penguin Group (USA) Inc.,
375 Hudson Street, New York, New York 10014.
JOVE is a registered trademark of Penguin Group (USA) Inc.
The "J" design is a trademark belonging to Penguin Group (USA) Inc.

PRINTED IN THE UNITED STATES OF AMERICA

20 19 18 17 16 15 14 13 12

Contents

Thank you readers!

You've overwhelmed me with the wonderful response to my beloved Winston brothers. Your letters and e-mails have been very much appreciated.

When I first decided to write Cole Winston's story as a novella, I never dreamed that so many of you would enjoy him and his interfering, zany brothers as much as I did. I must admit though, I hoped my editor would like Cole's story enough to want the other brothers.

To my relief, she did!

And so you got Chase Winston, the quiet bartender with the very kinky, and very hot, sexual predilections. Then the youngest brother, Mack Winston, surprised his family—and his woman—with a core of maturity and responsibility normally hidden behind a carefree façade.

I present you with Zane Winston in *Wild*, a Jove single title. Zane is well-known as the rowdiest Winston brother of them all—with good reason. Zane is sexy, outrageous and unstoppable. All he needs is a not-so-perfect woman to turn his orderly bachelor world upside down. And what a woman she is!

I hope you enjoy all the Winston brothers as much as I enjoyed writing them.

My best,

Lori Foster
www.lorifoster.com

P.S. Prepare yourself as I introduce a new Winston male in *Wild*. Joe Winston, a disreputable, rough and sexy cousin, is guaranteed to knock your socks off!

To Cindy Hwang,
From the first Winston brother to the last, working with you has always been a pleasure. Thank you for making this so much fun!

Tangled Sheets

Chapter One

She refused to spend her twenty-sixth Valentine's Day as a virgin.

Despite her circumspect upbringing, despite the well-meaning strictures of the maiden aunt who'd raised her, she was ready to become a woman, in every sense of the word. And Cole Winston—bless his gorgeous, sexy soul—was offering her the opportunity she needed to see her plans through.

Sophie Sheridan scanned the flyer again as she hesitated just inside the door of Cole's bar, previously called The Stud by some macho former owner, but changed to merely the Winston Tavern after Cole bought it. Heaven knew, the bar's reputation was notorious enough without a suggestive label. Though, to Sophie's mind, The Stud was pretty apropos, given what the Winston men looked like, Cole Winston especially.

All the neighboring shops had received a flyer inviting women to take part in a new Valentine's Day contest. Not that the Winston men needed an incentive to draw in the female crowd. Women loved to come here, to see one of the four brothers serving, tending bar, simply moving or smiling. They were a gorgeous, flirtatious lot, but Sophie had her eye on one particular brother.

The door opened behind her as more patrons hustled in, allowing icy wind and a flurry of snowflakes to surround her. For just a moment, intrusive laughter overwhelmed the sound of soft music and the muted hum of quiet conversation. Distracted, Sophie stepped farther inside the bar, then headed for her regular seat at the back corner booth, away from the heaviest human congestion. Since she'd met Cole some seven months ago after buying her boutique, he'd gone out of his way to accommodate her, to make certain her seat was available for her routine visit each night. He did his best to cater to all his customers' preferences, which in part accounted for his incredible success at the bar. Cole knew everyone, spoke easily with them about their families and their problems and their lives.

But he was so drop-dead sexy, Sophie spent most of her time in his company trying to get her tongue unglued from the roof of her mouth. It was humiliating. She'd never been so shy before; of course, she'd never received so much attention from such an incredible man before, either. Cole made her think of things she'd never pondered in her entire life, like the way a man smelled when he got overheated, so musky and sexy and hot, and how his beard shadow might feel on the more sensitive places of her body.

She shuddered, drawing in a deep breath.

While Cole believed she was timid and withdrawn, and treated her appropriately, Sophie had concocted some sizzling, toe-curling fantasies about him. Now, thanks to his contest, she just might be able to fulfill them.

Heat slithered through her, chasing away the lingering cold of winter, coloring her cheeks. Unfortunately, Cole chose that moment to set her requisite cup of hot chocolate in front of her. He'd put extra whipped cream on the top, and the smell was deliciously sinful. Almost as delicious as Cole himself.

"Hello, Sophie."

His low voice sank into her bones, and she slowly raised her gaze to him. Warm whiskey described the color of his eyes, fringed by thick, black lashes and heavy brows. She swallowed. "Hi."

Slow and easy, his grin spread as he looked down to see the flyer clutched in her hand. "Good." There was a wealth of male satisfaction in his rough tone, and his gaze lifted, locking onto hers, refusing to let her look away. "You going to enter?" he asked in a whisper.

Here was the tricky part, the only way she could think to gain her ends. Their relationship, already set by her tongue-tied nervousness, was hard to overcome. She couldn't merely go from reserved to aggressive overnight, not without confusing him and risking a great deal of embarrassment.

Her aunt Maude had drummed the importance of pride and self-respect into her from an early age. If she gambled now, and lost, she'd also lose the comfort of coming to his bar every night, the excitement of small conversations, and the heat of her fantasies. If he rejected her, she wouldn't simply be able to pick up and carry on as usual. Something very precious to her—their relationship— would have been destroyed. Everyone she loved, everyone she felt close to, was gone. She didn't want to risk the quiet, settling camaraderie she shared with him in the atmosphere of his bar.

But if she won, if she was able to interest him for even a short time, it wouldn't last. Cole was renowned as a diehard bachelor; he simply didn't get overly involved with anyone. At thirty-six, you had to take his dedication to living alone seriously. The man obviously *liked* being a bachelor, had worked hard at staying that way.

His rejection could put a distance between them she wasn't willing to chance. So she had to use deception.

"I couldn't," Sophie said, laying the colorful flyer aside. She licked her lips in nervousness and toyed with the cup of hot chocolate, making certain it sat exactly in the center of her napkin. "I'd feel silly."

Cole's smile was indulgent and blatantly male. He pulled a chair over from the next table rather than sitting opposite her in the booth. He straddled it, his arms crossed over the back. "Why?" He sat so close, Sophie could smell his scent, cologne and warm male flesh, a combination she hadn't appreciated or even noticed until meeting Cole. She breathed deeply and felt her stomach flutter, as if his scent alone could fill her up.

Cole tilted his head at her, cajoling. "All you need to enter is a photo. I can even take your picture here at the bar. There will be dozens of other pictures up, too, you know. Already, we've had around twenty women sign up. I'll hang all the pictures in the billiard room, and on Valentine's Day, we'll vote on the prettiest picture."

"There's no point in it," Sophie said, though she hadn't meant to. She wasn't fishing for a compliment, but she realized that was how it sounded when Cole made a *tsking* sound.

His hand cupped under her chin, lifting her face, and his look was so tender, so warm, her heart tripped over several beats, making her gasp. "You're very pretty, Sophie."

Oh, to have him mean that! But Sophie had seen Cole treat everyone in the bar in the same familiar way. He was simply a people person: open, solicitous, and friendly. He teased the older women until they blushed, left all the younger women giddy with regret, and the men, regardless of whether they were businessmen, laborers, or retirees, all liked and respected him. They gathered around him and hung on his every word. Cole liked people, and he made everyone, male and female, young and old, feel special.

The heat from his hand, the roughness of his palm, was a wicked temptation, inciting sinful thoughts. She wondered what it might feel like to have that hard palm smoothing over other parts of her body, places no one had ever seen, much less touched. Her breathing quickened and her hands shook.

Clamoring to get her thoughts in order, Sophie held up the flyer and tried for a bright smile. "I think this might be more suitable for my sister. I don't photograph well, but she's in town for a brief visit and might like the idea."

For an instant, Cole froze, then he dropped his hand and studied her. "You have a sister?"

"Yes. A twin actually." The words slipped easily past her stiff lips. "Though we're not that much alike in personality. Shelly is much more . . . outgoing."

"Outgoing?" He looked intrigued. Shifting slightly, he said, "A twin," and his tone was distracted, low and deep. "Tell me about her."

Sophie blinked at him. "Um, what's to tell? She looks like me, except she's not so . . ."

That small smile touched his mouth again. "Buttoned down?"

"Well, yes, I suppose." *Buttoned down? What did that mean?* "Shelly was always the popular one in school."

Suddenly, he shook his head and his dark, silky hair fell over his forehead. Sophie loved his hair, how straight it was, the slight hint of silver at his temples, the way it reflected the bar lights. She wanted desperately to smooth it back, to touch him, to see if it felt as silky and cool as it looked. She clasped her hands tightly on the table.

"You should both enter. Maybe even together. The judges would love it."

"Who . . ." She had to clear her throat. Cole suddenly

stood, and his size, his strength, always sent her brain into a tailspin. She peered up at him, liking the differences in their sizes, imagining how they might fit together. There was just so much of him to appreciate, to tempt. "Who are the judges?"

Now his grin was wicked. "Me and my brothers. I think it's justice, given the way the media has taunted us this last year. Did you see that most recent article?" He snorted in amusement. "My brothers ate it up."

Sophie smiled, too. All the Winston brothers were superb male specimens. Cole owned the friendly neighborhood bar, but his brothers, Mack and Zane and Chase, helped work it. Mack was the youngest, and still in college, but at twenty-one, he had the quiet maturity of a much older man. Zane, at twenty-four, was the rowdiest and split his workload between his own computer business, which was still getting off the ground, with the sure paycheck from his brother. Chase, at twenty-seven, only a year older than Sophie, shared all the responsibilities with Cole. Though Cole owned the bar, he consulted with Chase on all major decisions. Chase, unlike Cole, was quiet, and more often than not, worked behind the bar, handing out drinks and listening, rather than talking.

In the seven months since she'd first met them, Sophie found the brothers got along incredibly well, and combined, they were enough to send the female denizens of Thomasville, Kentucky, into a frenzy.

"They actually suggested we should go topless," Cole said.

Sophie covered her mouth in an effort to hold back her

mirth. The local papers had a fine time with their good-natured taunting of the Winston men. They teased them for their good looks and their overwhelming female clientele, constantly soliciting them to do an article on their personal lives. The brothers always refused.

Cole sounded disgruntled, but Sophie thought the idea had merit. Heaven knew, even with the business they had now, their popularity would likely double if the Winston men strutted around bare-chested. It was an altogether tantalizing thought.

"Zane has been threatening to take his shirt off all day," Cole added, "and the women have been egging him on. Knowing Zane, he just might do it. I have to make sure he doesn't end up doing a striptease and get us shut down."

This time there was no stifling her laughter. She, too, could picture Zane doing such a thing. He flirted outrageously, and like the other Winston brothers, had his share of admirers.

"You don't laugh very often."

Sophie bit her lip. His look was so intense and intimate, her belly tingled. He had the most unique effect on her, and she loved it. No other man had ever listened to her so attentively, shown such interest in her thoughts and ideas and feelings. He made her feel so special. She had no idea what to say, then didn't have to say anything as his concentration was diverted by Mack, who had sauntered up to his side. "The delivery guys are here."

Looking back at her, Cole nodded. "I'll be right there." He waited until Mack had turned away, then leaned down, one large hand on the booth seat behind her, the other spread on the table. "Enter the contest, Sophie."

His breath touched her cheek and she jerked. She stared at the table, her hands, anywhere rather than meet that probing gaze at such close proximity. She'd likely throw herself at him if she did. "My sister will be in later tonight. She'll enter."

He straightened slowly and she heard him sigh. "All right. I'm not giving up on you, but you can tell her to come see me when she gets here. I'd like to meet her."

Sophie watched him walk away, loving his long-legged stride, the way his dark hair hung over his collar, the width of his back and hard shoulders. As he maneuvered around the tables, women watched his progress, their sidelong looks just as admiring. He stopped to speak to many of them, leaving laughter and dreamy smiles behind, and Sophie knew he'd convince them all to enter. That was just the way he was, attentive to everyone, easy to talk to.

He'd meet her sister, all right. Sophie could hardly wait.

$\quad \sim \!$

"*Here.*"

Cole started in surprise as Chase shoved the icy cold can of whipped cream into his hand, drawing his attention away from Sophie. He raised a brow. "What?"

"You've been standing there salivating ever since she lifted her spoon. I always wondered why you put so damn much whipped cream on her chocolate. Now I know."

Cole didn't bother to deny the charge. Hell, he'd been half hard since Sophie had lifted the first spoonful to her mouth. Such a sexy mouth, full and soft and—he was obsessing, damn it.

He remembered the very first day he'd met her, when she'd bought the boutique a few doors down and across the street. She'd come in after work, looking prim and proper and very appealing, and she'd ordered hot chocolate, of all things, even though the weather in July had been steamy. Amused, he'd put an extra dollop of whipped cream on top, then watched in sensual appreciation while she'd savored it, her small tongue licking out over her upper lip, her eyes closing with each small taste. She'd been unaware of his scrutiny, and for seven months he'd been allowing her to torment him nightly with the ritual.

"Since she's finished that up, you want to go for broke and give her more?"

Cole shook his head, choosing to ignore the jest. "Too obvious. If she had any inkling how much I enjoy watching her, she would never order hot chocolate again."

"Or maybe she'd put you out of your misery and take you home with her."

Cole slanted his brother a look. Usually, Chase was the quietest, but he was damned talkative tonight. "Any particular reason why you want to annoy me right now?"

Chase grinned. "Other than the fact you're hiding over here in the corner, staring at her like a kid in a candy store with a pounding sweet tooth but no money to buy anything? Nope. There's no other reason."

"She refuses to enter the contest."

"Well damn." Chase stepped away for a moment to fill an order, then came back to Cole's side. "You couldn't talk her into it?"

He shook his head, distracted. "She has a twin."

"Oh ho, *two* Sophies. Now that sounds interesting. They're identical?"

Cole elbowed him. "Yeah. And get your mind out of the gutter."

"Too crowded, what with yours already being there?"

"Something like that. She says her sister will enter, but she doesn't want to." He sighed in disgust. "What is it about Sophie that makes me start fantasizing all kinds of wild things?"

"You tell me."

Crossing his arms over his chest and leaning back against the wall beside the ice chest, Cole considered her. "She's so buttoned down, so serene. Not once in the seven months I've known her has she ever missed a night, which means she must not be dating at all." He studied her dark brown hair, parted in the middle and hanging to her shoulders with only the gentlest of curls. It looked incredibly soft; he wanted to bury his nose against her neck, feel that silky hair on his face, his chest, his abdomen.

He wanted to see it fanned out against his pillows as he covered her with his naked body, wanted to see it tangled and wild as she reached for the pleasure he'd give her.

He shuddered in reaction. "Damn."

"Care to share those thoughts?"

"No." Narrow shoulders, but always straight and

proud, posture erect. Her skin could make him nuts, so smooth and pale. He wondered if she was that smooth all over, the skin on her thighs and bottom, her breasts, low on her belly. She would smell so sweet—he'd be willing to bet his life on that. Sweet and warm and sexy, just like the woman herself.

"Maybe her sister will give you a break. If they look the same, you could do a little imagining."

"I don't want her damn sister. I want her." He watched Sophie lift the mug of chocolate to her mouth now that the whipped cream was gone. She sipped, then patted her lips with a napkin. "It's more than just how she looks. It's *her*. She smiles at me, and all I can think about is warm skin, heavy breathing, and tangled sheets."

"You've got it bad."

"Damn it, I know it. But she shies away from me every time I try to get close. She's just plain not interested." He could easily picture the way her wide blue eyes would skip away, avoiding his, how her hands would twist together, how she'd bite her lip. God he loved how she bit her lip.

"Ask her why."

Cole glared at his brother. "Yeah, right. I can't even get her to enter the damn contest. How am I going to get her to open up her head to me?"

"There's a couple of days left. But if she doesn't enter, what are we going to do?"

Cole shrugged, angered by the prospect. "We'll pick a different winner. It's still a good contest. All the local papers have picked it up, so it's a great promo, even if we didn't need the publicity. And it'll only cost us drinks for a month."

"It'll also cost you a night on the town, lady's choice, because none of the rest of us are dumb enough to open that bag of worms. You're liable to find yourself with a permanent female escort."

Truth was, he wouldn't mind a permanent escort, if it was Sophie. He'd spent the better part of his life raising his younger brothers after his parents' deaths. He didn't regret the time he'd devoted to his brothers, just the opposite. Their closeness was important to him. But raising three boys, when he wasn't much more than a boy himself, had been a full-time job with no room for other relationships. He'd had to be content with fleeting female pleasure, the occasional night of passion.

Now Mack was in his last year of college, all the brothers were settled and secure, and Cole was finally free to live his own life. He wanted more. He wanted Sophie.

Damn her for her stubbornness, and for trying to pawn her sister off on him.

Cole walked away as Chase got sidetracked again with customers. He had some paperwork to do and might as well get started, but again, he paused in the hallway leading to his office and stared at Sophie. His plan had been so simple. Valentine's Day was a time for lovers, so therefore perfect for a contest that would bring the two of them together.

She was a shoe-in to win because his brothers knew how he felt about her, though they were amused because they thought it was mere lust. They didn't know he spent the better part of his day looking forward to seeing her when she closed her shop, when she'd spend a quiet hour sitting in her favorite booth, talking to him about everything and nothing. They didn't know he was obsessed with a woman for the first time in his life.

The winner of the contest not only got drinks at the bar free for a month, she would also have her picture taken with all the Winston men. The photo would be prominently displayed on a wall, and each year, another photo would join it as the contest became an annual event.

But best of all, the winner got a night on the town of her choice. Cole had visions of Sophie choosing a nice restaurant for dinner where they'd have plenty of time to talk without the bar's audience, followed by a little slow dancing where he'd be able to hold her close, move her body against his. He'd feel her thighs brushing his, her belly moving against his groin, her stiff nipples hot against his chest. And they'd eventually end up in bed with those tangled sheets he couldn't help seeing in his mind.

He didn't want to meet her sister. But at the same time, his curiosity was extreme. A woman who looked like Sophie, but wasn't. A woman who could be Sophie, but who wouldn't be so shy with him. He shook his head even as his body stirred. At that moment, Sophie looked up and their gazes locked. Even from the distance separating them, he felt linked to her, a touch that kicked him in the heart and licked along his muscles, a feeling he'd never experienced with any other woman.

Damn, he wanted her.

He wouldn't give up. Sooner or later, he'd get Sophie Sheridan exactly where he wanted her, and he'd keep her there for an excruciatingly long, satisfying time.

Chapter Two

Mack gave a long, low whistle that effortlessly carried through the closed office door. "Will you take a look at that."

Cole glanced up from his desk and paperwork, wondering what had drawn his brother's attention. It had been a long, frustrating night, and his eyes were gritty, his head leaden.

"Hubba hubba. Who is she?" Zane asked as he, too, came to loiter in the hallway. Cole frowned and pushed away from his computer.

"Don't you remember her? I'll give you a clue. Cole is going to choke on his own tongue—once he gets it back in his mouth."

"No!" There was a considering pause, then, "Well,

yeah, I suppose it could be her. But what did she do to herself?"

"Hell if I know. But she looks good enough to—"

Cole shot out of his chair, his curiosity too extreme to repress. He'd been determined to ignore the sister if and when she showed, and considering it was well after midnight, he figured he wouldn't have to worry about it.

He jerked the door open and Zane, who'd been leaning on it, almost fell on the floor. Cole helped to right him, then followed Mack's gaze across the room. Every muscle in his body snapped into iron hardness. He couldn't move. Hell, he could barely breathe.

Like a sleepwalker, he let go of Zane and started forward. He could hear his brothers snickering behind him, but he ignored it. God, she looked good. His heart punched so hard against his ribs he thought he might break something—and he didn't care.

As he got closer, she looked up, and her smoky blue gaze sank into his. She trembled, her chest drawing deep, quick breaths, and then she smiled.

"Sophie?"

A husky laugh sent fingers of sensation down his spine. "Of course not. I'm her sister, Shelly. And you must be the big, gorgeous owner Sophie's told me so much about." Her gaze boldly skimmed down his body, like a hot lick of interest, then back up again. "My my. I have to say, Sophie didn't exaggerate."

Cole was floored. Oh, he was interested; after all, he wasn't dead, and the woman standing in front of him, dressed all in black, was a surefire knockout. But she wasn't Sophie.

She could be Sophie, he thought, unable to keep his gaze from roaming all over her from head to toe, but the words out of her mouth were words he'd only imagined, not something Sophie would ever actually say to him. She held out her pale, slender hand, and he took it, painfully aware that he had all three of his brothers' rapt attention.

"Cole Winston," he said, and his voice sounded deeper than usual, huskier. Arousal rode him hard, making it difficult to form polite conversation. "Sophie told me you might want to enter our contest?"

Her hand lingered in his, small and warm and fragile. It felt just like touching Sophie, sent the same rush of desire pounding through him, and he felt like a cad, like he'd somehow betrayed her. Only Sophie's touch had ever sizzled his nerve endings this way, but now her sister's was doing the same.

"Yes."

That was all she said, and Cole stared. Amazingly, he could see her pulse beating in her slim throat, the fragile skin fluttering as if she were nervous. *Or excited.*

They were still holding hands. Cole cleared his throat. When he started to pull his hand back, she held on, stepping closer to him. She brought with her the scent of the fresh evening air, brisk and wintery, mixed with the warm, feminine scent of her skin, a scent he recognized. His nostrils flared.

"I didn't realize Sophie had a sister until today."

Her gaze lowered, and a wry smile curved her lips—

lips the exact replica of Sophie's lips. His muscles twitched.

With a slight shrug, she whispered, "My sister is a little shy."

The urge to taste her rushed through him. He hadn't felt this primal, this turned on, in a long, long time. Even though she wasn't Sophie, she looked the same, only wilder, more attainable, and his beleaguered male brain reasoned that she likely even tasted the same. He couldn't seem to stop himself from pulling her up to his side, wanting to feel her close, wanting to see how her body lined up to his. "Why don't I show you the rest of the bar?"

Very slowly, her thick lashes lowered. "I'd like that."

Long-repressed desire for Sophie twisted in his guts. Every image he'd ever formed in his mind slammed into him at once. Slumberous, sated blue eyes, taut nipples and trembling breasts, open, naked thighs. *Tangled sheets*. He stifled a deep groan and put his hand on her narrow waist through her coat.

They turned, and all three of his brothers jerked around, running into each other, tripping, trying to pretend they were busy doing something besides staring. He could feel their cautious glances as he led Shelly to the back room where the billiard tables were housed, but it was a peripheral awareness; all his attention was on the petite woman beside him, the sound of her anxious breaths reaching his ears above the din of normal conversation and music. There were few people still in the bar so late on such a cold and snowy night, and the two men playing pool took one look at him, grinned, and put down their sticks. They left the room without complaint.

"Can I take your coat?"

Shelly smiled, then slipped it off her shoulders. As Cole stepped behind her to take it, he leaned close, breathing in the scent of warm woman. His stomach muscles knotted and he locked his knees. He tossed her coat—black leather, long and sexy—over one end of a pool table. She turned to face him again, slowly, expectantly. Her sweater was black, emphasizing her pale skin and the richness of her chestnut hair, now pulled on top of her head with a gold clasp, showing her vulnerable nape and small ears, little wisps of baby-fine hair. He wanted to press his mouth there, to watch her shiver in sensation.

His gaze dropped to her breasts, lingered, and amazingly, her nipples puckered, thrusting against the soft, fuzzy material of the sweater. Cole didn't dare look at her face, knowing he'd be lost, his vague control shot to hell. A few glossy curls had escaped the clasp, and one curved invitingly just above her breast, taunting him, forcing him to imagine her without the sweater. Her breasts were small, but they tantalized him, looking soft and sweet, and he knew her skin would be very pale.

Unable to help himself, he stepped closer. With the coat gone, he saw she was wearing the skinniest pair of black jeans he'd ever seen, jeans that hugged her bottom and showed the long length of her legs. He'd often wondered on the details of Sophie's build. Her clothing was always somewhat concealing, so that while he knew she was slim, he couldn't detect all the curves and hollows of her woman's body.

Shelly's outfit left little to the imagination, and he wondered if Sophie was built the same, so slight, but so damn feminine. His hands shook.

"Do you play?"

It took a second for his brain to comprehend the words, and when he did, his body stirred. He could easily imagine playing with her, spending long hours toying with her body, learning every little secret, every ultrasensitive spot. He would explore first with his hands, and then with his mouth. He gave her a hot look that made her eyes widen and her lashes flutter. In nervousness? Not likely, considering her bravado.

She stammered slightly. "Pool, I mean. I've . . . I've never played, but I've often wondered . . ."

"I'll teach you," he heard himself say, even though he knew he should get away from her. She wasn't Sophie, no matter that he was so turned on he could barely breathe. He couldn't imagine Sophie ever being so coy, teasing a man in such a way. *Damn, he liked it.*

"Are you good?"

He'd turned away to move her coat and rack the pool balls, and now he froze, his eyes closing, sexual innuendoes tripping to the tip of his tongue. Hell, he could banter with the best of them, make sexual sport of any conversation, no matter how mundane, but he didn't want that with this woman. If he ever hoped to make headway with Sophie, if he ever hoped to have her body under his, open to him, accepting him in all ways, then he had to curb his desire now.

He wasn't a horny kid incapable of maintaining control. He was a grown man and he wanted Sophie, not just for a night, though that was his most immediate craving, but possibly for a lifetime. He wanted to sleep with her every night and wake with her beside him in the morning. He wanted to know every inch of her, heart and soul.

As tempting as he found Shelly, she still wasn't Sophie. It was the way she looked, being the mirror image of Sophie, that was playing havoc with his libido. Nothing more.

So he summoned a calm he didn't feel and turned to face the sister. Determination made his guts twist in regret because at the moment, despite all he'd just told himself, he had an erection that throbbed in demand, and it wouldn't be going away anytime soon.

"Actually," he said, keeping his gaze resolutely on her face, "I'm a little rusty."

Her eyes, turning a darker blue, held his. "Then maybe we can warm up together." Before he could find a retort, she selected a pool cue and came to stand very close to him. "How do I hold the stick?"

With his heart thumping in slow, hard beats, Cole turned her so her back was to him, then guided her to lean slightly over the table, positioning the cue, placing her hands just so. She took her first shot and barely disturbed the colorful balls. One rolled about an inch. Shelly chuckled. "Sorry. I suppose I didn't do it hard enough?"

Cole felt as if he were dying by slow degrees as he

once again racked the balls. "Try again, and this time, follow all the way through."

He straightened and she whispered, "Show me."

Damn. If he hadn't wanted to so badly, he could have said no. But for some reason, Shelly drew him as no other woman had, except for Sophie. It didn't make any sense. He hadn't even looked at another woman in a sexual way once he'd really gotten to know Sophie and realized how perfect they'd be together.

He walked behind her again, and this time, she bent without his instruction, her small bottom pressing into his lap while his body curved over hers. She wiggled, a soft sound escaping her, and he froze. Almost without his permission, his hands moved, from folding over her hands, to slowly slide up her arms to her elbows, then inward to hold her waist. She was so narrow, so warm. His palms rubbed over the softness of the fuzzy sweater, then higher, feeling her ribs and then the warm weight of her breasts against the backs of his hands.

He hurt; his stomach knotted, his chest felt tight, his erection throbbed. He had to stop or he'd totally forget himself. With a stifled groan, he straightened away from her and took two steps back. Slowly, Shelly laid the cue stick aside and turned to face him.

She tilted her head, eyes wide; something in her gaze looked almost desperate. He ignored it and drew on his nearly depleted control. "Maybe it would be better if I got one of my brothers to instruct you."

~✺

Distressed, Sophie *felt her stomach give a sick flip at his* words. He didn't want her, even with her being so obvious, even with her making herself more appealing, he didn't want her. She turned away and bit her lip to keep him from seeing her hot blush of mortification. She didn't blush well, never had. While another woman might get a becoming pink flush to her cheeks, Sophie could feel hot color pulse beneath her skin, from her breasts to her hairline, turning even her nose and ears red. Her skin was so fair that any blushing looked hideous, not attractive.

Zane stuck his head into the room. His gaze skimmed her, his brows lifted curiously, then moved on to his brother. He spoke quietly. "Mack left a while ago. The bar is nearly empty, and Chase is ready to give the last call. I'm going to head on home."

She felt Cole approach behind her. "All right. Drive careful. I hear the roads are crap from all the sleet and snow."

With escape uppermost in her mind, Sophie turned to face Cole again, a smile planted firmly in place, her blush hopefully under control. He was closer than she'd suspected, and she took a hasty step back. "Oh, I'm sorry." A nervous laugh bubbled past her lips. "I, ah, suppose that settles the pool lesson. I should let you men finish up here and go home."

Cole looked cautiously undecided. Good manners won out. "We have about half an hour. Enough time for you to enter the contest if you're still interested."

He kept watching her, his golden brown eyes direct, almost probing. Sophie prayed he wasn't suspicious. If he figured her out now, she'd just die. To that end, she sidled close once more, doing things Sophie had always wanted to do but would never have the nerve to follow through on.

One hand splayed over his chest, and she was stunned by the feel of his hard muscle, of the heat emanating from him in waves. There was no need to deliberately lower her tone; it emerged as a husky whisper as her body seemed to soak up his nearness. "Of course."

He covered her hand with his own, paused, then carefully removed it, holding it to his side. "The camera is in my office. You can wait here—"

"I'd rather just come with you." Self-preservation warred with curiosity. She needed to get away from him, to accept the pain of his rejection in solitude. But she'd always wanted to see his office, an extension of the man, knowing it would reveal so much about him.

He had a thick, overstuffed couch in his office. Many times she'd heard one of the brothers joke about taking a nap, especially Mack, who had his schoolwork to contend with but insisted on carrying his weight at the bar. Cole had done such a fabulous job with the brothers. They were all exceptional, responsible men.

So many times, Sophie had pictured him in that office behind the thick wooden door, dozing on the couch or sitting at his desk going over papers. She now wanted to know if the reality was the same as the fantasy, since the fantasy was evidently all she'd ever have.

Reluctantly, Cole nodded. "All right." He released her, putting his hand at the small of her back and guiding her forward. Just that slight touch, so simple, made her think of other things. His spread hand spanned the width of her waist. He was large all over, his hands twice the size of hers. With a small shiver, she imagined those large, rough hands on her body, covering so much of her skin with each touch. Her breasts throbbed and an aching emptiness swelled inside her.

The light was out in his office, and the cool dimness enveloped her as they stepped inside. She didn't quite know how she managed it, but she turned as he closed the door behind them and their bodies bumped together. Her feet seemed glued to the floor.

"Shelly . . ."

His voice was husky, not at all unaffected. She didn't need to breathe deep to inhale his hot male scent, not when she was already close to panting, her lungs expanding in sheer excitement at the touch of his hard-muscled body against hers.

Slowly, unable to resist, she went on tiptoe and nuzzled her face into his warm throat. God, it was as wonderful as she'd always imagined, his smell brisk and hot and stirring, his skin warm to the touch.

His hands clasped her upper arms, his fingers wrapping completely around her, biting into her flesh. "The light is on the desk," he muttered, but he sounded desperate, the words shallow around thick breaths.

Sophie tried to pull back, knowing this wasn't what he wanted, struggling to accept her defeat, but he lowered his head, cursing so softly, and his jaw brushed her temple. She swallowed hard at the near caress, aching for something she'd wanted for so long now. Sexual craving was new to her; she'd never experienced it for anyone but him, and the overwhelming need to indulge the craving and answer the burning in her body was making her crazed.

He shifted slightly and then her belly brushed his lower body and she felt the iron-hard length of his erection like a thunderclap. It burned into her, solid and unmistakable and with a small gasp, she pushed closer, her body seeking out more contact, reassured by the discovery.

Cole cursed again. In the next instant, his hand turned her face up and he groaned harshly, even as his mouth covered hers. Devouring, eating, holding her steady for the frenzied assault of his tongue and teeth. She'd imagined a kiss, but never this carnal mating of their mouths. Her heart rapped against her breastbone, her stomach curled tight. Helplessly, she opened her lips and accepted his tongue, all the while pressing into him, loving the feel of his excitement, the way his erection ground into her.

He pulled his mouth away, but it wasn't to stop.

"Cole," she whispered as his lips burned across her jaw, her throat, nipping and licking. His hands slid down her back, roughly grasped her bottom, and lifted her into his pelvis, his fingers plying her flesh as he moved her against him.

She held onto his shoulders, dizzy with a building urgency and a tender relief. *He wanted her.*

She moaned as he adjusted his stance, pressing her legs open to make room for his long, hard thigh, pulling her higher so she rode him. Embarrassment couldn't quite surface, even with the newness, the intimacy of it all. This was Cole, and this was what she'd wanted since the first night she'd met him. He was all the things her aunt Maude had ever warned against, every temptation imaginable wrapped up into a gorgeous package of throbbing masculinity. But he was also the most incredible man, gentle and proud and caring. Strong in all the ways that counted most. Every sinful fantasy she'd ever had winged through her mind, and she wanted every one of them to come true with him.

His open mouth pushed aside the neckline of her sweater so he could suck her soft skin against his teeth. Sophie wondered if he'd leave his mark, and hoped he would. She tilted her head to make it easier for him, and her toes curled inside her shoes at the delicious sensation of his warm mouth and tongue.

He groaned. "Damn . . ."

Somehow, he seemed to know how her breasts ached, and keeping her close with one hard hand on her buttocks, he lifted his other hand and enclosed her breast in incredible heat, his palm rasping deliberately over her nipple until she gave a raw moan of pleasure, then cuddling the soft mound gently. His mouth found hers again, swallowing her broken gasp when he lightly pinched her nipple, tugged and rolled. His tongue, warm and damp, slid into her mouth and she greedily accepted it.

They were leaning against the door, the heat thick around them, the darkness shielding, when the knock sounded and they broke their kiss, both of them panting for breath.

"I've locked everything up and I'm taking off. Just

wanted you to know." There was a low chuckle, then Chase added, "Carry on."

Cole's chest moved like a bellows. Her feet were completely off the floor as she straddled his thigh, her arms tight around his neck. One hand still held her behind, and it contracted now as he seemed to fight some inner battle. She could see the white gleam of his eyes in the darkness, could feel his scrutiny.

No, no, she begged to herself, holding the words inside with an effort. But then she was being set back on her unsteady feet and moved a good distance away—the entire length of his long, muscular arms. She felt cold, denied his body heat, and she wrapped her arms around herself. One of his hands still held her, making certain, she supposed, that she couldn't close the distance between them, while he raked his other hand through his hair. She heard Cole's head hit the door as he dropped it back, then twice more. His frustration was a palpable thing, shaming her, making her want to run.

He abruptly moved away from her and opened the door. He stepped out into the hall, and she could hear the murmur of voices as he spoke to Chase.

She wasn't at all surprised when Cole came back to tell her, his tone steady and detached, "It's time to go. Come on, I'll see you to your car."

He didn't touch her again, and she felt defeated. Until she remembered how wildly he'd responded to her. He wanted her. But for some reason, he didn't want to want her. Maybe, her thinking continued, it was because he feared she might require a commitment. Did he think because she was *Sophie's sister* he might be obligated to pay if he played? Did dallying with a friend's relative imply ties she hadn't considered? She'd led such a solitary life, she had no idea of the codes involved in male/female social relationships.

Sophie thought maybe he was only fearful of being trapped, and she felt newly encouraged.

The silence was almost oppressive as they slipped on their coats and Cole finished up a few last-minute things. The bar was pitch dark as they left, but when they stepped outside, the bright glow of a streetlamp lit the entire front of the building. Cole managed several locks, then turned toward her, and when Sophie glanced at him, again taking in his incredible body, she had to struggle for breath.

Cole was still excited. She could read it on his face: the color high on his cheekbones, the clenched jaw, the heat that burned in his eyes. Her gaze skimmed lower, beneath the hem of his coat, and she saw his erection still plainly visible beneath his fly. Oh, he wanted her, all right. All she had to do was reassure him, to make certain he knew there would be no repercussions to their lovemaking.

He took her keys from her and opened her car door. For the first time since leaving his office, he spoke. "You're driving Sophie's car."

Bolstered now by new confidence, Sophie smiled. "She insisted. We live on different schedules, with her an early bird and me a night owl, so there isn't a conflict. And," she added deliberately, hoping to entice him, "I won't be in town that long. Not more than a few days."

He didn't take the bait. "I see. Well, good night. It was . . . nice meeting you."

She almost laughed at that inane comment and the irony in his tone, but his face was hard, set in stone, and she didn't want to anger him. "Oh, we'll see each other again. You forgot to take my picture. I'll be back tomorrow night, okay?" Playfully, trying to be bold to ensure the credibility of her ruse, she reached out one leather-gloved finger and stroked his chest. "Maybe then we'll be able to stay on track. Or then again, maybe not."

His jaw locked, and as he turned away, she heard him mutter an awful curse. Sophie closed her door and started her car. Her heart was still beating too fast, her breasts still tingling, and there was a pulling sensation deep inside her, an acute emptiness that demanded attention. It felt delicious, and she wanted more. She wanted everything.

She wanted Cole Winston.

Chapter Three

It had been an awful night. Cole sipped his coffee and tried to order his thoughts, but lack of sleep and extended, acute sexual frustration made his brain sluggish, hampering his efforts. The events at the bar, the sensual overload, and then the smothering guilt had conspired against him to make him toss and turn in between dreams of making love to a woman who looked and felt and tasted like Sophie but reacted like Shelly. Every so often, the two had combined to provide dreams so damned erotic he'd awake with his own raw groan caught in his throat, his body sheened in sweat, every muscle hard and straining.

He could still taste her, still feel the damp heat of her lips and tongue, and the warm softness of her mound as she'd worked herself against him. Her breast had felt perfect in his palm, small and sweetly curved, the nipple thrusting, eager for his mouth. And he'd wanted so badly to suck on her, to draw her deep until she begged for more.

He swallowed hard and closed his eyes, heat washing over him in waves. His hands trembled as he groped for his coffee mug and took a scalding gulp.

He had to talk to Sophie. When he admitted to her how he felt, how damned attracted he was to her, how badly he wanted her, she might bolt. If she wasn't interested in him, he could lose her friendship, and that wasn't something he even wanted to contemplate. But at least his confession should take care of Shelly, removing her as a temptation. He couldn't go through that again, couldn't chance the strength of his control. Hell, he'd been a hair away from laying her across his desk and stripping those damn flesh-hugging jeans down her long legs. He would have taken her hard, in a hot rush, and he had a feeling she'd have liked it.

But he couldn't exchange one woman for another; it wouldn't be fair to any of them. And the simple truth was, he wanted Shelly because she was the exact image of his Sophie. But she wasn't Sophie, and he didn't want to blow a chance with Sophie by missing that distinction.

He glanced at the clock as he finished his third cup of extra-strong coffee. He was seldom up this early, not with his hours at the bar, but sleep had been impossible. The caffeine hadn't kicked in yet, but it was almost nine-thirty, and by the time he got to Sophie's boutique, she should be there. Shelly was right about that, Sophie was an early bird. He'd better go before he lost his nerve.

That thought made him laugh because no woman had made him nervous since he'd turned sixteen. But then, no woman had ever mattered like Sophie did. He'd been waiting seven months for her. Ridiculous. It was time he put an end to things.

A half hour later, Cole opened the oak and etched glass door of the boutique, hearing the tinkling of the overhead bells. It was a classy little joint, filled with feminine scents and at the moment, lots of Valentine decorations. A small blonde-haired woman was perched in the corner, preparing to dress a nude mannequin in an arrangement of filmy night wear. She glanced up, looking at him over the rim of her round glasses.

"I'll be right with you," she said around a mouthful of straight pins that she held in her teeth.

"I came to see Sophie. Is she in?"

The woman straightened with new interest and quickly folded the garment in her hand, laying it aside and placing the pins on top. "No, I'm sorry. She's running a little late today. She called to ask me to open for her. Was she expecting you?"

Cole shook his head. It wasn't like Sophie to be late, and a flash of concern hit him broadside. "She's not ill?"

"No, I gathered she's just extra tired today." The woman smiled. "I'm Allison, her assistant. Aren't you the oldest Winston brother who owns the Winston Tavern? I saw your picture in the paper recently."

Cole twisted his mouth in a wry smile, well used to the feminine teasing. "Guilty. I hope you ignored the article. The paper loves catching me and my brothers unaware."

Allison's grin spread as she gave him a coy, slanted look. "It was a very nice shot. I saved the article."

Her blatant flirting didn't bother him; he'd deflected plenty of female interest in his days, gently, so he wouldn't ever hurt a woman's feelings.

Unfortunately, he hadn't deflected Shelly very well.

Cole abruptly changed the subject. "Do you know when Sophie will be in?"

"Sorry, I don't. She just said *later* around a very loud yawn. I think she's zonked and getting a late start this morning, judging by how she sounded."

"She was probably up late with her sister." He frowned with the thought. What if Shelly had already related the events of the evening to Sophie? What if she'd told Sophie how he'd kissed her . . . and more? They'd probably sat up all night gossiping about him and his cursed lack of control.

Damn it, Shelly had no business interfering with Sophie's rest. He knew Sophie worked long hours, and if anyone was going to disturb her sleep, he wanted it to be him.

Allison laughed. "Nope, that couldn't be it because she doesn't have a sister. Sophie is an only child."

Cole was surprised that Allison didn't know her employer any better than that, but then he thought of how private Sophie was, how little she talked, and he understood. "Shelly is her twin. She's in town for a short visit."

Allison shook her head and put her hands on her hips. "I don't know who's been pulling your leg, but Sophie is all alone. She lost her folks when she was just a kid. Her aunt took her in and raised her, but she died, too, about a year ago."

His heart flipped, then began to slow, steady thumping. Every nerve on alert, Cole asked, "Are you sure about that?"

"Positive."

Bombarded by a mix of feelings, most of all confusion, Cole braced his hands on the countertop and dropped his head forward, deep in thought. *No twin.*

"Hey, are you all right?"

He nodded. Hell yeah, he was all right. He was damn good. It was just that . . . He looked up at Allison again, trying for a casual expression to hide the emotions slamming through him, most of all sexual elation.

He felt off balance. On top of the carnal images crowding his brain, a swelling tenderness threatened to overwhelm him. Sophie was all alone in the world, not a single relative around. He'd lost his parents, too, so he knew how devastating that could be. But he'd always had his brothers, and they were closer than most complete families. He wanted to protect Sophie, to comfort her, to tell her she'd never be alone again.

His mind immediately skittered onto more profound thoughts, like the heat and sexual urgency of the night before. A hot rush of searing lust forced him to grip the counter hard. If Sophie didn't have a sister, then his entire day was about to take on a new perspective. Anticipation churned low in his abdomen. "You know Sophie well?" He was careful to keep the question negligent, not to arouse suspicions.

Allison shrugged. "Sure. I've been with her since she bought this place, around seven months now."

"I remember when she opened it." Cole could feel the heated, forceful rush of blood in his veins. His body hardened, pressing against the rough fly of his jeans, but he couldn't help himself. He shifted uncomfortably, remembering last night, how he'd touched Sophie, kissed *Sophie*. He knew what her breast felt like, how it nestled so perfectly in the palm of his hand. He knew the texture of her tight little derriere, the taste of her skin.

And he knew that Sophie Sheridan, actress and fraud, wanted him—enough to pretend to be someone else. His knees nearly buckled.

He cleared his throat twice before he could speak. "Sophie and I have gotten to know each other pretty well. But I could have sworn she told me she had a sister."

"No." Allison, bursting with confidences, perched on a stool by the cash register and leaned her elbows on the counter. "Her aunt was all she had, and they were really close. They've always lived together because the aunt got sick and Sophie had to take care of her. But then she died last year. It was an awful blow to Sophie and she took her inheritance and moved here, away from the memories." Allison tilted her head. "You interested in her?"

Oh yeah, he was interested. He knew his eyes were glittering with intent as he smiled down at Allison, making her blush. "We've been close as friends, but I was hoping to give her a surprise for Valentine's Day, something a little more . . . intimate. Could you do me a big favor, and not mention that I was here or that I asked about her? I don't want to ruin the surprise."

Eyes wide, Allison made a cross on her chest with an index finger. "I won't say a word. Sophie deserves a little fun."

Oh, he'd give her fun, all right. He mentally rubbed his hands together in sizzling anticipation. Sophie Sheridan was about to get what she wanted.

No, not sweet shy Sophie, he thought, remembering how she'd refused to enter his contest, how she froze every damn time he touched her. The sexy Shelly. Cole grinned, already so aroused he didn't know how he'd get through the day. Only the thought that the night would be an end to his frustration kept him on track with his plan. He'd deal with Shelly tonight—and then Sophie would deal with him in the morning.

He'd give her a Valentine's surprise she wouldn't soon forget.

⋙⟶⟝

Sophie was dragging by the time she'd gotten off work. The combination of the late night, the stress of deception, and the anticipation of starting it all again had her weary, both in mind and body. Aunt Maude had believed in early to bed, early to rise, and Sophie had always adhered to the philosophy, happy to do her best to please the aunt who'd raised and loved her. Yet she'd been up till almost two A.M. last night, and even after she'd gotten to bed, she hadn't been able to sleep, too filled with repressed desire. She wasn't used to the churning feelings that had kept her awake, and rather than sleep, her mind kept wandering back, remembering the delicious feel of Cole's hard, warm body pressed close, his muscled thigh between hers, his rough palm on her breast. She shivered anew. It had been a long, disturbing night.

Allison had been helpful, but too cheerful all day, smiling and humming, and Sophie had been endlessly relieved when she finally hung the CLOSED sign in the front window.

Despite her tiredness, she was anxious to see Cole, now that they shared a measure of carnal knowledge. She knew what his body felt like, how ravenous he was when kissing, his heady taste.

When she walked into the bar, shivering from the icy night, Cole immediately looked up at her, snaring her in his golden brown gaze. She had the feeling he might have been watching for her, and her heartbeat tripped alarmingly. His smile was different somehow, warmer and more intimate. Sophie wondered if it was Shelly's effect that made the difference.

For an instant, she was jealous of herself.

When Cole picked up a mug to fill with hot chocolate, releasing her from his gaze, she went to the back booth. Her belly tingled and her breasts felt heavy as she waited for him to serve her. She'd be herself, she thought, keeping her conversation to a minimum, drinking her hot chocolate without exception.

Only he didn't just give her the chocolate and leave after a few polite words. He set the cup in front of her, then seated himself opposite her in the booth, propping his chin on one large fist and smiling directly into her stunned eyes. He surveyed her until she squirmed, all the feelings from last night seeping into her muscles like an insidious warmth until her breath came too fast and shallow and her nipples puckered almost painfully tight. She hunched her shoulders in an effort to hide them.

Cole grinned, his gaze still a little too warm, too intent, slipping over her face as if he'd never seen her before. Just to break the tension, Sophie nodded at the steaming mug. "Thank you. I've been looking forward to this all day."

"Hmm. Me, too."

She paused with the spoonful of whipped cream halfway to her open mouth. His tone had been a low hungry growl. "Cole?"

He reached across the table and his large hand engulfed hers, then gently guided the spoon to her mouth. His gaze stayed directed on her lips, expectant, and like a zombie, Sophie obediently accepted the whipped cream. Slowly, Cole pulled the empty spoon away from her closed lips then laid it aside, his eyes so hot she could feel them touching on her. Using his thumb, he carefully removed a small dab of the cream from the corner of her mouth, and the gesture was so sensual, Sophie experienced a stirring of need low in her abdomen. His rough thumb idly rubbed her bottom lip, and for a few seconds her vision clouded and she had to close her eyes to regain her equilibrium.

She felt nervous and too tense. Much more of this and she'd be getting light-headed, fainting at his feet.

He pulled away, and his voice was low when he spoke, almost a whisper. "Have you ever dated, Sophie?"

His hands rested flat on the table, and she watched him shift, those long fingers coming closer to hers. She tucked her hands safely into her lap. If he touched her again, she'd be begging him for more, ruining her entire charade. "Why do you ask?"

"Oh, I don't know." His wicked smile was too sexy for words, but also playful. "Meeting your sister last night made me wonder why the two of you are so . . . different."

"You liked Shelly, then?" She already knew the answer to that. If Chase hadn't interrupted them, she had an inkling their intimacy might have become complete. What they'd done had been so satisfying in a way, but also very frustrating. The incredible feelings he'd created had been escalating, building, and she wanted to know what would happen, what the fullness of it all would be. She wanted to feel his body bare of clothes, to trace the prominent muscles she'd felt with her fingertips, skin on skin. His scent was stronger at his throat, and she wondered how it might be in other places, across his chest and abdomen, and where that thick erection had thrust against her.

Her breath caught and held as Cole reached across the table and fingered a curl hanging over her shoulder. "Yeah, I liked Shelly. But I like you, too."

She made a croaking sound, the best she could do with her thoughts so vivid and him looking at her like that. His knuckles brushed her cheek as he continued to toy with that one loose curl. "Well? Do you ever date?"

"No. I . . ." She tried a slight smile, but her face felt

tight and strained. "You know how it is, how busy a business can keep you."

He nodded. "I raised my brothers, you know. Keeping them out of trouble and in school took up most of my time. I've just gotten to where I can have a serious relationship."

Sophie wanted to run away as fast as she could. Was he hinting that he wanted a relationship with Shelly? Good grief, she'd have to find a way to dissuade him of that notion.

Her jealousy swelled.

A smile flickered over Cole's mouth as he gave a playful tug on her hair. "Why don't you and Shelly get your picture taken together? I can't imagine anything prettier than that."

"Together?"

"Mmm. I could almost guarantee you'd win. And since you come in here every night, you could get your hot chocolate on the house."

And he could get his night on the town with Shelly. Words escaped her, so she merely shook her head. Winning the contest had never been her intent. She'd merely wanted to spend more time with Cole under the pretense of entering, using it as a way to introduce him to Shelly — on a temporary basis.

"All right. Suit yourself. But could you do me a favor? Ask Shelly if she can come in a little later tonight. Closer to closing. I have a lot of things to take care of and when she's here, I don't want to be distracted with work. Could you do that for me?"

Her mind raced. She'd probably have time to go home and catch a nap. She was absolutely exhausted, and as excited as she was about seeing him again, kissing and touching him again, she could barely keep her eyes open. A little sleep would refresh her and sharpen her flagging wits. "Yes. I'll tell her. There . . . there shouldn't be a problem. Her time is pretty free right now."

"Good. And Sophie?" He grinned, waiting for the questioning lift of her brows. "If you change your mind and decide to enter the contest, just let me know."

She could feel the embarrassed heat rushing to her cheeks and barely managed a nod. God, she hated it when she blushed. "Yes, all right. Thank you."

He walked away, whistling, and Sophie stared at her chocolate in abject misery. Most of the whipped cream had melted.

Well heck. She was horribly afraid her plans had just gotten irrevocably twisted.

Cole made it sound as though he hadn't stayed single by choice but rather by necessity. He'd even hinted that he wouldn't mind getting involved with a woman now.

And here she had stupidly given him over to her make-believe sister. Sophie covered her face with both hands. *The best laid plans,* she thought.

She finished up her hot chocolate and literally fled.

"*You're grinning like the cat who just found a bucket of cream.*"

"Yeah." Cole turned to Chase and grinned some more.

He'd been grinning all night, and with good reason. Damn, he felt good. *Sophie wanted him.* He kept reminding himself of that, but every time, it thrilled him all over. If he hadn't already known about her ruse, her last blush before rushing out would have done it. No one blushed like Sophie. He wanted to see her entire body flushed that way, hot for him and how he could make her feel. He'd been thinking and planning for hours now, ever since Sophie left, knowing that Shelly would return.

"So, what's up? You and Ms. Sunshine finally hook up, or was it that little rendezvous with the sister? That lady looked like she could put the grin on any guy."

Cole and Chase had always been as much like best friends as they were brothers, possibly because they were the two oldest, even though nine years separated them. They'd pretty much always confided in each other, but even so, if he'd had a choice, Cole would have kept Sophie's secret to himself. Problem was, Chase already knew she supposedly had a twin, so an explanation was in order. He sighed. "There is no sister."

Chase paused in the act of polishing a glass. "Come again?"

Damn, but he couldn't seem to stop grinning, the satisfaction almost alive inside him, bursting out. "Sophie doesn't have a sister." He said it slowly and precisely, relishing the words. "She's an only child."

Cole waited while Chase sorted that out in his mind, then a dumbfounded look spread over his face and he laughed out loud. "Well, I'll be." He gave a masculine nudge against Cole's shoulder. "Aren't you the lucky one?"

Relieved that Chase was going to view the circumstances in the same way he had, Cole nodded. "Damn right. But no one else knows."

"Not a problem. Mack and Zane were so busy tripping over themselves yesterday trying to figure out what was going on with you two, I just left them to their own imaginations. It's not often they get to see you tongue-tied around a woman."

Cole slanted him a look. "It wasn't my tongue that was knotted up. Hell, I think the Inquisition could have been easier than last night was."

"But tonight will be different?"

"Oh, yeah." Tonight he had no reason to resist Shelly's invitation. That expanding tenderness gripped him again, and his resolve doubled. When he thought of what Sophie was putting herself through, the elaborateness of her plan, he wanted to whisk her away and spend days showing her how unnecessary it all had been. Almost from the first day he'd seen her, he'd wanted her. All she had to do was smile, or order hot chocolate, and he was a goner. "If I don't miss my guess, Sophie is trying to get one thing without losing another."

"And you're both of those things?"

He nodded. "She's lived a sheltered life with an elderly aunt, and she hasn't ever dated much. She doesn't want to risk the comfort of coming here every night, which I gather is the sum of her social life, by causing an awkwardness between us. If we have an affair, things might change, at least that's how she likely sees it. But once I explain it all to her, she'll know how silly she's been."

"So you're going to admit to her you know she's an only child?"

"Hell no!" Cole scoffed at the very idea. Sophie, in all her innocence, was offering him a fantasy come true, and no way was he going to mess up her little performance. Besides, he wanted to see exactly how far she'd go with it. "I intend to show her that I want her, no matter who she is."

"Sounds like a dumb, hormone-inspired plan to me. And one guaranteed to tick the lady off."

"Like you're the expert?" Chase did even less honest dating than Cole. The death of their parents had hit him hard, and he'd been mostly reclusive ever since. Not that he was a monk, just very selective, and always very brief. Cole couldn't think of a single woman Chase had ever seen more than three times.

Chase shook his head. "It doesn't take a genius to figure out she'll be embarrassed. And women can be damn funny about things like that. You can accidentally bruise her while horsing around with some rough play, and she'll forgive you that. But hurt her feelings, and she'll never forget it."

Since that wasn't what Cole wanted to hear, he shrugged off the warning. Sophie had two sides, that was apparent now, and he intended to appease them both.

At that moment, she walked in, and incredibly, she looked even better now than she had last night. Of course, now he was looking at her with new eyes. This was his

Sophie, so shy and sweet, yet now looking so sexy his teeth ached. The combination was guaranteed to blow his mind.

She wore the long, black leather coat again, this time over a loose, white blouse that buttoned down the front, tucked into a long black shirt and flat-heeled black shoes. She looked sensuously feminine and good enough to eat.

"Here comes Mutt and Jeff, so you better get your eyes back in your head and your tongue off the ground."

At Chase's muttered words, Cole pulled his gaze away from Sophie—*Shelly*—and turned to his brothers.

Mack was the first to speak, though he kept his fascinated gaze on Sophie. "What's going on with her lately? She's looking too damn fine."

"I'll say," Zane added. "Not that she wasn't a looker to begin with, but she never seemed aware of it before. She was always so . . . understated. Now her sex appeal is kind of up front, right in your face." He chuckled. "I like it."

Cole didn't bother responding to either brother. "I'm going to take her picture, so I'd appreciate some privacy while I'm in my office with her."

Mack's grin was so wide, it lifted his ears a fraction of an inch. "You need privacy to take her picture?"

Zane slugged him, which gained a disgruntled look, and a reciprocal smack. As Zane rubbed his shoulder, he said, "Don't tease him, Mack. Hell, I'm just glad to see him finally cutting loose a little." To Cole he remarked, "You act more like a grandpa than a big brother."

"Gee thanks."

Mack chuckled again. "We promise to give you all the leeway you need. In fact, given it's Friday, I can close up with Chase if you like."

"I was going to ask. Thanks."

"Sorry I can't stay too, Cole, but I already have plans. If you'd warned me—"

Chase gave his brother a distracted look. "Zane, you always have plans. What's her name this time?"

Unabashed, Zane straightened in a cocky way and said, "I never kiss and tell."

Cole figured Zane was more than old enough to manage his own love life, so he thumped him on the back and said, "Have fun," as he walked away to meet Sophie. She was still standing in the middle of the floor, and he realized she wasn't certain where to sit. From the beginning she'd always taken the back booth, which was the most secluded. But tonight, right this moment, she wasn't supposed to be Sophie and she didn't know how to act.

Someone turned on the jukebox just as Cole reached her and he had to yell to be heard. "I see you got my message."

She stared at him, devouring him with her eyes, and now he knew how to interpret that look. His lower body tightened in anticipation.

"Yes. Uh . . . Sophie told me to make it a little later. How soon will you close up?"

"Chase will give the last call in a few minutes." A couple shuffled past them, clinging to each other, barely moving their bodies as they feigned an interest in the music. Cole grinned. "Do you dance?"

As he asked it, he caught her hands and tugged her closer. She blanched. "Ah, no I don't. . . . That is . . ."

"No one is paying any attention," he cajoled. He pulled her into his arms, at the same time looking over her shoulder and seeing the rapt faces of his brothers. No attention, indeed. He frowned and shook his head at them. They all three nodded back, displaying various degrees of humor and curiosity.

Sophie tucked her face into his shoulder. "I've never danced much."

"You're doing fine." He nuzzled her temple, enjoying the feel of her warmth and softness so close, breathing in the sweet, familiar smell of her. She brought out his animal instincts, and he wanted to somehow mark her as his. His arms tightened and his thoughts rioted with plans for the coming night. "I like holding you."

Shuddering slightly, she leaned back to see his face. "I like having you hold me. Very much." She bit her lip, hesitant, then blurted, "And I liked what we did last night. Why did you stop?"

Cole felt poleaxed by her direct attack. He hadn't expected it. Lifting one hand, he cupped her cheek. "It was time to close the bar."

Sophie shook her head. "No, it was more than that. You seemed angry." Color in her cheeks deepened, but she held his gaze. "I want you to know, Cole, just because I'm . . . Sophie's sister, that doesn't mean I'd expect any more from you than any other woman."

"Oh?" *Silly goose.* She was so sweet and innocent, he wanted to pick her up and carry her away someplace private, then spend the long night reassuring her, making love to her, tying her to him. He knew his brothers were all watching, all alert, so he controlled himself. "What do other women expect from me?"

She swallowed audibly, but those smoky blue eyes never wavered, and he realized he admired her guts as much as everything else about her. Carrying out her plan couldn't be easy on her, and it directly indicated just how badly she wanted him. Lord help him, he'd never make it through the night.

"Nothing more than a nice night or two together, I suppose. I won't . . . won't be in town long. For the few days I am here, I'd like to share your company. But you don't have to worry about me hanging around afterward. I have my own life to live and I'm not interested in complicating it with a relationship. You don't have to worry that I'll make a pest of myself."

His chest tightened with some strange emotion he'd never experience before. He brushed her bottom lip with his thumb, then whispered, "Come into my office where we can talk. I'll have Chase bring us something to drink."

She looked more than a little relieved by his offer and smiled her thanks before taking the hand he extended to her. Her fingers were still chilled from the outdoors, and he gently squeezed, giving her some of his warmth. His body thrummed with excitement.

He turned and caught the flurry of movement as his brothers quickly found something to do. Zane was pulling on his coat, ready to leave. Mack was red in the face, studiously inventorying their stack of shot glasses. And Chase merely smiled, giving them both a brief nod.

As Cole passed him, he said, "A couple of drinks, Chase?"

"Sure thing." There was so much wickedness in Chase's tone, Cole felt obliged to add, "Colas please." He didn't want to gave Sophie a hot chocolate, thereby giving up the game by showing her he knew her preferences. Beyond that, he wasn't at all certain his control was up to it right now. The way she drank hot chocolate was better than an aphrodisiac.

Luckily, Sophie didn't notice the byplay. Her gaze remained on her feet as they entered his office. This time, he'd left the light on. He wanted to see every small expression that might pass over her face. He locked the door and smiled at her. "Come here."

Slightly startled, her eyes rounded and her sweet mouth opened just before he covered it with his own. He vaguely heard Chase announcing the last call, and he felt his muscles tense. Soon they'd be alone; he'd have her all to himself, with all the privacy he needed to see about fulfilling every single wish she'd ever had.

He folded her closer, one hand cupping the back of her head, his fingers tangled in her silky hair, the other pressing low on her spine, urging her body into more intimate contact with his.

And just that easily, she melted. There wasn't an ounce of resistance in her. He parted her lips with his tongue, licking into her mouth, touching the edge of her small white teeth, stroking deep, claiming and exciting. Her hands fisted on his chest, pulling tight the material of his shirt.

"Cole . . ."

The knock on the door announced the arrival of their drinks. Cole took in her dreamy gaze, her flushed cheeks, and smiled to himself. "Don't move."

She merely nodded in response.

He opened the door and took the tray Chase handed him. "Thanks."

"Don't do anything I wouldn't do."

"What wouldn't you do?"

"Exactly." Chase slapped him on the shoulder and pulled the door shut.

When Cole turned back to Sophie, she was still standing in the same spot as if rooted there. He smiled, set the tray on the desk, and turned to her. He touched her cheek, her chin, smoothed her eyebrows. Her face was so precious to him. He kissed her again, then began maneuvering his way to the desk. She clung to him, following his lead, and when he lifted her to sit on the very edge, she did no more than sigh.

"I'm glad you wore a skirt, baby." He trailed kisses over her jaw and down her throat.

Breathless, she asked, "Why?"

He lifted his gaze, amused by her innocence, charmed by her heavy-lidded eyes and dazed expression. Slowly, he slid one hand down her side to her knee, then back up again, under her skirt.

"Oh!"

He grinned, but it cost him. Her slim thighs were

warm, silky, and as his fingers climbed, he realized she wore stockings. He muttered a low curse and took her mouth, bending her back on the desk, hungry for her. With her skirt bunched up it was easy to nudge her legs apart and nestle his hips there. He gave up the exquisite explorations of her legs to cup one small, perfect breast. "I can feel your heart racing," he said against her mouth.

She pressed her face into his chest. "I love having you touch me."

"Then you'll love this even more." He slid the top button of her V-necked blouse free. She sucked in a breath, then held it. The next button opened, and he could see the silky-smooth flesh of her chest, the beginnings of her cleavage. He traced a finger there, dipping and stroking both breasts, moving close enough to a nipple to make her shiver in anticipation. "God, there can't be anything softer or sweeter on earth than a woman's breast," he said as he continued to tease her. He shaped and molded her breasts in his palms, pushing them up, marveling at the resiliency of her soft flesh.

Sophie gave a quiet moan.

He tugged another button free. Her bra was white lace, barely there, and the sexiest damn thing he'd ever seen. He wondered if it matched her garter and panties.

Their foreheads were together, both of them watching the slow movement of his dark hand on her pale, delicate skin. He opened the last two buttons and pushed her blouse aside, lifting both hands to cup her breasts in his palms.

"So pretty," he breathed.

Her breasts trembled with her deep breaths; he touched the front closure of her bra with a fingertip.

And the music in the bar died. Sophie lifted her head, startled.

"Shhh, it's okay. They're just shutting down. It's time for everyone to go home."

She blinked, and her lips quivered. "Do we need to go, too?"

"Not if you don't want to." He kissed her, a warm, featherlight kiss. "But I'd like to take you home with me, sweetheart. My apartment is only a few blocks away. My couch is okay for a quick nap, but I don't have napping in mind, and I don't want anything about tonight to be quick." He touched her face, his fingertips barely grazing her downy cheek. "I don't mean to rush you. I know things are progressing awfully fast." His mouth tipped in a small smile and he added, "After all, we just met. But I want you, and you obviously want me. Will you come home with me? Will you spend the night?"

Her eyes went wide, her lashes fluttering. He could see the wild racing of her pulse in her throat. "Yes." She swallowed hard, then smiled. "Yes, I'd like that. Thank you."

Chapter Four

Cole grinned at her perfect manners, wanting to tease her but unable to dredge up an ounce of humor.

The rigidity had left Sophie's shoulders by the time they were in his car, but she was far from relaxed. He'd barely managed to talk her out of driving herself to his apartment. He knew she'd wanted her car there as an avenue of escape.

He wanted her to trust him, to give him everything.

She remained silent as he parked the car and led her to the second floor of his apartment building. He didn't mind. The silence wasn't overly uncomfortable, but rather charged with tension and anticipation. Something very basic and primal inside him wanted to see Sophie in his home, on his territory, in his bed. He wanted to stake a claim, and he intended to do it right. He'd never been a barbarian before, but right now, he felt like howling, like slaying dragons to prove his affections.

She looked around as he unlocked the door and led her inside.

"My place is pretty simple. I'm not one for much decorating, and until recently, one or more of my brothers lived with me. Mack only moved on campus this past year and he was the last to go."

He watched as her gaze skimmed over everything, the dark leather furniture, the light oak tables, the awards and trophies set on a table that one or more of his brothers had won in sports and academics.

The eat-in kitchen was barely visible through an arched doorway. The bedrooms were down a short hallway.

"It's very nice," she said.

He pulled off his jacket, then took her coat, tossing both over a chair arm. "Zane teases me about being a housewife, but I like to keep the place clean, and now, he's no different. Teaching those three to do laundry and mop floors and cook was a chore, but they finally picked it up. We used to have a regular cleanup day, and there were no excuses accepted for missing it. Well, except for the time Chase broke his leg. Then we let him off the hook."

He grinned at her, wanting her to relax, to get to know him better. He was telling her things he'd never discussed with any other woman, and truth be told, she looked fascinated.

"How old were you when your parents died?"

"Twenty-two. I'd just finished college. Mack and Zane were still in grade school, but Chase was in junior high."

"It must have been awfully rough."

He nodded in acknowledgment, unwilling to rehash the past and all the problems that had cropped up daily. "We got through it. They were good kids, just a little disoriented by it all. It took time to get readjusted, to get past the loss." He wanted to ask her about her own loss, but because he wasn't supposed to know about it, he couldn't, and it frustrated him. They should be using this time to build a closeness, not hiding behind secrets.

Abruptly, he asked, "Are you hungry? Or would you like something to drink?"

She hesitated only a moment and that intriguing blush turned her face pink. Then, suddenly, she launched herself at him. Her arms went tight around his neck, almost smothering him as he caught her. "All I want is to finish what we started at the bar." She pressed frantic kisses to his neck, his nose, his ear, making him laugh, and at the same time groan with an incredible rush of hot lust. "I want to lie down with you and touch you and—"

"Honey, shush before you make me crazy." To guarantee her compliance, he kissed her, holding her face still, thrusting his tongue deep, tasting of her, making love to her mouth. Her words had affected him, making his body ache in need.

He pulled her blouse from her skirt and quickly skimmed the buttons open, then pushed it off her shoulders. She helped, wiggling her arms free and trying to keep their mouths together.

Laughing again, he said, "Take it easy, honey. We've got all night. There's no rush."

He gentled her, stroking his hands up and down her bare back, placing small, damp kisses across her skin. Her hands clutched at his hips and he obligingly stepped closer to her, letting her feel his rigid erection, nestling it into her soft belly.

She made a small sound of mingled excitement and delight. "Cole?"

"Hmmm?" he muttered, distracted by the taste and texture and scent of her skin. The fact that this was his Sophie sharpened the pleasure to a keen edge.

"Will you take off your shirt, too?"

He hesitated, afraid he might lose control if she started touching him too much. But her eyes were soft and huge, inquisitive and excited, and he couldn't resist. His heart pounding, he unbuttoned his shirt and shrugged it off, then peeled his T-shirt over his head. He dropped them both on the floor. Sophie's gaze moved over him, warm and intimate.

"You can touch me, honey."

Still, she seemed timid, so he took her hand in his, kissed her palm, then laid it flat on his chest. Sophie licked her lips as she tentatively stroked him. "You're so warm and hard."

He laughed. Hot was a more apt description, and there was no questioning how hard he was. It felt like his jeans would split at any minute. He ruthlessly maintained his control and started on the side button to her skirt.

"Cole . . ." She stiffened, anxiety in her tone.

"I want to see you, baby," He searched her expression and read so much nervousness there, he paused. Cupping her face and leaning close, he whispered, "You're very sexy. I could spend a lifetime looking at you and it wouldn't be enough."

Her small hands curled over his wrists. "And we certainly don't have a lifetime, do we? I . . . I'm leaving in just a few days."

When would she give up that ridiculous tale? At this point, it almost annoyed him. It was so difficult not to call her by name, not to admit how much he cared. But this was her show, he reminded himself, and he was determined to let her play it as she chose, at the same time, helping to meet her goals, to give her everything she'd ever wanted. "Are you sure you won't be able to stay in town awhile?"

"No." She interrupted him quickly, firmly, then stepped against him to wrap her arms tight around his waist. "No, we can have tonight, but that's all I need. Just one night. An exciting experience for both of us, but no more than that."

His confidence started to dip. Had he misread her? Did Sophie truly only want a very brief affair?

Not even that, he thought, as her words *just one night* reverberated in his brain. Maybe, unlike him, she had stayed single by choice. God knew, the woman was more than attractive enough to draw men in droves. He'd seen the underlying sensuality beneath her quiet persona, so it stood to reason other men would have seen it as well.

Even Zane had commented that she was a looker, and he was a connoisseur of women.

Anger washed over him. Her ruse no longer seemed so touchingly sweet, and he was met with a new determination, one to make her so deliriously satisfied, so sated with his lovemaking, she wouldn't be able to deny him ever again. He would give her what she wanted and more. Before the night was over, she'd be as addicted as he.

One night hell.

"Take off the skirt, sweetheart. Let me touch you." The growled words hung heavy between them until finally Sophie released her death grip on him and lifted her head. Cole stepped back just enough to allow her to move freely.

Her eyes looked more gray than blue as they held his, looking for reassurance. At his smile, she carefully released the button to the waistband of the skirt and slid the zipper down. It immediately dropped over her slim hips to layer around her ankles. Cole took her hand and she stepped out of it, leaving her shoes behind as well.

The dark, sexy stockings covering her long, slender legs were enough to make him groan, but it was the sight of her narrow waist, her flat belly, that shook his control. Her panties were pale, and the small triangle of chestnut curls could be seen beneath the sheer material, taunting him, making his palms burn with the need to touch her

"Christ, you're beautiful."

He hadn't realized she'd been holding her breath until she let it out in a long shaky sigh. "I wasn't sure what you would think—"

"I think I'm one lucky bastard," he muttered, his tone none too steady. "Come here, honey."

He didn't mean to be rough, to startle her, but he didn't think he could take much more. He'd been imagining this moment for almost seven months, and the reality was much sweeter than any fantasy he'd dredged up. He supposed it was because he genuinely cared about her, because he liked and respected her, that sex between them seemed like so much more. To him, laying her down and burying himself in her would be more than physical, it would be emotional and mental, too, a bonding of more than just their bodies.

The softness of her skin drew him, and he touched her everywhere, his hands gliding over her shoulders, her waist, the back of her thighs above the stockings. He pulled his mouth away from hers as he slid both rough palms into her panties, cuddling her small buttocks. Sophie stiffened, and he kissed her ear, then nipped the lobe. She gasped and her fingers contracted on his arms.

"I like that," she whispered.

He smiled despite his roaring lust. "This?" he asked as he stroked her silky bottom again. "Or this?" His teeth closed carefully on her earlobe as his tongue teased. She arched against him.

"Yes, that."

"There are other places to nibble, you know. Places you'll like even more."

"Oh?" She was breathless, trembling all over. Keeping one hand on her bottom to hold her close, Cole slid the other hand back up her side until her reached her breasts. With only one flick, he opened her skimpy bra.

They both groaned as he cuddled the soft, delicate weight of one warm breast in his hand. She gave a rough purr of feminine pleasure but jerked slightly as he caught her stiff nipple between his fingertips and rolled.

"There's here, too." With that warning, he bent his head and caught the tip of her breast between his teeth, flicking with his tongue, just as he'd done to her earlobe. Sophie grabbed his head, her fingers tight in his hair as she cried out. Cole opened his mouth wide and drew her in, sucking strongly. His hands closed on her waist and he backed her to the nearest wall, then stepped between her thighs, deliberately forcing her legs wide.

His hand moved down her waist, over her belly, and his fingertips toyed with the edge of her panties. Sophie shivered and moaned, and he knew he was tormenting her as much as himself. Just as his fingers dipped inside he kissed her again, swallowing her moan of pleasure.

She was warm, wet, her tender flesh swollen, and his fingers gently caressed her until she was panting, her face pressed to his throat, her fingers grasping his biceps.

"Right here, honey," he whispered as he used his middle finger to ply her tiny, swollen clitoris.

"Oh God . . ." Her body jerked in reaction, pressing hard against him.

Cole kissed his way back to her ear, his teeth once again catching the lobe. His tongue stroked just as his finger did, and Sophie wasn't too innocent to realize the parody of what he did. She clutched at him and her hips began to move in tandem with the rhythm he set.

She was close, and he knew it. It surprised him, her immediate, unsparing reaction to him. It also made him nearly wild with lust. He'd always assumed Sophie had hidden depths, that once unleashed, her passion would be savage and uninhibited. His entire body pulsed with each small shudder she gave, each deep, raw moan. And when he whispered, "You would taste so sweet. Can you imagine my mouth here, honey, my tongue touching and licking—" she gave a stifled scream and climaxed.

Cole held her close, keeping the wild pleasure intense until she whimpered and slumped into him, utterly drained. Blood pounded through his veins, roaring in his ears. He scooped her up and hurried into his bedroom. He lowered her to the bed, laying her on top of the cool quilts, his own body coming down to cover hers.

He kissed her long and deep, caressing her breasts, her thighs, her belly. He leaned back to look at her, then removed her open bra and finished stripping her panties down her legs. She turned her face away, breathing shakily.

"You're perfect, sweetheart." What an understatement. He'd never seen a woman who stirred him like this one did. He kissed her breasts, sucking and nipping, his mouth gentle, his tongue rough. Sophie's body seemed to be designed with his sensual specifications in mind. He felt a near frenzy of need, but Sophie lay sated and limp beneath him, one hand in his hair, idly stroking. He shoved up to his side, pulled a condom from his jeans pocket, then held it in his teeth while he struggled out of the rest of his clothes.

His shoes went across the room when he kicked them off. He stood to shuck his jeans down his legs, and then turned back to Sophie. She immediately protested.

"I didn't get to see you," she said with a sexy pout.

Despite his need, Cole chuckled and moved her thighs apart, situating her for lovemaking. "Whereas I can see you very well. All of you," he added in a low, breathless growl, looking at her damp, soft curls and the tender flesh they protected. She still wore her stockings and the wisp of a garter belt, and she was so incredibly sexy he nearly lost his control. His fingers stroked over her again, easily now with her recent orgasm, feeling her slick dampness, her heat. Her modesty was gone and she simply allowed him to look, to touch. The sight helped to curb his rush. He could look at her forever and be happy.

She wasn't willing to give him forever. Damn this game.

She stretched like a small cat and smiled at him. "It's hardly fair, you know. I've been very curious about your body."

"You'll see me soon enough." He tore the silver package open and slipped the condom on. "But not now because I can't wait."

He caught her legs in the crook of his elbows and bent low over her, leaving her totally exposed and vulnerable to his possession. Sophie grabbed his shoulders to hold on, her eyes wide and dark, her breath coming in small, anxious pants. He probably should have taken more care, treated her more gently, with more restriction. Instead, he held her wide open and watched as he entered her body, as her delicate flesh gave way to his, slowly allowing him entrance. His muscles clenched even more, his heart thumping heavily. She was tight, resisting him, and he flexed his buttocks, forcing his way forward.

She said his name on a low moan.

"God, you're snug," he whispered through clenched teeth, and his forehead was damp with sweat. Sophie tipped her head back, biting her lip and squeezing her eyes shut. A rosy flush spread from her breasts to her throat and cheeks, not embarrassment, but sharp arousal. It fed his own. And then he sank into her, her body finally accepting his, squeezing him like a hot, wet, hungry fist.

He knew, of course, that she wasn't overly experienced, that she was mostly shy and withdrawn and therefore probably not all that practiced with men. But he hadn't expected her to be like this, so tight that he had to wonder if any other man had ever had her. The thought that he was the first, that she'd waited twenty-six years for him, broke his control, overwhelming him with a tidal wave of feelings he couldn't name and wasn't ready to deal with.

He withdrew, only to rock into her again, slow at first, but then harder and faster. "I'm sorry, baby," he said between rushing breaths, "I can't wait."

With no apparent complaints, Sophie reached for him, drawing his mouth down to hers, kissing him with a hunger that matched his own. Her small, feminine muscles held him tight, resisting each time he pulled away, then gladly squeezing as he pushed deep back into her, milking him, making him wild. When she pressed her head back, groaning in another immediate climax, Cole followed her. His mind went blank, his vision blurred, and his body burned. He felt a part of her, her scent in his head, his heart. He pounded heavily into her slim body until finally, he stiffened and his body shook as he emptied himself. He stayed suspended like that for long moments, then slowly collapsed against her.

Their rapid heartbeats mingled, and he could feel her breathing in his ear, soft, fast breaths. *God, he loved her.* The possessiveness nearly choked him; he wanted badly to whisper her name, to tell her how their lives would be from now on. To make her admit she cared also.

He'd gladly given up his personal life to care for his brothers. In that time, no woman had really appealed to him, to tempt him from his duty. But now he was free, and Sophie was here, as if sent by fate just when he was ready for her and needed her most. He wanted her, now and always. But he held back the words of commitment, unsure of her and how she would take such a declaration when she'd been so insistent on their time limit.

Slowly, carefully, he untangled his arms from her legs and heard her moan as her legs dropped. He'd been too rough, moved too fast for her, but she hadn't complained.

He managed a kiss to her neck by way of apology, but his mind was too sluggish, too affected, to do more than that. Her fingers sifted through his damp hair, and he could feel her smile where her mouth touched his shoulder.

"I hadn't imagined anything like that."

How the hell could she form coherent words? Cole struggled up onto his elbows and looked down at her, still breathing hard. She appeared smug and very satisfied. "So you thought it was okay?" he teased.

"Incredible."

He felt like a world conqueror at her words. He brushed his fingertips over her swollen lips. "I'm glad. I think you're pretty damned special, too. I always have."

She stilled for just a moment, her eyes wary. Her tongue came out to touch nervously on her lower lip, and she accidently licked against his finger. They both shuddered in reaction. "We only met a few days ago."

He was still inside her, her naked breasts flattened against the hardness of his chest, their pulses still too fast, and she continued the ridiculous game. She should have been admitting the truth to him by now. He'd all but told her how he felt.

Unless, of course, she didn't feel the same. If what her assistant, Allison, had said was true, her life had been so quiet, so sedate, she may have just hungered for a quick bite of adventure. Did she truly want him as a one-night stand? He'd assumed she'd concocted the absurd plan because she was unsure of herself and him. But it was possible the opposite was true, that she didn't hope for more involvement, but rather a guarantee of less. His stomach cramped at the possibility.

"Cole?"

"I was just thinking. It seems like I've known you a long time."

"Maybe that's because you've known Sophie. But we're nothing alike."

He smoothed her dark hair away from her face, wishing there was some simple, magical way to figure her out. He'd never suspected that his Sophie might be so contrary and complex. "I don't know about that," he whispered. "Sophie is—"

She laughed, interrupting him and quickly changing the subject before he could say the words that he desperately wanted to say, words he hoped would reassure her and gain a reciprocal declaration. "Are you ever going to get around to taking my picture?"

Momentarily distracted, he teased, "Like this?" He looked her over leisurely, the wild tangle of her hair, her sated gaze, the way her limbs were entwined with his. His hand smoothed over her hip. "You'd be a winner for sure."

She smiled. "How about just a head shot?"

He pretended disappointment. "I suppose it'll have to do." He pulled away, letting his hand linger on her thigh for a heart-stopping moment. "Don't move."

"I'm not sure I even can." But she did turn toward him, propping her head up on an elbow. "Where are you going?"

"I have a camera here."

Cole disposed of the condom, then slipped on his jeans before rummaging in his closet for the instamatic camera. He looked up to see Sophie posed there, her hair wild, the quilts rumpled beneath her, one long, stocking-clad leg bent, the lacy garter still in place. A new wave of heat hit him. She was his. One way or another, he'd make her admit it.

"I should have gone slower, played longer," he said as he surveyed the feast she made.

"Why didn't you?"

He shook his head and came to sit on the edge of the bed. "Because you made me so crazy I couldn't even think straight, much less wait very long. I meant to make our first time together really special."

She laughed. "You haven't heard me complaining, have you?"

He'd never imagined Sophie with that particular impish smile. He kissed her, loving her more with each passing moment. "So you feel satisfied?"

She stretched again. "Absolutely. It was more than I'd ever imagined. So stop worrying."

"All right." It was easy to convince him since he didn't want to waste a single second with her by debating the issue. The night was still young enough, he'd have plenty of time to prove his point to her.

He lifted the camera to his eye, sending her squawking and screeching, grabbing for the sheet. "Cole, wait! I have to comb my hair. I'm a wreck."

"No, you're beautiful." She crossed her arms over her breasts and laughed at him, and that's the picture he took. When it slid out of the camera, he lifted it out of her reach, then stood to put it on his dresser.

"Don't you dare consider hanging that anywhere!"

"I'm keeping that one for myself."

She relaxed again and studied him, her expression going soft and curious. "Why?"

"So I can look at you whenever I want." That was the truth, though not nearly close to how deeply he felt about it. "Now, if you want to put your blouse on and comb your hair before I take the entry picture, that's fine, but I swear you don't need it."

"I'm going to do it anyway."

He chuckled at her show of prim vanity. "All right. I'll go get us something to drink. You have about three minutes."

*He was back in two, and Sophie had just begun to un-*tangle her hair. She still felt languorous and warm and sated. She wanted nothing more than to curl back up on the bed with Cole and do all those things they'd already done, plus more. The bed smelled like him, and she could have snuggled into it forever. She pondered the possibility of stealing one of his pillows, but knew she'd be found out. She glanced at the clock and wanted to cry over the amount of time that had already passed them by.

Though she was enjoying their easy banter and intimate conversation—something she hadn't expected—she hadn't had near enough time to explore his body. It fascinated her, his perfect collection of hard bone and strong muscle. The few quick looks she'd gotten had made her insides feel like they were melting. She literally wanted to kiss him all over.

"What are you thinking about? There's a wicked gleam in your eyes."

Startled, Sophie looked up at him. He set a tray with two mugs of hot chocolate and a can of whipped cream on the dresser. His chest was bare and as he moved, muscles flexed and rippled. His jeans hung low, thanks to the fact he hadn't buttoned or zipped them, and his bare feet were large, braced apart, the tops sprinkled with dark hair.

She wanted to groan in pleasure; she wanted to tell him to stand there for about a year or so and let her look her fill. "I was thinking of your body, and how unfair it is that I haven't gotten to touch you much."

He froze for an instant, then shuddered. His eyes narrowed and grew dangerously bright. "You'll get your turn, if you're sure you want it." He loaded one mug of hot chocolate with whipped cream, forming a small mountain, then carried it to her with a spoon. Sophie scooted up against the headboard and balanced the warm cup between her palms. Leaning forward, she licked at the cream, more than a little aware of Cole's gaze.

His hand touched the side of her face, smoothing her hair back behind her ear. "I'd like to make love to you until morning, honey, if you're sure you're up to it."

Dark color slashed high on his cheekbones and his eyes were bright, glittering. He looked very aroused, and Sophie set the mug aside on the nightstand to give him her full attention. "I'd like that, too. I want this night to be enough to last a long, long time."

"You're not too sore?"

Such a strong wave of embarrassment washed over

her, she felt even her nose turn red. "Of course not." It was a partial lie; she did feel achy in the places she flatly refused to mention. But it didn't matter, not when compared with the pleasure of getting to hold him again.

"You were so tight," he whispered, his hands still touching her as if he couldn't help himself. "I know you haven't had much hands-on experience. No," he said, placing a finger over her lips when she started to object. "I'm not judging or asking for details. But I know women's bodies, babe. And you were either a virgin, or you've been a hell of a long time without a man. You were so damn tight I almost lost my mind. But either way, I don't want to hurt you."

Sophie felt touched to her soul. He was so wonderfully considerate, so decidedly male. Protective and virile, and she could gladly spend a lifetime with him. He'd hinted several times that he wouldn't mind continuing his relationship with Shelly, and she was so very tempted. But how could she ever manage such a thing? Keeping up the game for only a few days had worn on her. Already, she'd missed more sleep than ever before. Her boutique demanded all her attention in the mornings, so she couldn't keep up the late hours with Cole along with her normal shift at the shop. And the longer she was with him, the more risk she ran of being found out. If Cole knew she acted out both roles, what would he think? She shuddered at the mere possibility.

Softly now, because tears were so close, she whispered, "I want anything and everything you can give me tonight. What little discomfort I have doesn't matter at all, not in comparison to how you make me feel."

The muscles in his shoulders and neck seemed to tighten even more. Abruptly, he stood and grabbed up the camera. "Give me a smile, honey."

She did, though she knew it was a weak effort. His obvious arousal triggered her own. Once the photo was taken, he looked at the picture, nodded in satisfaction, then put it and the camera aside. "Now."

Shakily, her smile barely there, Sophie asked, "Now what?"

"Now we finish our drinks—after you get rid of that shirt."

Once again, he unbuttoned her blouse, playing with her, kissing each spot of skin that was uncovered, teasing her. Sophie relished his attention to detail. He also knelt in front of her to remove her garter and stockings. "I want you completely naked," he explained, and she hadn't cared to argue with him, too excited by the husky timber of his voice.

To her surprise, once that was done, he didn't attempt to make love to her again but instead wanted to assist her with her mug of hot chocolate. Sophie giggled every time he carried a spoonful of whipped cream to her mouth, but he was persistent, cajoling, and before the drinks were done, she had caught on and teased him unmercifully, licking at the spoon and sometimes his fingers, making him groan in reaction. She'd never been a flirt before, but she liked it.

And judging by his reactions, he liked it, too.

She thought of all the nights she drank hot chocolate at his bar and knew she'd never be able to order the drink there again. The chocolate always gave her a boost to get through the rest of her evening after a long workday, sort of like the caffeine from coffee did for others. She drank it year round, but now, she would imagine this scene, and if Cole so much as looked at her, she would recall his touch, his kiss. Though this was happening to Shelly, Sophie would be affected. No, she would never drink hot chocolate in front of him again. But it was worth it to lose the one small, routine comfort, when compared with the excitement of their present play.

"God, the way you do this ought to be outlawed for the sanity of mankind."

She merely smiled.

"You're such a tease," he whispered.

To which she replied, "Me? You're the one who still has his jeans on."

He leaned forward and kissed her, his tongue smoothing over her lips, then dipping inside before he pulled away. "An easy enough problem to fix." He stood and unselfconsciously shucked off the last of his clothes. Sophie caught her breath at the sight of him. He was already hard, thrusting outward, and her body warmed at the significance of that.

"I started something earlier that I didn't get a chance to finish."

She couldn't imagine what. Everything had felt very finished to her; her nerve endings all came alive as she remembered the ways he'd touched and kissed her. Her eyes rounded when he scooped her up and laid her flat on the bed, one of her legs across his lap, the other behind him. Without a word, he leaned over and very gently nipped her ear, his tongue touching, stroking. One hand closed on her breast, and his fingers smoothed over and around her nipple until she squirmed.

Her body thrummed in immediate excitement. She closed her eyes, thrilled by his touch, how quickly he could bring her to a high level of excitement. She'd never imagined anything like this in her life.

He moved from her ear to her throat, then her shoulder, which she hadn't realized was so sexually sensitive to his touch, but every time he kissed her skin, every little lick, sent a riot of sensation through her body, seeming to concentrate between her thighs.

"There's a lot of things I'd like to do to you, honey."

"Yes." Whatever he wanted was fine with her; he seemed to know things about her body she'd never guessed.

"You taste so sweet," he whispered as he neared her breasts. His breath was fast, his mouth hot as he covered her nipple and tugged. Her back arched, but he soothed her, murmuring to her until she relaxed again, though her heartbeat still galloped.

"Relax and let me make love to you, baby."

Relax? Her entire body felt too tight, too sensitive. Then his teeth closed on her nipple, just sharp enough to alarm her. He tugged and she cried out, but he didn't stop, gently tormenting her. She started to grasp his head, but he caught her hands in one fist and pinned them above the pillow. His rough, raspy tongue smoothed over and around her nipple until she cried, then he switched to the other breast.

He was in no hurry now and she could do no more than accept his unique brand of torture. Still, she tried to protest when he left her breasts to kiss her ribs, but he wouldn't be deterred. Sophie moved against him, wanting to feel him push inside her body, to fill her. She ached for him. The feelings were even stronger now that she knew what to expect, what to anticipate.

She stiffened when his mouth moved to the top of her left thigh and her breath caught in her chest. His fingers slipped between her thighs and cupped her. "Remember what I told you earlier, babe?"

One finger found her most sensitive spot and gently rubbed back and forth. Sophie couldn't find enough breath to answer him.

"Do you remember?" He lightly pinched her, tugged, stroked, and Sophie couldn't keep the long moan from escaping between her tightly clenched teeth.

"That's it. You do remember, don't you? Here, and here . . ." He kissed her ear again, her nipple. "And here." In the next instant, his mouth replaced the fingers between her legs and she couldn't believe it, couldn't control her reactions or her small screams. Her hands pulled free and knotted in his hair, keeping him close, and he moved closer still, tasting her, licking her, nipping with his teeth. He gently sucked as he worked one rough finger into her, then another. Pushing deep inside, slowly, adding to the building pressure and pleasure.

The contractions hit her hard and she screamed out her climax, vaguely aware of his hum of satisfaction, of the way he pressed his own body firmly against the mattress. Her hips bucked and he resettled her, his long fingers biting into her hips, holding her still. It seemed to go on and on and he wouldn't relent until she pounded on his shoulders and shuddered and begged.

Seconds later he was over her and he cupped her face between his palms, his fingers still damp. "Look at me, Sophie."

She managed to get her eyes open though it took a lot of effort. His words were indistinct to her muddled brain, but she knew he wanted her attention. Cole looked fierce, his face flushed darkly, his nostrils flared as he struggled for breath. And then he drove into her and once again her body reacted, her heels digging into the mattress as she strove to get as close to him as possible. Her climax, so recently abated, so utterly exhausting, came back to her in a flash of undulating heat and pinpoint sensation. She clung to Cole while he ground himself against her, his eyes never leaving her face, their gazes locked. It was a connection that went beyond physical, that joined their hearts as well as their bodies.

He groaned harshly and cursed and then she felt him coming, knew he'd locked his legs against the intensity of his climax. And he said her name again and again, as if he couldn't help himself. "Sophie, Sophie . . ."

This time when he collapsed, he turned so she faced him on her side, sparing her his weight. One heavy thigh draped over her own. His body was damp with sweat and radiated heat. For long minutes neither of them spoke. They allowed their heartbeats to slow, their bodies to cool.

Something, some vague unease niggled at the back of Sophie's mind, but she was too drained to identify the cause. She tried to ignore it, but it remained, vexing her like a dull toothache, prodding at the recesses of her mind.

Cole kept her close, locked in his arms, and then he whispered, "Sleep." His fingertips touched her nose, her cheekbones. "You look tuckered out, honey. Give in. I'll wake you when it's time to go."

Sophie sighed, comforted by his scent and the leisurely way he stroked her. She felt safe, protected. He snagged the quilts and pulled them over her, tucking her in. Within minutes she could feel herself drifting off, the long, restless nights two days past suddenly catching up to her.

Cole's hand cupped the back of her head, his fingers kneading her scalp, and that was all it took. She was aware of one last lingering kiss to her forehead, and then she was asleep.

Chapter Five

At first she was only aware of warmth and comfort, a coziness she'd never experienced before. She'd never awakened in a strange bed, and doing so now momentarily disoriented her. She sighed, mentally forcing herself from the depths of the deep sleep she'd enjoyed. Cole's scent and warmth mingled around her, stirring her senses. Even without full awareness, things felt almost perfect, except for one tiny problem. She frowned and concentrated on getting fully awake.

But the second she opened her eyes, she knew what had gone wrong.

Oh God, he'd called her by name.

Sophie was afraid to move, almost afraid to breathe. Cole lay heavily beside her, his even breaths touching against her temple, disturbing the fine hairs there. He had one heavy thigh draped over her legs, one arm limp around her waist, the other cushioning her head. Their combined body heat had worked to glue their skin together and she knew, if she moved, he'd awaken.

Then the questions would begin.

She closed her eyes as dread filled her. *He knew!* The last time they'd made love, he'd called her Sophie, not just once, but over and over again. He knew she wasn't Shelly, but he'd made love to her anyway. She couldn't begin to comprehend the ramifications of such a thing. She was naked, in bed with the man she'd spent seven months fantasizing about, the man she'd slowly fallen in love with. They'd made love repeatedly and her body ached in tender places, reminding her just how new this all was to her, and how well he now knew her body.

Carefully, moving like a ghost, she turned her face to look at him.

His dark lashes cast long shadows on his cheekbones and beard stubble covered his lean jaw, chin, and upper lip. How long had they slept? His dark, silky hair fell over his forehead, and Sophie was amazed at how the sight affected her.

God, she loved him.

She closed her eyes as pain swelled inside her. Cole knew who she was, and now she had to deal with that. But she needed time. She couldn't sort out her thoughts with him so close, his naked body warming her own.

At that moment he yawned and stretched. Sophie froze, frantically praying that he wouldn't awaken. He put one arm above his head and rolled onto his back.

Her insides quivered in relief; she felt almost light-headed. Not daring to move, she waited several moments, but he slept on. He, too, was exhausted. And his normal routine was to sleep later, since the bar kept him out at night. Slowly, holding her breath, she slid one leg to the edge of the bed.

When he remained motionless, she moved her other leg. Luckily, his bed was firm and didn't sag or rock overly with her motions. It took her nearly three full minutes, but finally she was standing beside the bed, staring down at him. He muttered in his sleep, scratched his bare chest, then sighed heavily.

What had she done?

Escape was the only clear thought in her mind. She needed time, time away rom him, from his magnetism. She had to think. On tiptoes, she gathered up her clothes and slipped out into the hallway. There she dressed hastily and grabbed up her coat. She didn't bother to look into a mirror, already knowing she looked a wreck. A night of debauchery had to leave a woman somewhat disheveled, but there was nothing she could do about it now, so she didn't want to dwell on it.

The lock on his front door gave a quiet snick as she slipped it open, and her heart almost punched out of her chest. But there were no ensuing noises, so she assumed he slept on.

She ran the few blocks back to her car still parked at the bar, the cold slicing into her, almost unaware of the tears on her face. Fortunately for her peace of mind, the streets were all but completely deserted. There was no one to witness her humiliation as she stumbled up to her car, then dropped her keys twice before finally getting the door unlocked.

She drove like a madwoman, anxious to be home in the comfort of familiar surroundings where she could sort it all out in private. When she finally pulled into the parking lot, her car was still cold and she was racked with shivers. It was almost six-thirty.

She couldn't bear the thought of working today, not sure if Cole would feel obliged to come and see her after the way she'd run off, more afraid that he wouldn't bother at all. The humiliation was too much. She called Allison and asked her to cover for her the entire day. It would mean paying the assistant overtime, but Sophie didn't care.

Once Allison had agreed, Sophie stripped off her clothes, took a warm shower, which did nothing to shake off the awful chill deep inside her, then she crawled into bed. She had to decide what to do, how to explain, what excuse she could use for such a dastardly trick.

But first, she cried.

*So what's wrong with you? You've looked ready to commit murder all night. The customers are giving you a wide berth."

Without answering, Cole stalked away from Chase. He felt heartsick and so damned empty he didn't know how to deal with it.

Of course, Chase wouldn't let it go, following Cole as

he headed for the office, throwing the door back open and walking in without taking the obvious hints. He pulled out a chair and sat down. "Give it up, Cole, and tell me what's wrong."

His eyes burned and his gut clenched. Furious, he turned to Chase and said, "You want the goddamned details? Fine. She walked out on me."

"Sophie?"

Cole threw up his hands. "No, the First Lady. Of course I mean Sophie."

Carefully, Chase asked, "So you went after her and stopped her and told her how you feel, right?"

Sending his brother a look of intense dislike, Cole said, "I was asleep. She snuck out on me."

"Oh."

"After I woke up this morning, I went to her boutique, but her assistant said she called in sick. I don't have her home phone number or even know where she lives." He laughed, the sound devoid of humor. "After seven months—*after last night*—I don't have her damned address."

"Ask the assistant."

He growled, then said in a mock woman's voice, "It's against policy to give out personal information, but I promise to tell Sophie you asked."

Chase scowled. "She refused to give you Sophie's number?"

"Yeah. No matter what I said, she wouldn't give in."

"So that's it? Hell, I might as well throw dirt on you. If you're giving up now, you're dead and buried."

"I'm not giving up, damn it! I just don't know what to do at this precise moment. Waiting doesn't sit right. I have no idea what Sophie might be thinking."

"All right. I'll take care of it." At Cole's incredulous look, Chase added, "I'll go over there and talk to the assistant. I'll get Sophie's number for you."

"And how, exactly, do you plan to do that?"

"Never mind. Just figure out what you want to say to her when you do call her. If you blow this, I'm going to be really disappointed in you."

Mack and Zane approached the office just in time to hear Chase's comment. "Disappointed in Cole about what?"

Chase left the office to fetch his coat and get on his way. The three brothers followed him like he was the Pied Piper.

"What's going on with you two? Where's Chase going?"

When they were all behind the bar, Cole turned to his brother Mack. "On a blind mission, though he doesn't believe that just yet. But he will, after he meets Allison."

Zane stepped up, a look of confusion on his face. "Who's Allison?"

"Sophie's assistant."

"Oh yeah. I remember her."

Both Cole and Chase turned to stare at him. They started to ask, but thought better of it. The details of Zane's love life were often too boggling to deal with. Mack snickered.

After a moment, while Chase tugged on his coat and

gloves, Zane asked, "Did you and Sophie have a falling out or something?"

"It's none of your business, Zane."

He shrugged at Cole. "Fine. But I just wondered if there was some reason you weren't serving her. If you'd rather I'd take her a drink, just say so. But I don't like ignoring a woman."

Cole's head snapped up and he stared over at the familiar booth. There sat Sophie, hands primly folded on the table, her expression cautiously serene, though her face was pale and her eyes were red. His heart twisted, then lodged in his throat.

Chase asked, "How long has she been sitting there?"

"About ten minutes now. Usually Cole serves her right off, so I didn't know . . ."

His words dwindled off as Cole climbed over the bar instead of going around it, sending several customers jumping out of his way, awkwardly snatching up their drinks so they wouldn't get spilled. Cole's stride was long and forceful, his gaze focused on his approach to Sophie's table. With each step he took, his pulse pounded in his ears until he almost couldn't hear. When he reached her, she looked up and he saw her eyes were puffy. God, had she been crying? He searched her face; words, explanations, all jumbled in his mind so that he couldn't get a single coherent thought out. Finally he just leaned down and kissed her. Hard. Possessively. He kept one hand on the table in front of her, one on the back of her seat, caging her in, keeping her from pulling away.

But she didn't try to pull away. Her small hands came up and grabbed his shirt, tugging him closer still.

He heard a roaring in his ears and realized it came from the bar. Lifting his mouth from Sophie's, he looked around and saw a majority of male faces laughing and cheering—led by his damn, disreputable brothers, of course.

He grinned, then faced Sophie again. She started to speak, but he covered her mouth with a finger. "I love you, Sophie."

Her eyes widened.

He leaned closer still, speaking in a rough whisper. "I've waited seven months to spend the night with you, and it was worth it. But I'll be damned if I'll wait anymore. I love you, I want you. Now and forever, regardless of what name you go by, or how you dress. You're mine now. Get used to it."

He waited, but her big smoky eyes never wavered from his. She was completely still except for the pulse racing in her throat. Cautiously, he lifted his finger. "Well?"

She swallowed audibly. "All right."

By small degrees, his frown lifted and his mouth quirked. She'd said yes. "You want me, too?"

"I've wanted you since the very first time I saw you."

He kissed her again, then asked, "Why the hell did you run from me today? Christ, I almost went nuts when I woke up and you were gone."

"I'm sorry. I felt stupid—"

"Damn it, Sophie—"

It was her turn to shush him, and she used her entire

hand. Their audience chuckled. No one could hear what was being said, but Sophie's actions were plain enough. Cole grinned behind her palm.

"I felt stupid for pretending to be someone else instead of just being brave enough to tell you how I feel. So I decided to stop being a coward. Aunt Maude always told me adults should own up to what they do, to be responsible for their actions and accept the results. She also told me I should never be afraid to go after what I want."

Through her muffling fingers, he asked, "You want me?"

She nodded, tears once again in her eyes. "I love you."

His long fingers circled her wrist and he pulled her hand down. "I wish I could have met Aunt Maude. I have a feeling we'd have been good friends. Will you tell me all about her?"

She nodded, then forged onward. "I realized you must care about me, too, because you kept hinting about wanting a relationship. At first I thought you wanted Shelly. I was jealous."

His look was affectionate, full of love. "Goose."

"But then I finally remembered that you knew Shelly and I were the same."

"Not at first, and it almost made me demented. I wanted Shelly because she looked like you, made me feel like you do. I couldn't understand it because you're the only woman who makes me insane with lust and sick with tenderness." Then he growled, "Not to mention what you do to a mug of hot chocolate." He pulled her from her chair and swung her in a wide circle to the sounds of raucous cheers. "Will you marry me, Sophie?"

Very primly, she replied, "I was hoping you'd ask."

At that moment, Chase set two hot chocolates on the table. He winked at his brother. "Hey, might as well go for broke."

⟡

The Valentine *contest went off without a hitch. Sophie* was chosen unanimously by Cole's three desperate brothers, who wanted nothing to do with an arranged date for themselves. The local newspaper explained it away by saying Sophie and Cole had fallen in love during the contest, which put the perfect slant on the whole Valentine ambiance and gained them an enormous amount of publicity, some of it even covered by a local news station. Sophie, as the lucky winner, got incredible publicity for her boutique as well. Allison had her hands full fending off reporters who blocked the growing influx of new customers. She complained heartily, but Cole figured she was well up to the task.

Cole announced to the reporters that since he was soon to be a married man, next year one of his brothers would serve as escort for the winner. That brought about some bawdy comments from the women customers and some hearty groans from his brothers, who pretended to be terrified by the prospect but who nonetheless preened under the weight of feminine attention.

Sophie stood by Cole's side, elegant and serene and beautiful. He felt like the luckiest man alive. The contest really had been the perfect idea for both of them, even if they'd each indulged in ulterior motives.

He glanced up and saw the contest photo on the wall. As per the contest stipulations, Sophie had posed with all the Winston men. Their much bigger bodies crowded around hers, dwarfing her petite frame. She was laughing, and all the men looked smug.

In his nightstand drawer at home was a different photo, the one he'd taken of Sophie while her hair was still tousled and her cheeks flushed from his loving. But that one was private, for his eyes only. Forever.

Next year, he thought, grinning as he watched his brothers give one interview after another, the contest might work out as the perfect idea for another Winston man. He wondered which of them would be the lucky one. Then Sophie nudged his side and he forgot about everything but her. He led her to his office where solitude awaited—along with a carafe of hot chocolate and a can of whipped cream.

Tangled Dreams

Chapter One

Even though it was an incredibly busy night at the bar, even though he could barely hear the newest order over the din of loud conversation, music, and laughter, he heard her. Her every thought. Chase watched her, saw that her mouth wasn't moving, that she wasn't actually talking, but he could still listen to her.

She was on the other side of the bar, standing by a group of Halloween decorations that his sister-in-law had designed out of a bunch of pumpkins he and his brothers had carved. The haystack and jack-o'-lanterns were festive and provided an amusing backdrop to the serious expression on Allison Barrow's face. He'd known her several months now, ever since his brother had married her best friend and boss, but he'd never before noticed how cute her round, wire-framed glasses looked on her small nose or the fact that she had a tendency to straighten them needlessly.

He noticed now. But why?

His youngest brother, Mack, bumped into him. "Hey, Chase, orders are piling up here. You want to stop day-dreaming and help me out?"

Chase gave Mack a distracted glance. "Come here a minute, will you?"

Mack paused. "What?"

"Over here. Come on. Now stop right there." Chase positioned him exactly where he'd been standing. Mack was in his last year of college, still studious and alert. Surely he'd pick up on something. "Now, look over there at Allison. See her, right past the redhead with the skinny guy in a suit? By that Halloween display?"

"Yeah, so?"

"What's she saying?"

Mack turned to stare at Chase in disbelief. "What's she saying? How the hell should I know? I can barely hear you, and you're only two inches away from me."

Frustrated, unable to really explain, Chase said, "Well, look at her, dammit, and try."

With a sound of disgust, Mack again stared toward Allison. Chase saw his gaze warm a little, then go over her from head to toe, and for some reason, that annoyed him. Now that he'd really noticed Allison, he didn't particularly want Mack doing the same. He'd always thought Allison was cute, in an understated, sort of just-there way, but suddenly she looked very sexy to him. She was twenty-five, on the short side, dark blue eyes, medium blonde hair. Nothing special. Certainly not the type of woman to appeal to his baser side. But tonight he couldn't pull his attention away from her. He suddenly heard her every thought when he'd sure as hell never been a mind reader before. And he only heard Allison, no one else. There was something going on between them, and it didn't make any sense.

"Well?" Chase prompted.

"She looks different, doesn't she?"

"It's the clothes," Chase explained, having noted the difference himself. It had taken him several minutes to finally pinpoint what made her look so unusual tonight, so . . . sensual. "She's wearing some sort of old-fashioned, vintage dress."

In truth, she looked like a woman straight out of film noir. The dress was a deep purple gray, and even from a distance, Chase could see that the color did things for her eyes. Or were her eyes just brighter tonight, more alert?

There was subtle black beading on the top of the dress that caught the bar lights and drew his attention repeatedly to her less-than-outstanding bustline. At least, he'd never thought it outstanding before. But now . . . Now he was imagining her naked and almost going crazy because of it.

The waistline was tight, showing off her trim build, and when she turned, Chase not only saw that she had on seamed stockings but also that the damn dress had a flat bustle of sorts, a little layering of soft material that draped real nice over her pert behind, a behind that would feel just right against his pelvis if he took her from the back . . .

"It looks . . . I dunno, kind of sexy on her, doesn't it?"

"Mack." Pulled from his erotic thoughts, Chase said it as a warning, surprising himself and his brother. His tone had smacked of possessiveness, and he didn't like it, but he also didn't like another man, not even his brother, thinking Allison was sexy. He wasn't quite used to himself thinking it yet. "Pay attention."

"To what? From what I can tell, she's not saying anything. She's just standing there all by herself, looking sweet. In fact, she looks a little lost."

Chase rubbed his face. "So you don't hear anything?"

With a strange look, Mack asked, "What exactly am I supposed to be hearing?"

Damn. There was no way Chase could repeat the thoughts he'd picked up on so clearly. They were fairly . . . intimate. Explicit thoughts. Sexual thoughts. *About him.* He almost groaned. "Never mind. Forget I said anything."

Mack frowned at him. "Hey, you okay?"

"Yeah, fine. Go on before we get mobbed by disgruntled customers. You take that end of the bar, and I'll handle this end."

With one last curious look at his brother, Mack sauntered off. The bar, owned by the brothers, was especially packed tonight. It had gone from being a popular watering hole to a regular hangout. People not only drank there, they danced and played billiards and pinball. Cole, the oldest brother and recently married, was thinking of expanding into the empty building next door. He'd discussed his plans with Chase just the other day, and Chase was all for it, especially if it meant they'd hire in some help. The bar was plenty prosperous enough now to support several additional employees, and with Zane, the third brother, getting his own computer business off the ground, and Mack finishing up college, it was certain the two younger brothers would likely work less and less at the bar.

Cole had originally bought it to support the family after their parents had died. He'd worked damned hard, making ends meet and taking care of three much younger brothers. Chase, as the second oldest at twenty-seven, was still nine years younger than Cole, with Zane twenty-four and Mack just turned twenty-two. Chase had always tried to help out as much as possible, and he and Cole were friends, as well as being as close as brothers could be, but none of them had expected the bar to eventually be so popular. It had given them a great start in life and had guaranteed employment for the younger brothers, but it had served its purpose and it was time to think of the future.

Their clientele was as much female as otherwise, being that until Cole's recent marriage, they'd all been bachelors—according to the local papers, the most popular bachelors Thomasville, Kentucky, had to offer. A lot of women lamented Cole's altered state, which sent an overflow of attention to the remaining brothers. Chase smiled. He wasn't all that interested, being something of a recluse and extremely particular in his sexual appetites, but Zane and Mack sure appreciated all the female adoration.

The six to eight o'clock rush was finally starting to

wind down when Chase was hit with another of Allison's vivid internal dialogues. He'd been fending off the stray thoughts, doing his best to ignore them, but there was no way to keep this one out. A tray in his hands, a dishrag over his shoulder, he paused on his way to the sink, like someone had frozen him in mid-step.

Such nice shoulders. So sexy. Probably hard and smooth to the touch. And hot. They'd move when he thrust, the muscles shifting . . .

And then a visual image joined the words, an erotic picture of him making love to Allison. It was carnal, sensual, and showed him exactly what she'd look like naked, laid out beneath him, straining against him while he drove into her. Her small breasts were flushed, her pale pink nipples were puckered tight. Her eyes were closed, her blonde hair fanned out on a pillow, her hands desperately clutching his shoulders . . .

The tray almost slipped out of his hands, and he barely managed to catch it. He shook his head, trying to clear it, totally overwhelmed by a wave of raging lust and heated need. He turned to stare at her.

She was looking at him, and as he stared, gaze intent, her face turned pink and she ducked her head. Like a sleepwalker, Chase plunked the tray on the bar, threw the dishrag to the side, and started toward her.

She looked up at him, her eyes now rounding with alarm, and she took a hasty step back, but the haystack and pumpkins were there, crowded into the corner, making it impossible for her to flee. Which was just as well, because if she'd run, he'd have simply chased her down. All he could think of was getting his hands on her.

Chase stalked her, keeping her in sight, stepping around those people loitering or dancing in the middle of the floor, dodging tables and ignoring greetings. He didn't like being played with, and while he didn't know how she did it, he knew Allison was in some way responsible.

He stopped right in front of her and she looked up at him, one hand pressed wide over her heart as if to keep it contained in her chest. He started to question her, but then he noticed her lips, soft, pink, parted slightly, and he wanted so badly to kiss her he couldn't think straight. He could almost taste her on his tongue, hot and wet and woman sweet. His hands shook—hell, his whole body shook.

Like a wild animal scenting a female in heat, it took all his concentration to control his basic urges. He'd *never* felt this way before, not even with the most accommodating women, and they were rare indeed. His desires were usually specific, a little risqué to the average woman, something that needed to be catered to in order to achieve mind-blowing pleasure. He simply didn't get overwhelmed with lust at the mere sight of a woman.

Anger washed over him, making him tremble. He didn't want to notice her, dammit. She'd never affected him this way before, so why now? How did she do it? He stared down at her, at that tempting mouth, and every muscle in his body tensed. He cursed softly.

Oh God. Maybe I should have chosen Zane. He'd have

been willing at least, and so much easier. He wouldn't question what was happening . . .

"Like hell!" Chase took her shoulders and shook her slightly. Through clenched teeth, he growled, "You're right, Zane wouldn't hesitate; he'd probably already have you in the back room with your little bustle in the air. But I'm not Zane, and I didn't start this, you did."

She stared at him, her shock apparent, her face draining of color.

Jealously made him a little rougher, a little less discreet than he'd normally be. He took care to keep his private life private. Not that he was a monk, but he sure as hell wasn't the outgoing, obvious ladies' man that his younger brother Zane was. His hands tightened on her narrow shoulders and he leaned low to say, "You can just get thoughts of Zane right out of your head."

She blinked up at him, the pulse in her throat going wild. "What . . . what are you talking about?"

They were so close, her glasses fogged just a little, then slipped down the bridge of her nose. Chase could see small flecks of gold in her deep blue eyes, like little explosions of heat. His jaw worked for a moment, then he said with just a touch more calm, "How dare you even consider my brother?"

She gasped, putting both her palms on his chest. The touch burned him, making the lust that much worse. He wanted to howl. He had never in his adult life had this happen, had lust rage over him so suddenly, so uncontrollably. Hell, of the four brothers, he was the quietest, the most discriminating in outward appearances. And control, especially with a woman, was something he insisted on.

She glanced around, her movements nervous, then whispered in a rush, "Chase, what in the world is wrong with you?" Her face was flushed, her eyes round, and she looked embarrassed and alarmed and very worried.

Chase, too, glanced around. Several people were looking at him, including his damned brothers. *They must have radar,* he thought, wondering how all three of them had known he was going to make a fool of himself. But the fact that he had, that it was over a woman, was rare enough that he knew they wouldn't ignore it or let him forget it. He simply didn't cause scenes, ever, but especially not over women.

Turning back to Allison, striving for a pleasant look rather than that of a crazy man, he said, "I'd like to talk to you. In private." The words slipped out through his teeth and the parody of a smile he'd forced to his mouth.

She rolled her lips in and bit them, her gaze still wary, then nodded. But she looked far from willing. She looked nervous as hell. He could *feel* her nervousness, damn her, just like he'd felt everything else.

Holding her arm in case she changed her mind, Chase led her past the bar toward the back office. Mack stood behind the bar, shaking his head in wonder. Cole, standing in his path, frowned in concern, and Zane, surrounded by a group of women, grinned like the village idiot. Ignoring the two younger brothers, Chase stopped in front of Cole and said, "I need a few minutes of privacy."

Looking between him and Allison, Cole narrowed his eyes.

There was no way Chase could explain, so he said simply and firmly, "I'll be back out as soon as I can," and his tone alone forestalled any arguments.

Cole looked hesitant, then finally he nodded. "Take your time. We can handle things now."

"Thanks." Chase turned away, and Allison stumbled along beside him. He realized it looked like he was dragging her along, but that was only because she was holding back a bit. Chase glanced down at her. "You're causing a scene."

"Me?" They were now out of sight of the main room of the bar, and she again held back as Chase opened the office door. "You're the one doing the caveman routine. What in the world is the matter with you?"

He snorted. "Like you don't know." Hell, she'd been thinking about him all night, taunting him with those personal, private, *sexual* thoughts of hers. He didn't know how he knew it, but he did, and his conviction was so strong he didn't doubt it for a moment. He gently propelled her into the office and shut the door.

The lock turned with a quiet click.

Only one light was on, a small lamp sitting on the desk. Chase watched as Allison backed up a few steps, then stopped and braced herself. For what?

"Allison . . ."

You can do this, you can do this, you can . . .

"Do *what?*" Chase barked, advancing on her, again losing his temper. Startled, she jumped back and her knees hit the soft, slightly worn sofa that Cole had installed years ago when long nights sometimes made it necessary to nap at the bar. Allison lost her balance and she tumbled gracefully onto the sofa, the soft, flared skirt of that killer dress fanning around her. Her spine pressed hard to the back of the sofa in alarm. She started to jump up again, but Chase stepped so close she couldn't, not without plastering herself against him.

And judging by her expression, she didn't want to do that.

She eyed him, then whispered, "I don't know what you're talking about."

He leaned down, one hand on the back of the sofa next to her head, the other on the arm next to her side, pinning her in. "You want me. You've been thinking about me all night, distracting me, invading my head. Now you're trying to give yourself a pep talk and—"

Her eyes flared wide like saucers, and she fumbled with her glasses. Her mouth moved, but no words came out. Finally, she sputtered, "How on earth do you know that?"

He frowned, tilting his head to study her carefully. Her old-fashioned dress was a major turn-on for him, and he fully appreciated the feminine, sultry picture she presented. It affected him somehow, but he couldn't say exactly why.

"Chase?"

She sounded honestly surprised, and then he felt her shock roll over him and knew she'd had no idea he'd been listening in on her ruminations. She hadn't silently talked to him on purpose, he'd just suddenly been able to read her. *Why?*

Chase touched her cheek, feeling the heat of her blush. She was mortified to discover he knew her thoughts. Some of his anger evaporated, and he wanted to reassure her somehow, but first they had to figure out what was going on.

Standing up straight again, he said, "Don't move."

She shook her head, mute. Her thoughts were such a jumble he almost smiled. Poor little thing. She was as confounded as he. And now that he knew she wasn't controlling the situation, wasn't controlling him, he could almost appreciate the novelty of it.

He touched the tip of her nose, then a loose blonde curl by her temple. He liked touching her, he thought, then immediately withdrew. He didn't want to like touching her. "This is going to take some time to sort out. I'm going to go get us a couple of drinks, then we'll talk, okay?"

Her chest rose and fell rapidly, making the beaded bodice glitter. She looked away. "Okay."

"Allison?"

Her gaze came back to him reluctantly.

"It's all right." He searched her face, noticing how pretty her eyes looked, how they weren't just a dark blue, but a multitude of blue shades, complex and original. "That you want me. I mean."

Her lashes lowered, her hands fisted in her lap, and she whispered, "Oh God."

Smiling now, feeling like he was finally getting the upper hand, Chase walked out. Damn, he didn't know what was going on, but one thing was certain: Allison hadn't denied wanting him. She hadn't denied anything. She'd been too upset and embarrassed and confused to do more than stare up at him, letting him absorb her thoughts, letting him experience her desire.

And her desire sparked his own.

He was so hot, he thought he could breathe steam. His muscles were tensed, his abdomen tight. He felt like he'd been indulging in an hour of specialized foreplay, and in a way, he supposed he had, listening in on Allison's thoughts, seeing her small fantasies. They'd been almost real, and had affected him like a touch.

This whole thing went beyond the realm of reality. If someone had tried to tell him any of this was possible, he'd have laughed. Mind reading? Ha. He hadn't believed such a thing existed, but now he knew it did.

Even stranger than that was Allison, suddenly looking so appealing, suddenly wanting *him*. He'd always been polite to her but distant, because he'd instinctively felt she wouldn't meet his needs. She was mostly quiet, a little perky but in a cute, friendly way, not overtly sexual. A small woman with sweet features, not a single risqué or daring thing about her. She didn't in any way look like a woman who would indulge his sexual demands. So he'd been merely polite and she'd always been the same.

Now he knew her quiet facade hid some heated urges, and though they weren't on a par with his, they intrigued the hell out of him.

Hurrying, he went behind the bar and grabbed two colas. Cole tried to talk to him, but he put him off. Hell, there was no way to explain the unexplainable. Cole would think he'd gone off the deep end.

Mack and Zane started whispering, their heads together, but he ignored them, too, not even bothering to give them a second glance.

Even this far away from Allison, he still knew what she was thinking, and he wanted to get back to her, to reassure her. She was afraid of what he'd think, racking her brain for an explanation he'd accept. Her uncertainty was understandable, even endearing, given the bizarre situation.

For whatever reason, she suddenly wanted him, and he didn't really think he should turn her down. Hell no. Whatever was frightening her—and she was frightened—he'd take care of it.

Cole walked up to him again. "Chase . . ."

"It's under control, Cole. Don't worry."

Cole searched his face, not looking the least bit convinced. "But . . . *Allison?*"

Chase grinned. "Yeah, I know. Pretty surprising, huh? Maybe there's some black magic at work, considering it's almost Halloween, or there's a full moon out tonight or something. Who knows?"

Cole didn't respond to the joke. "Do you know what you're doing, Chase?"

Considering that a fair question since he wasn't behaving at all like himself, Chase shrugged. "I'm working it out. That's all I can tell you for now."

Cole still looked concerned, but he let it go, saying only, "Just remember she's my wife's friend and assistant. I don't want to end up in the doghouse because of you."

Chase laughed. As he headed back to the office, colas and napkins in his hands, he dodged under a black paper cat and an orange paper jack-o'-lantern hanging from the ceiling. Maybe Halloween really did have something to do with this sudden power of his to read Allison, to see things in her he'd never seen before.

If so, he intended to enjoy it while it lasted.

But first, he wanted some answers.

Chapter Two

Allison paced the office as she waited for Chase to return. She'd never been in here before, and beyond her nervousness was a curiosity that kept her looking around. Cole mostly used the office, since he was the bookkeeper of the bar. Chase generally contented himself with being a bartender—and an unusual one at that. He wasn't chatty, was more of a listener than not. He had the incredible knack for keeping disagreements at a minimum, negating the need for a bouncer. The bar was a lively place, but it was friendly, and totally acceptable to a family man or woman.

The office was large with a massive desk at one end and a plush sofa against the adjacent wall. A few chairs were scattered about with a filing cabinet or two. Photos of the brothers at various ages hung on the wall, and with her heart pounding, Allison went to peer at an aged photo of Chase. He was younger, but even then she could see the hidden fire in him, the repressed energy that everyone else seemed to miss, accepting him as the *quiet brother*. She shook her head. He was still incredibly gorgeous and her stomach knotted. It suddenly seemed like much too much.

"Darn it, Rose, I knew this was a bad idea. He's actually angry that I want him. Why wasn't Jack good enough? He couldn't read my mind, and we both know he was more than willing, even if he didn't exactly make my pulse race the way Chase does. He had no idea what you were planning. It would have been so much—"

The door slammed and she turned to see Chase, drinks in his hands and a frown on his face. "First my brother Zane, and now some bozo named Jack. How many men are you daydreaming about?"

He was angry again—

"Damn right I'm angry!"

Her own temper sparked, obliterating some of her nervousness. "Stop doing that! Stop reading my mind."

He stared at her, and very slowly his frown smoothed out. He looked disgruntled as he stepped into the office and set the drinks on the desk. "I can't help it. It's like you're screaming into my head."

"But why?" Her hands twisted together in nervousness. "I don't understand."

"Hell if I know. You came in tonight and just like that, I heard you thinking about me."

If her face got any hotter, her ears were going to catch

on fire. Mustering her courage, determined to see this through—a thought he obviously read, judging by his smile—she admitted, "I've done that before."

"Thought about me?"

She swallowed hard and nodded. "Yes."

Eyes narrowed sensually, he stepped closer. His voice was low and heated when he asked, "Sexual thoughts?"

Her stomach did quick little flips of excitement. "Yes."

"I never guessed."

"I know. You've never even noticed me." That was painfully true, and there'd been many a night when she'd gone home feeling heartsick because she was all but invisible to him.

Chase reached out and touched her cheek again. "I'm sorry."

Darn it, she had to censor her thoughts a little better or she'd never be able to get through this.

Chase grinned. "Don't bother on my account. I kind of like reading your mind."

With the most ferocious frown she could muster, she said, "Well, I don't like it!"

He looked very annoyed again. "Because you're also thinking about Zane and this Jack person?"

"No!" She shook her head, flustered to the core. Seeing no hope for it, she admitted quietly, "I don't want Zane or Jack. Not like . . ."

His gaze softened. "Like you want me?"

"Yes. But none of it matters. I don't need to be a mind reader to know you couldn't care less about me. I'm sorry if my thoughts are suddenly intruding in your head, but I don't really know what I can do about it."

His frown was back, only now it looked more confused than angry. "You want me, but you don't want to do anything about it?"

Allison turned away. This was the tricky part—

Chase swung her back around and up close to his chest. His hands held her firmly, not hurting, but making certain she couldn't move away. Allison thought he'd shake her again, and she braced herself, but no sooner did she think it than he narrowed his eyes and sighed. "Dammit, I would never hurt you, okay?" When she didn't answer right away, he added, "I promise. Trust me."

Heart tripping at his deep, compelling tone, she said, "Okay."

"Good." There was a wealth of satisfaction in his heated gaze, but also determination. He tugged her the tiniest bit closer, until she gasped. "Now let's get something straight. I don't want you to try planning and plotting against me. It's only tricky if you're not honest with me."

Being so near to him was muddling her brain, making logical explanations difficult. "I . . . I can't be honest with you."

"Why not?"

"You won't believe me, and you'll think I'm nuts, and you won't want anything to do with me, but I need you to . . ." She closed her mouth, appalled by how much she'd just blurted out.

His gaze moved from a fascinated study of her eyes, to her mouth, then down to her breasts. His fingers on her arms turned caressing, persuasive. In a soft, gentle tone, he said, "This whole situation is nuts, so I doubt you can add much lunacy to it. And to be truthful, I'm finding I want a lot to do with you. Maybe it's just a masculine gut reaction to knowing how much you want me, but I've had a hard-on since you first started thinking about me. And it's you I've got pictured in my brain, not any other woman."

Allison groaned. His words were like an aphrodisiac, making her blood race, her toes curl. Rose couldn't have planned this any better if she'd tried. But it was all wrong. Even if he was now willing to do what she needed him to do, it wasn't because—

Chase leaned down and pressed his mouth to her temple. "Tell me what you need me to do, honey."

Honey. He'd never called her that before. She liked it. "I'm glad."

Her head dropped forward to bounce against his chest and she groaned again, this time thoroughly flustered at her wayward thoughts.

Chase chuckled, nuzzling against her crown. "I'm sorry. Would you rather I didn't answer your thoughts?"

She shook her head. This situation was so bizarre, it bordered on comical. But then, everything that had happened to her since moving into the house was beyond belief. "No. It's just . . . disconcerting."

His hands stroked up and down her back, and her eyes closed as she basked in the heat of his touch. He kissed her brow and said, "To me, too, you know. My brothers are probably out there huddled together, coming up with every wrong conclusion there is. It's for certain they're not anywhere close to the truth."

Alarmed, she pushed back to look up at him. "You're not going to tell them, are you?" It was bad enough that Chase had been drawn in, but she didn't want or need anyone else to find out all her secrets.

Chase cupped her cheek, his touch so tender she could barely find her breath. "I don't know. I'm not even sure yet what's going on. But if it'll make you feel better, for now I won't say anything."

Her eyes closed in relief. "Thank you."

"What secrets do you have?"

Darn. She hadn't meant to let that slip. Then realizing she might as well have spoken out loud, she said, "Just give me a little time, okay?"

"Time for what?"

"Time to figure out how to tell you, how to get used to this, how to prepare myself."

He didn't look like he wanted to agree. In fact, he looked very disagreeable, but he finally nodded. "Answer a few questions for me, then."

"If I can."

"Who's Jack?"

That was easy enough, though not a very desirable topic. "He's a man I've been dating. He wants to get serious, but I don't."

He looked far from pleased by her explanation. "Why?"

"He's not . . . right for me."

"In what way?"

Chase made it very difficult to talk when he kept touching her, his big hands smoothing over her shoulders, her back. And he stared at her mouth, making her self-conscious.

And he damn well knew it.

He shook his head. His voice was deep and affected, husky with desire. "I'm sorry. It's just that I can't stop thinking about kissing you—and a lot of others things. Things that'd likely have you hightailing your pretty little behind out of here as fast as you can."

Ignoring most of what he said only because it didn't make sense to her, she asked, "You . . . you really want to kiss me?"

"Oh yeah." His voice dropped even more and he stared at her lips. "But I can tell you don't really want me to. Yet."

Allison tried to step away, but he wouldn't let her go, so instead she covered her face. "This is so difficult."

She found herself hauled up against Chase's chest, his arms wrapped tight around her, comforting her. "I don't mean to make it—whatever *it* is—harder for you, honey. But I can feel your confusion. You want me, but you don't want to want me. Have I got that right?"

She sighed. He smelled so good, and it felt so good to be this close to him. More than anything she wanted to be with him, in every way imaginable.

He drew in a deep breath. "*Every* way?"

She stared at him, speechless. That had sounded too

ominous by half. Still, she would have agreed, but there were stipulations that she couldn't ignore.

His eyes narrowed. "What stipulations?"

Darn it, she had no privacy at all! It took all her control to hold back her fist. She wanted really badly to punch him.

Chase held her tighter. "None of that."

This time she didn't even question his right to know her thoughts. Thoroughly disgruntled, accepting there was no way she could sort out her thoughts in her own head, she groaned and pushed back to glare at him. "Do you think I should be happy to want a man who doesn't want me?"

"But I just told you—"

"Right. That you ... have an erection." Her face burned, but she didn't look away from him. "I know. But that's not because of *me*. Chase, you don't even know me, and you've never wanted to know me."

He was quiet, watching her closely.

"I think in the eight months that Sophie and your brother have been married, you've said about a dozen sentences to me, all of them mundane cordial niceties. How're you doing? Nice weather we're having. That sort of thing. Now, just because you know I've fantasized about you a little—"

"A lot."

"Okay a lot—"

One corner of his firm mouth kicked up. "Tell me some of the fantasies."

His voice was low, commanding, making her insides

tingle. She frowned severely. "No. Besides, you'll probably know them soon enough as it is."

His brows lifted. "You've got plans, do you?"

She opened her mouth, then saw his taunting smirk and wanted to slug him again. "No! I meant that you'd probably just read my mind and know them, though I swear I'm going to do my best *not* to think about you at all."

"Party pooper."

"It's not funny, Chase."

He grinned and kissed the end of her nose. "From my perspective it is. There's not a man alive who wouldn't pay good money to be where I am right now. It's not often a fellow can actually understand a woman or know her thoughts."

She snorted. "Like you can even begin to understand."

He ignored that. "And I really am curious about these fantasies, but I'll wait, if you insist. Now, about that other nonsense you rattled off."

Her wariness returned. "What nonsense?"

"Me not wanting you. Okay, so I'll admit I'd never really paid much attention to you before. I never pay much attention to any woman, at least not for long, but especially not a woman who's a friend and assistant to my sister-in-law. I have no intention of getting involved long-term with anyone, and your relationship with Sophie puts you just a little bit too close to home for comfort. You're not the type of woman for a one night stand, and one night stands are about the only speed I go these days, so I ignored you. It really didn't have anything to do with you."

She stared at him, disbelieving such words had actually come from his mouth. "My goodness. All that? So your disregard for me was actually something of a compliment, because I'm above such casual notice?"

"Don't be snide."

"Snide? I don't believe a thing you said. Since I've known you, I've seen you with three women, and if they were any indication of the type of female you gravitate toward, then I have no problem at all understanding why you've always ignored me, and it didn't have a lot to do with my friendship with Sophie."

He'd stiffened at her first mention of the women. "Meaning?"

"Meaning the women you go for are always beautiful and . . . and well stacked." She winced at her own word choice, but it was absolutely true. While she was full through the hips, lacking in the upper works, and of a very ordinary appearance overall, Chase had shown a preference for tall, slim, busty women—none of which could be applied to her.

He chastised her with a shake of his head. "Women are so damn weird."

"Weird!"

"And so hung up on their bodies. Allison, there's absolutely nothing wrong with how you're built."

Her mouth twisted. She obviously didn't have a single sacred thought.

"No, absolutely not, especially when you're thinking all kinds of ignorant things."

"Ignorant things? Chase, I have mirrors in my house, and I know what I look like."

"You look fine, better than fine, and it wasn't the look of those women that drew me."

"Then what?"

He hesitated, studied her closely, then smiled. "Not yet, honey. But maybe, given half a chance, I'll explain it to you someday."

The deliberate secrecy annoyed her. "See? You're obviously just not interested."

His own temper sparked at her stubbornness. "Then explain why I still have a damned erection!"

He no sooner shouted that than a tentative tap sounded at the door. They both turned, appalled. Chase recovered first, saying in a bark, "What is it?"

There was barely repressed laughter in Mack's voice when he called out, "Uh, there's a guy here looking for Allison."

"Uh-oh." She cleared her throat as Chase turned slowly to glare at her, then she answered Mack nervously, saying, "I'll, uh, be right out."

Chase looked like a thundercloud. "Who the hell is looking for you?"

"Jack?" She posed her answer as a question, not sure how he'd react.

Working his jaw, Chase stood silent for a moment, then finally said, "You'll tell him to leave."

"No, I will not! Chase, we agreed to meet here tonight before I knew any of this would happen. I need to talk to him, to tell him—"

"That you want me."

"No! I'm not going to tell him that."

"Then I will."

He turned toward the door, and Allison launched herself at him, wrapping her arms tight around his waist and digging in her heels. "Wait! You don't understand!"

Chase easily pulled her around in front of him, then pinned her to the door with his hands on her shoulders, his hips pressed to her belly. Her heart skipped two beats, then went into frantic overdrive. His breath fanned her cheek and his gaze was hot. With his lips almost touching hers, he said, "I don't want you to see anyone but me."

His scent enveloped her, his nearness made heat bloom inside her. She'd wanted this for so long, but not this way, not when he'd more or less been coerced.

"No one is coercing me, Allison. I want you, plain and simple."

"There's absolutely nothing simple about this and you know it." Still, did she have any choice? Rose was counting on her, and so was Burke. She licked her lips and could almost taste him. "There's a lot I have to explain to you yet."

His hips pressed closer, letting her feel the long, hard length of his erection, making her gasp. "Like who the hell Rose and Burke are?"

Her glasses were crooked and she straightened them, staring at his throat rather than meeting his eyes. "Yes. And . . . and why I think you should come to my house and. . . . and make love to me."

She peeked up at him. The heat of his gaze burned her up from the inside out. And then he kissed her, his mouth voracious, his tongue stroking. She clutched at him, overwhelmed and turned on and unable to rationalize what was happening. Unexpectedly, he caught her hands and pinned them over her head, then groaned deeply.

When he pulled away just the tiniest bit, he said roughly, "Get rid of the other man, Allison."

She practically hung there in his grasp, on her tiptoes, her arms stretched out, his pelvis pressed to her, keeping her still. "I . . . I will," she managed to stammer around her excitement. "But I have to do it right."

"Tell him to get lost."

"That would be cruel." She said it as a gentle reprimand, then quickly added, "He's a nice man, Chase. And he's serious about me. He asked me to marry him, so I can't just dump him like that."

Chase stared at her for a long moment, and she could see he fought an internal battle. Finally his eyes squeezed shut, and he whispered, "I've never been jealous before. I don't like it."

"You have no reason to be."

He kissed her again, softer this time, consuming, with so much tenderness it felt like her heart was swelling in her chest, nearly choking her.

"Don't let him touch you. Promise me."

"No." His kiss and his words left her nearly panting. "No, I won't."

With a sigh, he carefully, slowly released her wrists and stepped away from her. "Let's go before Mack starts telling everyone that I have a hard-on and I'm shouting about it."

Horrified by such a possibility, she asked, "He wouldn't, would he?"

"Hell yes, he would, if he thought it'd embarrass me. That is, he'd tell Zane and Cole. And they're the two I'd most prefer didn't know."

But when they stepped back into the bar, all three brothers stood there, grinning like magpies, and Allison knew Mack had already blabbed. Luckily, it was only Chase they seemed intent on teasing. But then Jack spoke up from behind them, drawing everyone's attention.

"Allison? What the hell's going on?"

She looked at Jack, silently begging for him not to start anything, but it was Chase who answered those thoughts, saying forcefully, "Forget it, honey," as he stepped forward. All three of his brothers crowded behind him.

Jack stiffened his spine. He was every bit as tall as Chase, topping six feet, but was Chase's exact opposite in every other way. While Chase was dark with golden brown eyes, Jack was blond with bright green eyes. They looked like two wolfhounds ready to bite each other. Allison was mortified.

"Cole, do something!"

He blinked at her, then turned to his brother. "Knock it off, Chase."

Both Chase and Jack ignored him. Cole shrugged at her, as if saying, *I tried.* But then he suggested, "At least make it private, Chase. You're embarrassing her."

Chase nodded agreement to that and turned to go back in the office. Jack followed him against Allison's protests.

Exasperated, Allison hurried in on Jack's heels, and shut the door behind her. "This is not necessary."

Chase said, "I think he disagrees."

In his most provoking tone, Jack said, "You're right, I do."

Trying desperately to salvage the moment, Allison said, "Jack, it's not even what you think."

Chase snorted. "Unless he's an idiot, it's exactly what he thinks."

Allison whirled to face him. "You promised, damn it!" Chase didn't even look at her, his attention fixed on Jack.

But he did say, "I promised to give you time to talk to him. But I didn't say anything about letting him yell at you."

"Allison?"

Jack sounded out of patience, and she turned to him again, saying in a whisper, "It was Rose's idea. I swear. I'll explain later . . ."

"Rose?" Suddenly Jack's expression relaxed and he even chuckled as he glanced at Chase with an amused look. "So you're letting Rose call the shots again, huh?" He shook his head, laughing at her.

Chase took an aggressive step forward. "Allison, maybe it's time you told me who the hell Rose is."

With a lift of his brows, Jack said, "I can explain, though I doubt you'll believe it any more than I do."

He was still amused, and seeing no hope for it, Allison decided she had nothing to lose. She frowned at both men. "Jack, you can forget our date tonight. In fact, you can forget any dates!"

Jack glared. Anger crowded his features, then a near panic. "Damn it, Allison . . ."

She crossed her arms over her chest.

Jack glanced at Chase, then narrowed his gaze on her face again. "I'll call you later when you've had a chance to calm down." And in a huff, he stormed out, slamming the door behind him.

Chase shook his head. Now that Jack was gone, he looked relaxed and under control again. His gaze lit on Allison, and he teased, "I thought you claimed he was a nice guy."

"And you!" She was practically fuming, she was so mad. Nothing had gone as expected, and she'd had more surprises tonight than one woman could bear. "I've decided you're not worth the trouble, no matter what Rose thinks!"

She turned to the door, ready to make a grand exodus, but Chase's hand flattened on it before she could get it open. Speaking close to her ear, he growled, "I don't get off till late tonight, so it'll have to be tomorrow morning. But we'll get together at ten to talk. Which is damned early for me, so I hope you appreciate the concession to my sleep."

"I won't—"

"We have a lot to discuss, and I think I'm showing a great deal of patience, all things considered."

She wanted to tell him to go to hell. She wanted to go hide somewhere, considering how horrible the evening had turned.

"But you won't, will you, honey?"

She turned the doorknob and he let the door open. As she stepped out, thoroughly defeated, she growled, "I suppose not. Good night, Chase."

"Ten o'clock, Allison. Don't make me wait."

Arrogant, obnoxious, controlling jerk . . .

She heard him laugh, and she groaned. Fleeing seemed her only option, and she did so quickly. But as she left the bar, she felt all four brothers watching her, and she knew, from here on out, nothing would be the same.

Chapter Three

Chase was distracted as he finished closing down the bar. It was almost two in the morning, and he and Zane were alone. Mack had taken off hours ago to catch some sleep before his morning classes, and Cole always left early these days, now that he had a wife waiting at home for him. Chase grinned, thinking about Sophie. She was awfully sweet, and the way she'd played Cole just before they were married was something he'd never forget, the stuff fantasies were made of. Cole hadn't stood a chance, and Chase considered him damn lucky to have her.

But thinking of Sophie and Cole reminded him of something that had been niggling at the back of his mind ever since Allison had stormed out of the bar, her thoughts confused and her frustration level high. Hell, his frustration was through the roof. He was still mildly aroused, even though she was gone. He couldn't get her out of his mind, and though he couldn't read her so clearly now that she wasn't close, he still got the occasional glimpse of her thoughts and it kept his desire on a keen edge.

Small talk with customers had been almost impossible tonight.

Zane came out of the back room, whistling. Out of all the brothers, he was the rowdiest. Zane seemed to have a little wildness in him that no one would ever be able to erase. Cole had never really tried, preferring just to temper that energy whenever possible. It had never bothered Chase before, but now, he kept thinking of how Allison had briefly considered Zane, and it bothered him a lot.

Zane looked up and caught Chase staring. The whistling stopped. "What'd I do?"

"Nothing. At least, I hope not."

Reaching for his coat off a hook in the hallway, snagging Chase's also, Zane started forward. "What does that mean?"

"I want to ask you something, Zane, and I want a straight answer, okay?"

Zane tossed Chase his coat, then propped his hands on his hips. "At twenty-four, don't you think I'm a little old for a lecture?"

"I wasn't going to lecture you."

"Oh." He grinned. "Well, good. Because I wasn't going to listen."

Chase perched on a bar stool and stared at his brother. "You remember back when Cole and Sophie first hooked up?"

"How could I forget?" Zane lifted himself onto the edge of the bar. "Hell, Cole was so damned amusing, I worked extra hours, neglecting my own business, just to get to watch him fumble around."

Chase grinned, too. "He did have a hard time of it, didn't he?"

"Aw, well, Sophie made it worth his while."

"You knew Allison back then, didn't you? I mean, even before Sophie and Cole hooked up." He'd sort of blurted that out, but he was getting edgier by the minute, prompted by some unknown discontent, like something was wrong, but he didn't know what.

Zane shrugged. "I know just about every woman in town, Allison included, but probably not the way you're thinking, judging by your frown." He grinned. "I asked her out, but she turned me down flat."

That surprised Chase. "She did?"

"Yeah, several times, in fact."

So Zane had asked her out more than once? He didn't like that. "You never said anything."

"Like you expected me to brag that I was turned out cold? Get real. Besides, from the way the two of you carried on today, I have to wonder if she wasn't hung up on you way back then. You can be damn blind when it comes to women, Chase."

"What's that supposed to mean?"

"It means a lot of women try to get your attention, but you don't take the bait."

Because they were nice, conservative women who

most likely wouldn't meet his appetites. He shook his head. "I date."

"Yeah, about five times a year." He snorted. "That's barely enough to keep a man alive. I figure every so often your libido takes over, and you cave. Other than that, you're a man of ice."

"Maybe I just don't like to spread myself so thin."

Zane chuckled. "You were sure spreading it around today. The way you corralled Allison into the back room reminded me of a stallion herding a mare. Not at all subtle."

Chase made a disgusted face and muttered, "Yeah, well, I don't know what got into me today." But even as he resolved to regain his iron control, his uneasiness grew, prompting him to leave. He stood up and pushed in the bar stool.

Zane slid off the bar and buttoned up his coat, preparing to follow Chase out. "If I'm not mistaken," Zane said, "I think it's called lust. And about time, I'd say."

Suddenly, Chase had to see Allison. The urge to go to her was overwhelming, as bad as the turbulent lust had been. He had to fight to keep from rushing out, making a fool of himself again. Only the fact that he didn't have her exact address held him back. He glanced at his brother and wanted to wince. Zane was giving him a rather knowing look.

"I don't suppose you know—"

Zane chuckled. "She lives on State Street, not too far from here. It's a big old cream-colored clapboard farmhouse, and you can't miss it because the roof sticks up way higher than any of the others."

Narrowing his eyes, Chase asked, "How do you know?"

"Well, I haven't been there wooing her, if that's what you're worried about. Besides, like I already told you, she wasn't interested in me. From what I understand, she inherited the house from an old spinster aunt. I helped out about a month ago when Cole and Sophie moved her in there."

"Thanks." Chase headed out the door, driven by some vague urgency he couldn't suppress. He tossed a quick look at Zane. "Lock up, will you?"

Zane blinked in astonishment. "You're not going over there now, are you?"

Chase didn't answer him. He didn't have time. Before he was completely through the door, he was flat-out running. He had to get to Allison. Why, he didn't know, but the panic was real, making his heart race and his jaw lock. Within minutes he was in his car, driving too fast, and just as he turned the corner on State Street, he was able to clearly hear her again, her every thought, her every word. And what he heard caused him an unreasonable amount of anger.

It's not that I mind you being here, really. It just makes me a little nervous because it's not something I'm used to. Especially when I'm trying to bathe. Couldn't you go away for just a little while until I finish up?

Someone was with her while she was trying to take a bath? And he refused to leave?

Allison's nervousness was real, flooding his senses. In fact, her nervousness bordered on fear, and Chase was suddenly so enraged, a red haze crowded his vision. He parked his car in the driveway with a screech, thankful that she didn't have any near neighbors on the older, quiet street. He jumped out of his car, stormed up the paved entry walk to the immense wooden front porch decorated with a huge jack-o'-lantern and some cornstalks, but as he started to pound on the door, he noticed a narrow window to the side of the front room was opened just a crack. In late October, the evening air was cool enough that all the windows should have been shut, especially considering she was a woman alone, on a dead-end street, and it was nearing three in the morning. His instincts kicked in.

Chase crept to the window and slid through it silently. Once inside, he closed and latched it, then looked around. He seemed to be in a parlor of sorts with carved, embroidered furniture, plenty of crocheted doilies, and lamps with fabric shades. Even though the room was dim, enough light came from the hall chandelier to let him clearly see the flocked, flowery wallpaper. He felt like he'd stepped back in time.

The house was dated enough to boggle his senses.

He explored cautiously, leaving the parlor and sneaking a peek into the adjacent rooms, one a library lined with dark, heavy wooden shelves, the other a more modern family room with a TV and overstuffed couch. The rooms were long and narrow with arched doorways and heavy drapes, and they opened to a central hall. At the end of the hall he could see a spacious country kitchen, and next to it, a small bath with black and pink ceramic tile on the floor and walls. Right inside the front door, to the left, was an incredible winding, ornate wooden staircase that led to the second floor.

Hearing a creak from above, Chase looked up. From the sounds of it, Allison was up there talking quietly with someone.

Jealousy, hot and dark, raced over his nerve endings, along with the need to protect. He could still feel her unease, and when he found out who was responsible, they'd be sorry. He crept upstairs. Each damn step seemed to groan beneath his weight, the typical speakings of an old house. The urgency suddenly quieted, replaced by annoyance—not his annoyance, so maybe it was hers?

The stairway ended with another hall. At one end was a large, narrow, diamond-paned window showing the dark night beyond, with two bedrooms, one on either side of the hall, in between. At the other end was a master bedroom and a larger bathroom, and that's where Chase headed. He could hear Allison clearly now, and his brows drew tight. Who the hell was she talking to? He paused outside the bathroom door and listened.

"Really, the idea is ludicrous. I can't sleep with Chase when he doesn't truly want me. And before you say it, you know it's just that darn trick you played on me, letting him read my mind, that has him reacting right now." She groaned. "When I think of all the stuff I imagined, it's *so* embarrassing. If it wasn't for that, he'd still think I was invisible.

"Oh, no. That dress had nothing to do with it, though I

admit I liked wearing it. It made me feel sexy, whether it actually worked or not." She laughed slightly. "The underthings were great. I loved them."

Chase peeked around the open door, his eyes narrowed. But there was no one in the room. Just Allison. Naked. In a tub of bubbles.

Her blonde hair was pinned on top of her head, little ringlets falling free, and her bare arms rested along the sides of the free-standing, claw-footed white porcelain tub. Her eyes were closed and her soft mouth smiled.

She sighed deeply, and one small pink nipple appeared above the froth of bubbles. Chase stared, mesmerized, unable to speak, barely able to breathe.

"I appreciate your efforts, guys, I really do. But I'm not at all sure I can go through with it, so let's just forget about Chase, okay?"

Chase stepped completely into the bathroom, his body pulsing with need. "Let's don't."

With a loud squeal and a lot of thrashing and splashing, Allison turned to see him. She knelt in the tub, her hands crossed over her chest, her eyes wide. She didn't have her glasses on and she stared at him hard.

Automatically, he said, "It's me, Chase."

"I know who it is! What in the world are you doing in here! This is my bathroom. How did you get in?"

He opened his mouth, but she interrupted him, shouting, "Never mind that! Just get out!"

He frowned. "Who were you talking to, Allison?"

She groaned. "Oh God, I don't believe this. I don't believe this, it isn't happening. . . . "

"Are you going to get hysterical on me?"

"Yes!"

She glared up at him, her big blue eyes rounded owlishly as she tried to see him without her glasses. She was still crouched in the tub, the bubbles reaching her hips, and her hands somewhat inadequate to completely cover her breasts. She was small, but the soft, white, rounded flesh showing from around her crossed arms was very distracting. And here she'd thought herself lacking . . .

Chase cleared his throat. "I'll step out in the hall, but make it quick. You have some explaining to do."

He walked out and dropped back against the wall, his eyes closed, his stomach muscles pulled tight. He'd left the bathroom door open and heard her growl, "Don't you dare peek!"

He just shook his head. "Hurry up, will you? My patience is pretty thin right now."

There was a flurry of splashing and mumbled cursing, then Allison, leaving a trail of water, padded barefoot out of the bathroom, an ancient embroidered chenille robe wrapped tightly around her, her glasses once again in place. Bubbles clung to the end of a ringlet over her right ear, and her throat and upper chest were still wet. The robe covered her, but the neckline dipped low enough that he could just make out the edging of white lawn underwear. Again, something vintage? When she stomped over to face him, the robe parted over her legs and he saw old-fashioned drawers that just reached her knees. His heart rate accelerated, but she quickly pulled the robe closed again.

She greeted him with a pointed finger poked into his chest. "How dare you barge in here, intruding on my privacy!"

Chase grabbed her hand, pulled her close, and gave in to the need to kiss her. She was still warm and damp, and she smelled like flowers. He held her head between his hands, urging her to her tiptoes, then kissed her long and soft and deep, eating at her mouth, capturing her tongue and drawing it into his own mouth. She groaned softly, and the hallway lights blinked happily around them.

"What the hell?" Chase looked up, but there was no one there. "What happened to the lights?"

Her hands remained fisted in his shirt, her expression dazed, her lips still parted. Around panting breaths, she said, "Hmmm?"

"The lights blinked, almost like a strobe."

"Oh." Very slowly, she pushed herself away from him, then straightened her glasses. She looked around with a frown. "It's an old house. The wiring is sometimes . . . temperamental."

Chase stared at her, saw her trying to gather herself, and shook his head. "Damn, honey, you look sexy as hell." He lifted an edge of the robe. "What have you got on under there?"

Her eyes widened and she clutched the robe. "Chase, stop it."

He stepped toward her, and she backed up. "Who were you talking to, Allison?"

"Myself?"

He shook his head. "I'm not believing it. Try again."

"You can see there's no one here."

"The window downstairs is open."

"It is?"

"Yes." He couldn't quite keep his gaze on her face, not after seeing her practically naked—and liking very much what he saw. He was so hard he hurt, and his imagination was going wild, thinking of all the things he'd like to do to her. "Don't you think that's a little risky, being you're here alone?"

"I didn't open the window, Chase."

His brows pulled down again, because she sounded totally unconcerned as she said that. Then she added, "What are you doing here, anyway? It's kind of late for a social call, isn't it?"

Why was he here? Damn, how could he tell her he'd been worried? That he'd felt something was wrong? He started to say just that when suddenly the lights flickered again, almost going crazy, and seconds later there was a crash downstairs. Chase grabbed Allison's arm, shoved her into the bathroom, and shouted, "Lock the door," before rushing down the stairs. His instincts were screaming an alarm, and he didn't wait to see if Allison would do as she was told. He just took it for granted that she would.

Bounding down the steps two at a time, an awkward task given the lights danced wildly, he reached the bottom in just a few seconds. He heard another noise, like a distant thump, and followed the sound into the parlor where he'd entered. As he bolted into the room, he saw that the wind had picked up a heavy curtain hanging over the window he'd climbed through minutes before.

He distinctly recalled closing and locking that window. Someone had just left the house.

He moved silently across the room, his gaze searching everywhere, checking out every corner. But the fact that the window was open when he got here, and then opened again, led him to believe someone had been in the house and had now left. Otherwise, how did the window get open, when it locked from the inside and he himself had just locked it?

He turned to go back to check on Allison and ran right into her. She would have landed on her sweet behind if he hadn't caught her upper arms and steadied her.

"Dammit! I thought I told you to stay upstairs." He wasn't at all pleased that she'd disregarded his orders.

She glared right back at him. "This is my house. And besides, I knew nothing was wrong. A house this old makes all kind of noises. There was no reason to be alarmed."

He wanted to shake her. This propensity he had for losing his temper and rattling her teeth was disturbing in the extreme. He'd never really lost his temper with a woman in his life, and he'd sure as hell never taken to shaking them. In fact, he took extra pleasure in maintaining icy control, in holding the reins of command gently. It was a big turn-on for him.

But Allison made him forget all that.

He leaned down close until their noses almost touched

and said in a low growl, "Someone was just in your house."

She scoffed.

"Dammit, Allison, how much proof do you need? When I got here, the window was open, which was how I got in, by the way. But then I closed and locked it. Only now it's wide open again and a table's knocked over and there's a broken dish on the floor. So unless you're going to tell me this house is inhabited by ghosts, you'll have to admit—"

"It is."

Her blurted statement and small wince had him verbally backing up. "It is, what?"

She drew a long breath and he felt her shoring up her courage, preparing herself, then she whispered, "It is inhabited by ghosts."

He had the horrifying suspicion she was serious. "Come again?"

With another deep breath, she looked up at him, then said, "The house comes with two ghosts. If you'd like, I could introduce you to Rose and Burke."

Chapter Four

Allison waited anxiously while Chase did no more than stare down at her. He looked skeptical and a little concerned. Finally he said, "Are you all right?"

"Chase." She took his hand and led him to a couch, forced him to sit, then turned on a few lamps. He was right. There was a knocked-over table and a broken dish. She frowned and said to the room at large, "Very funny, Rose. If you wanted to scare him off, you're succeeding."

"Uh, Allison—"

She waved him to silence, propped her hands on her hips over the soft robe, and looked around. "Well, Rose? You got him here, so the least you can do is come out and show yourself. What? No more blinking lights? No more parlor tricks?"

Nothing. She frowned again, then glanced worriedly at

Chase. He watched her like she'd grown an extra head. She raked a hand through her disheveled bangs, somewhat embarrassed. Darned aggravating ghosts.

"Uh, listen honey." Chase spoke very gently, very softly. He patted the couch cushion beside him. "Why don't you sit down here for a minute and I'll go see if I can get us something to drink."

When she shook her head at him, he left the couch to stand beside her, trying to urge her to the seat he'd just vacated.

She made a sound of disgust. "It must have been Burke. Rose is pretty nice most of the time, though she's sometimes a little crotchety. But Burke"—and here she raised her voice to make certain he'd hear—"can be a real pain!"

A cold draft filled the room, making her shiver. Chase looked around, then chafed her arms roughly to warm her. "Do you have another window open?"

"No, that's just Burke. He hates it when I insult him."

He eyed her dubiously. "On second thought, I don't want to leave you alone. Why don't we go into the kitchen together?"

Allison laughed. "Chase, you can read my mind. Can't you tell I'm not making it up?"

She might have been made of fine china, the way he now handled her. "I can tell you think you're actually talking to ghosts." He put a rather brotherly arm around her and urged her into the hallway. "But don't worry about that right now. Let's just go to the kitchen, and while you get something to drink, I'll check the other windows. There's definitely one open. Your hair is blowing around."

She lifted one hand and shoved a loose curl behind her ear. Her gaze searched every corner of the hallway and all the rooms as she passed, but Rose and Burke were hiding for some damn reason.

"Shhh. It's okay. Here, just sit a minute while I go check the windows and doors."

Allison sighed. "I'm not going to break, Chase."

"I know that." Then he very carefully smoothed her hair in a way that reminded her of a puppy being petted. "I'll be right back, honey." He jogged out of the room.

Allison looked around her empty kitchen and wanted to scream. She said aloud, "Well, I hope you're happy now. He thinks I'm loony. And I seriously doubt discrediting my mental faculties is going to inspire him to lust."

A warm breeze blew over her, taking away the chill. "Thanks. I hate being cold." Then she covered her face. "Guys, this is never going to work. I know you thought it would, but—"

Chase walked back in, a severe frown on his face. She knew he wanted to say something about her conversation with ghosts that he didn't believe in, but he refrained. "Everything on this floor is closed up and locked. I didn't check upstairs yet, but the breeze seems to be gone."

She eyed him carefully. "Of course it is."

"Actually, for such an old house, the locks are pretty secure. Were they changed recently?"

A safe enough topic, she decided. "My aunt, who I inherited the house from, had never married. She lived alone here, and it made her nervous. I think she updated the locks every two years, and she had them all checked regularly." Allison added with a grin, "Living with ghosts made her really nervous. She didn't accept it nearly as well as I have."

Pulling a chair up close so that their knees almost touched, Chase seated himself. He took her hands and stared her in the eye. "Forget your ghosts for a second, okay? You have a real problem."

"What?"

"Honey, I opened the front door and right off the edge of your porch, there are footprints in the dirt. Big prints. Not yours." He glanced down at her small bare feet, then with another frown, added, "Someone went out the window in a hurry, then leaped off the porch. Not a damn ghost, a flesh-and-blood man. Someone was here in the house with you."

Every small hair on her neck stood at attention while she stared frozen, straight into Chase Winston's dark, serious gaze. So that was why she'd been feeling so nervous and why Burke and Rose had invaded her bath.

Chase made an impatient sound. "Allison, I don't understand—"

She waved him to silence, finally ungluing her tongue from the roof of her mouth. "Don't you see? Usually they respect my privacy. They're around, but they don't intrude—at least, not much—and certainly not when I'm changing clothes or bathing. But tonight they kept hanging around the bathroom, and even though they're just ghosts, it really did make me nervous. I mean, I was *naked.*"

Chase blinked slowly. "Yeah, I noticed."

She ignored that and continued to reason things out. "At least, I thought that was why I was nervous. But now I think it must have been the intruder. Rose wanted me to be nervous, to understand . . . Oh God." The enormity of it hit her. "Someone was in my house!"

Chase bit the side of his mouth, and she could feel him thinking, sorting out what he'd say, how to address what he considered sheer fancy on her part. Finally, he lifted a hand to her cheek and tried a small smile. "Honey, you're telling me there're ghosts in your house, but that doesn't bother you. It's only the idea of a real man—"

"Oh, for pity's sake, Chase. You're a real man, and I'm not afraid of you. But then you don't sneak in through windows!"

His thumb brushed over her temple, distracting her. "Actually, I did."

She struggled to get her mind back on track and away from that big, warm thumb. "You know what I mean. You came because you were worried about me. Hey! That's it. Just like Rose transferred my thoughts to you at the bar, she must have let you know about the intruder. Can you just imagine what might have happened if you hadn't shown up?" She shuddered in very real fear. "I guess I owe Rose my thanks."

Chase appeared to be considering everything she'd said. "Okay, let's deal with that first. Why did you leave the window unlocked?"

Allison huffed. "I'm not an idiot, Chase."

"But . . ."

"I didn't leave the window open," she insisted. "And before you even think it, Rose or Burke would never do such a thing."

Chase lifted his gaze to the ceiling. "I wasn't going to suggest they might."

"Oh, that's right. You don't believe in them."

"What I believe is that someone broke in here, and they got in through the window. It didn't look to me like they'd broken in, rather they just opened the window because it wasn't locked."

"But they're always locked."

"This one wasn't."

She pondered that. How could such a thing have happened? The lights flickered again and both she and Chase looked up at the old Tiffany-style chandelier hanging over the kitchen table. Allison pursed her mouth. "See there? I think Rose or Burke have an idea, but because they're fickle and determined on their own course, they won't just come right out and tell me about it."

"They, uh, talk to you, do they?"

"I don't know if I'd call it talking. I mean, I hear them, but I don't know that they're actually saying anything. You understand?"

His expression was ironic. "Certainly. What's not to understand?"

She narrowed her eyes at him. "You claim to hear me when I'm not talking to you."

"But you're not a ghost."

"So?"

He opened his mouth, then closed it.

Satisfied that he'd listen, Allison stood to pace. "The thing is, they didn't come right out and tell me, but they did do the next best thing, which was to send you here." Then she glanced at him again, and the look on his face didn't encourage her. "I'm sorry you're out so late tonight. You must be exhausted after working all day."

Chase looked like he either wanted to strangle her or lay her out on the table and do wickedly sexy things to her. She gulped, knowing which she'd prefer.

"I know which I'd prefer, too," he said pointedly, staring at the way her robe gaped at her throat, "but I think we need to get a few things straightened out here first."

"Like my sanity?"

"I'm not suggesting you're insane—"

She began pacing again. "I'm not confused or making it up or imagining it, either. You saw the lights. Well, they do that to show they're agitated or excited. Which proves Rose and Burke are real. Or, that is, they're as real as ghosts can be."

"Because of some flickering lights? Honey, I hate to tell you, but this old house probably has lots of glitches in it. It's ancient enough to be falling apart. Damn, just look at the kitchen."

There was a touch of criticism in his tone as he looked around at the kitchen she loved so much. She saw his gaze linger on the old-fashioned free-standing sink with the hand pump at one end. Protectiveness for her house rose like a tide within her. "I happen to love my house."

He shook his head. "It looks to me like it needs some major fixing up."

No sooner did the words leave his mouth than a large plastic bowl filled with fruit toppled off the top of the rounded refrigerator to pummel his head. Chase jumped up, cursing and looking around, his body tensed. A plump orange rolled across the floor, stopping when it hit Allison's bare foot. She bent to pick it up. Several apples, a banana, and a few grapes were littered around him. Chase's look of insult was replaced by disbelief. "How the hell did that happen?"

"Burke?" When Chase scowled at her, she shrugged. "He loves this house. He bought it for Rose after they married, sort of a little love nest, though in this day and age the house would be considered huge. But anyway, Burke doesn't take kindly to someone insulting it, so if I were you, I'd be careful what I said."

"Dammit, Allison, that's ridiculous. Besides, I wasn't insulting the house, only commenting on the obvious."

"I guess Burke didn't like your comments."

He shook his head. "The floor slants, that's all. Even the walls are crooked. The bowl was bound to topple sooner or later. It was just coincidence that it happened to fall on me just then."

"If you say so."

He crossed his arms over his chest and leaned back against the refrigerator. It was such an old, squat appliance, his head was above the top now that he was standing. "I'd just gotten off work when I had the feeling you were upset about something. What are you doing up this late, honey?"

She fidgeted, wondering how much to tell him, but one look at his face and she knew he'd just read her mind if she attempted to hold anything back. Still, it was so embarrassing . . .

"Out with it, babe. All this hedging will just make it worse."

She bit her lip, knowing he was right but resenting him all the same. She should have had at least until tomorrow to get her thoughts together. "I couldn't sleep. I kept . . . kept thinking about you and that you'd kissed me and how wonderful it was." His gaze darkened, and his look became almost tactile. She shivered again, this time in reaction. Then she added softly, "And I kept thinking that it was all wrong."

His shoulders tensed while he looked her over from head to foot. "What's wrong about it?"

He sounded gentle again, but determined. Allison cleared her throat. "You don't really want me, Chase. I think Rose has done something to you to make you think you do. It's kind of a long story—"

"Do you have to be at work early tomorrow?"

"No. Not until noon. Sophie's opening it up tomorrow."

"So, we have plenty of time for you to explain this long story to me then, right?"

Unfortunately, she couldn't think of any reason to refuse him.

He smiled. "First, I think we need to call the police about the break-in."

"No!" Even as she said it, the lights flickered crazily.

Chase's expression hardened as he glared at the lights. "Allison, a man was in your house. If I hadn't shown up when I did, you might have been hurt—"

"It was probably just a prankster, you know, a kid messing around because of Halloween."

"It isn't Halloween yet."

"But you know that sort of thing always starts early. And now he's gone, and I'll be sure to double-check the windows every night from now on, so there's really no reason to worry. And no reason to bother the police."

Chase wasn't an easy man to fool. He leaned over and trapped Allison against the butcher block counter. "What's going on, Allison? Why the aversion to the police?"

With him this close, she could see how thick his eyelashes were, could smell him . . .

"Dammit, forget my eyelashes! I'm not trying to seduce you. At least, not yet. I want to know why you won't call the police."

She looked at his incredibly sexy mouth, saw it quirk slightly, then blurted, "Rose and Burke hate having people rummage through the place. It makes them nervous."

His eyebrows shot up incredulously. "Nervous ghosts?"

"Well . . . yeah."

Straightening again, he rubbed the back of his neck. But Allison's gaze dipped over his body—so gorgeous—

and her attention got stuck on the fact that he was hard again. His jeans fit him snugly and the soft, faded material hugged that part of his body, making heat explode inside her, her stomach twist in need.

He groaned. "You're making me crazy, babe."

"I . . . I think you need to see something." She gulped. "Before we go any farther, I mean."

He leveled a look on her, hot and expectant.

"It's . . . it's upstairs. In my bedroom."

He smiled.

Shifting nervously, Allison said, "I'll just go up and get dressed, and then I'll show you—"

Chase took her arms and half lifted her off her feet. He shook his head. "I like you just the way you are," he whispered, then kissed her gently, showing a lot of restraint. "You look sexy as hell with your hair pinned up, that soft robe giving me sneak peeks every now and again of that sexy cotton underwear, and your glasses perched on your nose that way."

She clutched the robe shut to rid the possibility of any further sneak peeks, then asked with a squeak, "You like the corset cover and drawers?"

"What I've seen of them, yes. Do you intend to model for me?"

Her brain went blank at the idea of dropping her robe for him. He grinned, and she quickly asked, "You think my glasses are sexy, too?"

Pulling her up flush against him, he said, "I think everything about you is sexy, and your damned ghosts don't have a thing to do with it."

"But . . . my glasses?"

He smiled again. "Let's go upstairs, honey. I think I've waited long enough."

Eyes wide, she said, "But I have to show you something before you start getting . . . um . . . amorous."

One large hand stroked her waist. "I'm already amorous."

"Chase . . ."

"You can show me what you think is so important, but it won't make any difference."

Allison turned to nervously lead the way to her bedroom. Under her breath she muttered, "Wanna bet?"

But Chase heard her, and he rewarded her sarcasm with a small smack on the bottom, then left his hand there, caressing. It took all her resolution to climb the stairs. And once they were in her bedroom, she avoided looking at him, knowing if she did, she'd jump his bones and they'd never get around to the important stuff.

Hurrying to her nightstand, she opened the top drawer and pulled out an old, red leather-bound journal. She thrust it toward Chase. "I haven't shown this to anyone else. But I think you should read at least part of it before we do anything."

He stared at the book, stared at her, and then stared at the huge, four-poster mahogany bed, and he sighed. Taking the book, he said, "I sure don't have any complaints on your bed, honey. It looks plenty big enough, and the four posters are giving me some interesting ideas." He looked at her, searched her face, then asked, "How about you?"

She gulped. "How about me, what?"

Nodding toward the bed, he asked, "Any interesting ideas?"

She could just tell he was reading her mind, and what was in it was too explicit for words. Ideas? Heck yes, she had ideas, and all of them had him naked for her pleasure.

Chase grinned, then sat on the edge of the mattress. "Not exactly the images I'm having, but we'll work on it." He held up the book. "Just as soon as I finish this."

He settled himself comfortably with a pillow behind his head, at his leisure. With one last glance at Allison, standing there with her mouth open, he murmured, "You're just damn lucky that I'm a fast reader."

And there was a promise to those words that had her catching her breath and shivering from the inside out. "I think I'll go get us those drinks we kept talking about."

"And something to eat? I'm starved."

"I'll see what I can dredge up." She fled the room, unable to look at him as he read the damning words in the journal that told what his purpose tonight would be.

Chapter Five

Allison made four peanut butter and jelly sandwiches and poured two large glasses of milk. Rose and Burke were mysteriously absent, and she had the feeling they were watching Chase read. She felt so bad for them, she sincerely hoped Chase would be able to accommodate what needed to be done.

She'd been downstairs over twenty minutes and decided putting it off any longer was just plain cowardly. Still, she dragged her feet as she went up the steps. Sure enough, when she entered the bedroom, she saw both Burke and Rose hovering over Chase, who still had his nose buried in the journal. Now, however, he'd taken off his boots and had his sock-covered feet crossed at the ankle, with one long arm behind his head. He was so tall, his stretched-out form went from the head of the bed to the very end, when she often felt lost in the incredible size of it.

When she stopped in the doorway, his gaze lifted to her, but otherwise he didn't move. His expression was speculative and lazy.

She cleared her throat, ignoring Rose and Burke. "I, ah, made you some peanut butter and jelly sandwiches. I hope that's okay?"

He laid the open book on the mattress, spine out, and rolled to his side, propping his head on a fist. He still didn't say anything.

"Um, interesting reading?"

"Very."

"How far did you get?"

"Far enough to know now what it is you want me to do."

"Oh." Her face heated and she inched closer to hand him the tray of sandwiches.

Chase set it in the middle of the bed, then patted the other side, indicating she should sit down with him. Very tentatively, she slid onto the mattress. She smoothed the robe over her outstretched legs, kept her back straight, and settled her hands in her lap. Just to give herself something to do, she picked up half a sandwich and took a small bite while staring at her bare feet.

Chase, knowing exactly how nervous she was, waited until she had her mouth full to say, "I'm supposed to be your *grand passion*, right?"

And Allison promptly choked.

Chase made no move to assist her, instead picking up

his own half of a sandwich and eating it in two bites while watching her struggle for a breath.

Allison wheezed and snuffled and when she could finally talk without rasping, she asked carefully, "Did you get to the part about the jewels?"

"Um-hmm. Burke gave Rose jewels as a sign of his love, but when he died with the measles, and she, too, got sick from never leaving his bedside, nursing him until his death, she hid them in the house so none of her damned relatives could steal them. They were, in Rose's words, a symbol of *grand passion*, and neither she nor Burke wanted them getting into the wrong hands."

Allison toyed nervously with a curl that had escaped her hairpins to hang to her shoulder. "That's right. And in fact, Rose did die of the same thing, only she went a little faster than Burke did because she was already so weak from taking care of him." She glanced at him. "Isn't that sad?"

Chase shrugged. "I suppose a wife who loved a husband would do exactly that. Or vice versa."

His answer obviously pleased the ghosts, considering how the lights twinkled happily and a warm glow seemed to fill the room. This time, Chase didn't even seem to notice the lights. All his attention was on Allison.

She cleared her throat. "They're not really a symbol of everlasting love or anything like that." She peeked at him through her lashes. "But Rose and Burke at least want the female relative who inherits the jewels to be . . . um . . . *passionate*. So far, there's been no one they feel fits the bill, so they've kept the jewels hidden, and they've been stuck here, not wanting to leave until the legacy of the jewels has been passed on."

"So it's an actual legacy of passion?"

Allison wasn't sure if he was teasing or not or if he believed any of it or not. His expression gave nothing away. "When they both died, they left the house to one of Burke's sisters, Maryann. But Maryann's young husband had already died, and she never remarried. Her only daughter, Cybil, inherited next, but she never even seemed interested in the idea of marriage. Rose didn't consider either of them women of . . . um . . . *fire*. Like herself. The women didn't believe in the ghosts and weren't that interested in men. It's Rose's worry about the jewels getting into the wrong hands that's keeping them both gounded on this plane instead of finding peace."

Chase ate another sandwich and drank half his milk, still looking at her in that watchful, curious way, as if waiting to pounce on her. "Rose didn't have any other relatives that suited her?"

Allison shook her head, and two more curls tumbled free. She tried to stick them back up, but somewhere along the way, she'd lost a pin or two. Chase's gaze skimmed her hair, lazy and hot, then came back to her face.

"I, ah . . . no, Rose's relatives all thought she'd married beneath herself, and most of them disowned her. That's why the jewels were so important. Burke had to work really hard to afford something for her that he thought her family would find adequate. But Rose never wanted anything material from him. Still, he bought her this house and the jewels and—"

"And they had a very passionate marriage."

Allison ducked her head. "Yes." Then in a smaller voice, she added, "That was all Rose ever expected from him. But he was an entrepreneur, and it wasn't long before they were actually doing pretty well. Rose had always believed in him, so she wasn't surprised. And it didn't make her love him more. And by then her family all wanted her back, but she was devoted solely to Burke and didn't want to associate with a family that hadn't accepted him based on the wonderful man he was rather than his material worth."

The last sandwich was gone, wolfed down by Chase. She'd only eaten a half. Chase finished his milk, then set the whole tray aside on the nightstand. He reached for Allison, and she stiffened, both in excitement and wary nervousness. She squeezed her eyes shut.

Chase paused, his hand now gently rubbing her arm. "I take it you're willing to fulfill the role of the passionate heir?"

Not quite meeting his gaze, she said, "Rose thinks I would suffice, though truth is, I've never considered myself a particularly passionate woman."

"No?" His fingers trailed up and down her arm, then across her throat.

Allison swallowed hard. "You'd probably find out soon enough, considering things are progressing right along here, but I'm actually still a . . . a virgin."

Chase froze, then with a growl he dropped back on the

bed and covered his eyes with a forearm. "I don't damn well believe this."

Allison peered over at him. He seemed to be in pain, his body taut, his mouth a firm line, his jaw locked. "Chase, are you all right?"

His laugh wasn't at all humorous. "A damned virgin," he muttered.

"Well, I'd hardly consider myself damned. I just never met anyone . . . um, except you . . . that I wanted to get all that involved with. Sexually I mean. And being as you weren't interested . . ."

"This is incredible. A *virgin*."

"You don't need to drive it into the ground."

Just that quick, Chase was over her, causing her to yelp in surprise before her breath was completely stolen away by the look in his eyes and the pressure of his wide chest over hers. He caught her hands in one of his and raised them over her head, effectively pinning her in place so she could do no more than blink. Through clenched teeth, he muttered, "Do you have any idea what I wanted to do to you?"

She opened her mouth but could only squeak.

Chase gently smoothed her hair away from her face, the careful touch in direct contrast to how he held her and the roughness of his tone. "You know so little about me, sweetheart."

Suddenly the lights turned dazzling bright, making them both squint against the glare. Allison turned her head to look in the corner at Rose—and her mouth fell open in shock. "Oh my God."

Chase shielded his eyes with a hand and barked, "What?"

She turned back to him, so surprised even the light couldn't bother her. "Is it true?"

"Is what true, damn it?"

"What Rose just said."

"I didn't hear her say a damn thing. Are you telling me the ghosts are here with us now?"

He couldn't see them. Allison registered that fact and wondered how she'd ever convince him. Then just as quickly she realized that if what Rose claimed about him was true, he probably wouldn't need much convincing.

Chase pressed his chest closer, effectively pulling her from her thoughts. With a near sneer, he asked, "And what exactly is it that Rose has said about me?"

She almost couldn't utter the words. It took two swallows, and a great deal of effort to whisper, "She says you're . . . you're kinky."

"Kinky!"

Allison nodded. "She says you like to . . . to dominate in bed." Chase's expression was almost comical in his disbelief. "She says that's why you're so choosy about who you sleep with, why you ignored me, because you didn't think I'd get into sex games with you or that I wouldn't indulge your preferences for a little bondage and—"

Chase laid a hand over her mouth, halting the flow of words. He whispered, as if he didn't want anyone else to hear, "There really are ghosts?"

Allison nodded.

The look of disbelief left his face to be replaced by outrage. He glared and thrust himself away from her, rolling off the bed and onto his feet in one quick, fluid movement. He searched the room, but the lights were dim again and Rose and Burke were hiding. Chase turned his accusing gaze on Allison, who hadn't moved a single muscle. She was still too fascinated by the idea of being at Chase's sexual mercy. She didn't know exactly what he'd do or how much mercy he'd have, but she was more than a little anxious to find out.

"Oh no you don't! Don't start trying to distract me again with sex." He pointed a finger at her. "You expected me to make love to you tonight, and you knew all along they'd be watching? You set me up as entertainment for them? Rose and Burke can't just be normal ghosts, oh no, they have to be damned voyeur ghosts!"

A pillow shot off the bed to hit Chase square in the face. He slapped it aside, but another took its place. Chase cursed and said, "Oh great. Now I've pissed off a ghost! It doesn't get much better than this, does it, Allison!"

Still lying there, feeling a lot more confident about the situation now, Allison grinned and said, "Then you believe in them?"

Running an agitated hand through his hair, Chase said, "Why not? It makes as much sense as anything else."

She looked ready to giggle. Chase realized he was behaving in an absurd way. There was Allison, spread out on a bed, looking so damned ripe and ready it made his teeth ache. And he was provoking ghosts.

It also dawned on him that she didn't seem overly repelled by the idea of him dominating her. In fact, if he was reading her right—and he knew he was—she was intrigued. *Well, how about that.*

Another pillow hit him.

"I think Rose wants you to apologize. She said she kept her eyes closed whenever Burke made love to her, so she sure as certain doesn't have any urge to watch you."

A reluctant smile curved his mouth. The uniqueness of the situation was finally starting to sink in. "She said that, did she?"

"Yes." Allison hesitated, then added, "But Burke says it isn't true, that she used to devour him with her eyes when they made love. He says Rose has the most beautiful, expressive eyes in the whole world."

Despite himself, Chase was touched by the sentimental words. *Ghosts.* And not just any ghosts, but passionate ghosts who joked and teased and loved. Who would have believed it? Allison had to be telling the truth because how else could she have known? And the damned pillows had literally flown off the bed without her help. She'd done no more than lay there, watching him. Waiting.

In a way, he was grateful, because Rose and Burke had given him Allison. Without their interference, he never would have seen the depths of her, and seeing her now, so anxious to take part in everything he wanted to do with her, he couldn't imagine not being with her.

He stepped over closer to the bed. "Tell me something, honey. Did you think to try this with Jack?"

She wrinkled her nose but apparently felt there was no point in lying. "I needed to do something passionate so

Burke and Rose could move on. They don't mind being here, but they're not settled. Only they didn't want me with Jack—and I have to admit I'm glad. He's a nice guy, despite how he acted at your bar, and he's been very considerate, very helpful to me. But I couldn't quite get into the idea of . . . of . . ."

Chase felt his heart swell at her pink cheeks and stammering tone. Very gently, he said, "You couldn't imagine being passionate with him?"

She nodded, then added in a whisper, "I tried to think about him that way, but it always ended up being you in my fantasies. And somehow Rose just sort of knew that. She insisted I should go after you, even though I told her it was useless. She even selected the stuff I'd wear—"

"Ah, that killer dress from yesterday?"

She nodded. "Rose found it in the attic."

"Was it hers?"

"No. She told me she really likes this modern, shorter style though." Allison smiled. "To Rose, it seems really risqué."

He lifted a brow and looked her over slowly. "To me, too."

"Really?" She gulped, then forged on. "Rose even picked out the stuff I'm wearing now, but at the time, I didn't know you'd ever see me in it."

He knelt on the bed beside her and without a word, unknotted the fabric belt to her robe to pull it open. He stared down at the soft-as-silk cotton chemise and drawers. There was a flawless rose crocheted on the neckline of the chemise right above a row of tiny shell buttons, and more roses on the front of each leg. The drawers closed up in front with a wide, intriguing flap—big enough for a man's hand. Chase breathed hard. "You can tell Rose I heartily approve."

Allison smiled. "You just told her yourself."

He stared down at her soft breasts, her small nipples hard and straining against the cotton material. He felt his nostrils flare, felt a twisting in his guts. Without lifting his gaze, he said, "Beat it, guys. Allison and I have some business to attend to."

The lights dimmed so that only a soft glow touched the bed, then a slight warm breeze passed over him and he knew Burke and Rose had given them privacy. He wasted no more time. Straddling her hips, he stared down at her body, at the way her chest rose and fell with her deep breaths. He unbuttoned his shirt and shrugged it off.

Allison groaned at the sight of his bare chest and started to reach for him. He smiled and caught her hands.

"No, I have a certain way I like to do things, sweetheart. And seeing as we'll be doing this a lot—"

"We will?"

"Oh yeah. Definitely. So we might as well start out right." He pulled her into a sitting position and removed her glasses, tossing them aside, then stripped the robe off her shoulders. Holding her wide gaze, he pulled the soft, chenille belt out of the belt loops.

He could feel her trembling, both alarmed and excited. "Don t ever be afraid of me, Allison," he ordered quietly. She licked her lips, eyeing that soft belt, then nodded.

"Good girl." Her acceptance pleased and provoked him. "Now, lie back down."

She was practically panting, her eyes unblinking, her lips parted. Chase couldn't help but smile at her. "Put your arms over your head, as far as you can. Try to reach the top of the bed."

She gulped, but she slowly did as he ordered. Blood rushed through his veins at her compliance. And better still, he could feel her excitement, almost as great as his own. It was like she was his exact match, a perfect soul mate, and his body and mind recognized that fact, making all the feelings more acute, more important.

Taking his time, making the anticipation build, he held her wrists together and looped the belt around them, then tied it to one of the sturdy posts at the top of the bed. When he was confident that the knot would hold, he trailed his fingers down her bare arms to her armpits, then over her collar bone. She shivered slightly, twisting, and he whispered, "No, don't move."

She stilled instantly.

He eyed her taut form. "Are you uncomfortable?"

"No."

That was the tiniest voice he'd ever heard from her, and he recognized the aroused tone. He touched the rose on her bodice. "I'm going to look at your naked breasts now, Allison."

She started to close her eyes, but again, he reprimanded her. "I want you to watch me," he instructed gently.

Her teeth sank into her bottom lip, but she kept her gaze on his face. The tiny buttons slid easily out of the silk loops, and little by little, he bared her. Her breasts were small, some of the fullness removed by her stretched-out position. He felt her touch of embarrassment but refused to allow it to interfere with her enjoyment.

Closing his fingers around one taut nipple, he said, "You're more beautiful than any woman I've ever seen."

She started to speak, and he pinched lightly, tugging. Her words evaporated into a gasp.

"You like that?"

"Yes."

He lifted his other hand, plying both breasts. Her back arched, ignoring his order to remain still, but he let the small disobedience pass. She looked sexy as hell writhing under his hands, and he enjoyed watching her, enjoyed feeling her waves of carnal pleasure pass through him.

Without a single word of warning, he leaned down and replaced one hand with his mouth. She cried out at the sweet, soft tugging and the stroke of his tongue.

"Shhh." He blew softly on her now wet nipple.

"Chase, I can't stand it."

"Yes you can."

He felt her frustration explode, felt her body tensing even more. She was drawn so tight, her entire body jerked when he lightly nipped her with his teeth. He tightened his thighs around her hips, holding her still, forcing her to his will.

He switched to her other breast, treating it to the same sensual torture. Around her nipple, he whispered, "I learned early on how much I love controlling a woman this way, being in charge of her pleasure, mastering her with sex. But I love controlling you even more."

She groaned and tried to lift her legs but couldn't. He smiled. "None of that now. I told you to be still."

"Chase . . ."

"It's all right. Let's see what we can do about these bottoms."

Sitting up, he positioned himself so that her upper thighs, clamped tightly shut, were accessible to his hands. Through the soft cotton, he stroked one finger over the center seam of the drawers.

Allison's head twisted from side to side and she tugged on the bindings of her wrists. It was an instinctive reaction, he knew, to try to free herself even though she didn't really want to be free. He could feel everything she felt, and it doubled his pleasure knowing his own unique form of foreplay drove her crazy with need. She was already wet, the drawers damp where his finger continued to stroke. He was careful to barely touch her, to avoid letting her get too close to the edge.

Her belly hollowed out and her breasts thrust upward as she tried to strain closer to his taunting finger. He watched her face as he asked, "What do you want, Allison?"

"I don't know," she answered on a wail.

"Yes, you do. Don't lie to me."

She squeezed her eyes shut and he lifted his hand. "I told you not to do that."

Gulping air, she forced her eyes open again. "I want you to touch me."

"Like this?" His finger slid down, dipped, came away.

A great shudder passed over. "No. Under . . . under the drawers."

His body rocked with his heartbeat. He slid his hand inside the seam, barely touching her. "Like this?"

She tried to thrust against him, but he pulled away again. "Oh, please."

"Tell me, honey."

"I want . . . I want your fingers inside me."

Her face was bright red, both with frenzied need and embarrassment. Chase was so pleased with her, he leaned down and kissed her mouth hungrily, thrusting his tongue deep, his control almost shattered by her innocently whispered words. When he pulled back again, she stared at him expectantly, her breath held. He opened the seam of the drawers, laying the material wide.

Her feminine curls were dark blonde, damp, and he wanted to taste her very badly. He locked his jaw against the temptation and insinuated one long finger between her folds, feeling her wetness, the warmth of her. His penetration was eased by her excitement, but the tightness of her nearly did him in.

Allison let out a low, keening cry as he forced his finger deeper. "Is this what you wanted, baby?"

She didn't answer, her hips working against him, almost lifting his weight from the bed. He pulled back, watching her face closely, then thrust again, hard and deep.

She screamed with pleasure. *His name.*

Cursing viciously, Chase levered himself to the side.

He pushed her legs wide, then held them there when she instinctively tried to close them again. The material of the drawers was in his way and he ripped it open wider, wanting to see all of her, vulnerable, open and ready for him.

Allison was stunned. He could feel her sudden confusion and anticipation. He slipped his finger into her again, then added another. Her hips bucked, and that was all the provocation he needed. Bending down, he took her in his mouth, his tongue hot and rough and insistent. He found her small clitoris and sucked gently.

Allison climaxed with a shock of incredible pleasure that shook her whole body, and he felt it all, felt her trembling, her emotional turmoil, her greed. He cupped her hips, lifting her tighter against his mouth, refusing to let her orgasm fade despite her cries and weak struggles. When finally she stilled, going boneless beneath him, he climbed off the bed and furiously stripped off his jeans and shorts.

"Allison?"

Her eyes barely opened—until she saw he was naked. Then her big blue eyes flared wide, looking him over in great detail. "Are your arms okay, sweetheart?"

She squinted at him, trying to see him more clearly, and he smiled. "I want to touch you, Chase."

"That's not what I asked."

Her legs shifted restlessly, then she nodded. "I'm not in any discomfort, if that's what you mean."

"Good. And don't worry. You'll get your turn. But for now—" His gaze burned over her again. Her legs were still open, her damp curls framed by lacy cotton. "—For now, I like you just the way you are."

He slid a condom on and moved over her. After gently lowering himself onto her, he held her face and said against her mouth, "I like making love to you like this, Allison. Will you mind if we do this often?"

She blinked at him, then mutely shook her head.

"Good. I think I'd enjoy keeping you tied to my bed forever."

"Chase . . ."

He could feel the questions she wanted to ask, questions about the future. But he couldn't even explain to himself what he felt, the rightness of being with her, the intensified pleasure of his naked body touching hers. She felt like his soul mate, like just being with her would be enough to make him whole. He realized how alive he'd felt since last night, when he'd first started sparring with her, wanting her, trying to understand her and get to know her better. He felt unbearably possessive, and he knew the feeling wouldn't go away anytime soon. Probably never.

He kissed her to stop any further questions and calm his own tumultuous thoughts, then reached down and carefully opened her to his first thrust. The bed rocked gently and she moaned into his mouth.

"So tight, honey. So damn wet. God, you feel good."

Her body resisted him at first, then, as if being welcomed home, she accepted him, his size and length, letting him in until he filled her completely. She gasped, arching her neck back, her tied hands curling into fists. Her muscles clenched and unclenched in small spasms, her entire body trembling. It was incredible and mind-blowing, and he couldn't pace himself, couldn't hold back to tease further.

He met her eager gaze as he balanced himself on his elbows and tried to control the depth of his steady thrusts. His jaw locked with the effort, his shoulders straining.

The damned bed, apparently on uneven legs, rocked back and forth with his every movement. He slid his hands over her breasts, felt her nipples tight against his palms, felt her hips lifting, seeking, her muscles squeezing around his erection as he thrust harder and faster, and he was gone, closing his eyes against the too intense pleasure of it.

Nothing in this life had ever felt so right.

He knew then that he couldn't ever lose her.

Chapter Six

*Long minutes later, Chase became aware of Allison shift-*ing beneath him. Good lord, had he fallen asleep? Appalled, he lifted himself to stare down at her. Her face looked so precious to him, glowing, flushed, happy, and also a little timid. He smiled and kissed her gently, then smoothed her mussed hair, now more unpinned than not. "Are you all right?"

She ducked her head shyly and attempted a restrained stretch. "I'm wonderful."

He looked up at her wrists, then reached to untie her. Lowering her arms carefully, he began to rub them, easing any tenderness she might feel. "I've never made love to a virgin before." He grinned at her. "It was a uniquely satisfying experience."

She gave him a quick glance. "I've never been tied up

before. I doubt I would have enjoyed it with anyone else but you."

"And with me?"

"It was . . . incredible. You're incredible."

Chase rolled to his back and pulled her on top. She wasted no time in doing some of the exploring she'd missed out on due to her restraints. Her hands coasted over his chest and she sighed in wonder. "You are one devastatingly beautiful man, Chase Winston."

Satisfaction settled into his bones. Life didn't get any better than having a naked Allison sprawled over him, his body replete from loving her, his mind at peace with the knowledge that she was his.

When she bent to press her soft lips to his chest, he laughed and resettled her against him. "Behave, woman. It's almost four in the morning. Don't you think we need some sleep?"

She made a pouting face at him. "I thought you said I'd have my turn."

"You will. Tomorrow."

She looked his length over greedily. "Will I get to tie you up?"

"Hell no." The frown she gave him now was mutinous, and he kissed her thoroughly in between chuckles. "The effect isn't at all the same, I promise. Besides, there are a few things I still want to do to you."

"Chase . . ." Her eyes were suddenly glowing warmly again.

He touched her cheek. "You're an intelligent, independent, sexy woman, Allison Barrows. I wouldn't have you any other way. Except," he added when she looked flustered at his praise, "in the bedroom. In here, I'm in charge. And I already know how much you like it, sweetheart, so don't bother protesting."

Allison picked up a pillow to smack him with it. The bed teetered. Chase caught the pillow, then frowned. "Has this damn bed always been uneven?"

Still looking disgruntled that he could so easily know her thoughts, she muttered, "Not that I've noticed. But then you probably weigh a hundred pounds more than me. I don't think I could make this bed move if I tried."

Chase sat up and rocked experimentally, then felt the enormous bed wobble again. With a dark suspicion, he climbed off the mattress and looked down at the thick posts supporting the massive bed. Placing one hand on the edge of the mattress, he pushed. The bottom left leg of the bed lifted and fell because it was almost a quarter inch short. Chase noticed a small corner of cloth poking out. He bent down, but it was stuck inside the bottom of the leg. "Allison, come here a minute."

"What is it?" She peered over the side of the bed, squinting in an effort to see clearly without her glasses. Her gaze was on his naked body, not the bed.

Chase shook his head in amusement, then tugged on his jeans so her attention wouldn't be divided. "See if you can pull that piece of material out when I lift the edge of the bed."

Chase was momentarily diverted from his quest when Allison scrambled off the mattress, breasts bare, drawers gaping open and hanging low on her lush hips. He felt a fresh wave of heat and almost forgot his purpose, especially when she went on all fours in front of him, then looked up. "Well?"

Damn. The erotic images that crept into his mind were probably still illegal in some states. It took all Chase's resolution to reach down and heft the edge of the heavy bed. He barely managed to lift it two inches, but Allison quickly tugged out the thin piece of white lawn. It had something written on it.

"What did you do with my glasses?"

Chase reached for the small square of material, but she held it out of reach. "I got it. I want to look first."

"Allison . . ."

She narrowed her eyes at him, still sitting on the floor. "You can control the sex, Chase, but that's all."

With a slow, satisfied grin, he picked up her glasses, then sat on the floor beside her, his back to the bed. "That's all I want to control, babe, so I guess we're in agreement." He slipped the glasses on her nose while she watched him warily.

"Somehow I'm not sure I won that one."

He leaned closer, eyeing a pert breast. "Later, when I'm showing you a position I'm particularly fond of, you'll be more certain."

She reluctantly pulled her gaze away from him and stared at the scrap of material. "Oh my God! Do you realize what this is?"

"Since you won't let me look, no."

"It's the directions to where the jewels are hidden!"

Despite himself, Chase felt the rise of enthusiasm. "A map?"

"Not really. I mean, it just directs us to a certain spot in the basement. And judging by how complicated this is, without the note, we'd never find the jewels."

The laughter erupted, so hearty he almost fell over. Allison smacked his shoulder. "What?"

"Don't you see?" He wiped tears from his eyes and chuckled some more. "The note is hidden in a leg of the bed, and the only way anyone would know about it is—"

Her eyes widened. "If they indulged in some pretty passionate activity in that bed! Otherwise, the bed is so heavy, it would never rock, and no one would ever notice the hidden note."

"Exactly. You have to admit, Rose was pretty damned clever."

Allison jumped to her feet. "Come on."

"Whoa." Chase held her hand and pulled her back to stand between his wide-spread legs. "Don't you think you should put something on first?"

"Why?"

"Because if you don't," he said succinctly, leaning forward to kiss her belly, "I won't be responsible for the fact that we never make it to the basement."

"We won't?"

He stared at one taunting nipple. "No, we won't."

Allison grinned. "You make me feel very sexy, Chase."

"That's because you are very sexy. Incredibly sexy."

"And here I'd always heard virgins weren't supposed to enjoy their first time."

Chase cupped both her breasts, his interest in cold jewels fading quickly. "You're not the average virgin, honey."

She flashed him a coy smile and stepped away toward her closet. "Or maybe you just have a rather unique way about you that . . . stimulates my sexier side." She wiggled out of her drawers and pulled a dress off the rod. She slipped it on over her head. Chase stared.

It was another old-fashioned dress, fitted across the top, calf-length. It had no collar, just sort of scooped down in a narrow *V* over her naked breasts. There were about a zillion little tiny covered buttons down the front that fit into narrow, covered loops. Chase watched her start buttoning and knew it would take an excruciatingly long time to get her back out of that dress. To him, it looked like an opportunity for endless foreplay.

He already looked forward to the effort.

She pulled out chunky heeled shoes, then said with a wink, "These are my Brighton Beach hooker shoes."

Chase narrowed his gaze. "You're naked underneath."

"I know." And just that easily, she sauntered out of the room. "Come on, Chase. I'll show you the way to the basement."

Chase grinned as he followed her, watching the tantalizing sway of her behind in the full skirt.

Allison had the foresight to grab a flashlight from the kitchen. Once in the basement, they had a hard time maneuvering across the packed-dirt floor. The one bare bulb hanging at the bottom of the stairs wasn't adequate to light their way. The basement was musty, the walls damp. They followed the directions carefully, counting off steps, making abrupt turns, steering around the odd pipe. They came to a stop in the far corner where the rough edge of a protruding, homemade laundry chute was just visible from the ceiling beams. Chase stared down at a rusted tub beneath it.

Fascinated, Allison paced around him. "That's the old laundry chute, from when Rose used to have to do the wash with a wringer-type washer. Burke built it for her. When they first got this house, they couldn't afford a maid of any kind, so he tried to make it as organized for her as he could. The chute starts under the sink in the hall bathroom, but a former heir had it boarded up when a modern laundry room was built off the kitchen."

"We need something to climb on," Chase said, moving to stand just beneath the chute. He aimed the flashlight at the square of linen in Allison's hand. "It says the jewels are directly up from here."

The flashlight beam bounced over the long, deep chute, then inside it. About two feet up, taped flat against the inside, was a narrow box. "Well, I'll be damned," Chase whispered slowly.

"Is it the jewels?"

"I think so."

Chase felt Allison's excitement roll over him, and then a thought occurred to him. "Where are Burke and Rose? There hasn't been a single light flicker or breeze or anything. Not since . . ."

Allison froze. "Not since you asked them for some privacy."

Chase gently touched her cheek. "Maybe they realized things would work out."

Allison bit her lip, her eyes huge behind her glasses; then she whispered, "Will they?"

They both jumped when a third voice intruded, amused and condescending. "Don't tell me you actually believe in that ghost nonsense."

Allison whirled around. "Jack?"

Chase stepped forward, forcing her behind his back. Jack stood at the bottom of the steps beneath the feeble bulb. In his hand was a gun. Very calmly, Chase asked, "Visiting again?"

Jack merely smiled. "Yes. That was me you found in the house tonight. I thought Allison would be in bed, and God knows, I never figured on you visiting that late. But not only did you visit, you stayed." His expression hardened and he glared at Allison, who stood on tiptoe to peek over Chase's shoulder. "After you sent me off without the slightest regret, I never suspected it was so you could have another man over. Somehow I had the impression you were a nice girl."

Allison gasped, but it wasn't the insult that shocked her. "How did you get in? I locked the front door behind you myself!"

"Ah, but first we went to the parlor and talked, and while you were busy explaining to me why we couldn't see each other anymore, I unlocked the window. You thought I was staring despondently, when I was actually planning." He smirked. "Your door is now a little damaged by the way."

"But why?"

"For the jewels, of course. You told me they were here somewhere, I want them. They must be worth a fortune."

Chase said nothing. He was busy watching the bulb over Jack's head dim slightly, then turn bright again. A small smile touched his mouth. "You want the jewels, you bastard? Fine they're up there."

He pointed at the chute, but Jack just shook his head. "I think you can fetch them down for me. And Allison can come over here by me to wait."

"No."

Jack raised the gun. "I'm not asking, bartender. I'm telling you."

Before Chase could stop her, she darted around him toward Jack. He saw her glance up at the light. He hoped like hell they weren't both nuts, trusting in ghosts that might not even be around anymore.

Once Allison was pinned to his side, Jack said, "Well hurry it up. Get the damned jewels."

Not willing to waste a single moment with Allison so close to the other man, Chase turned over the heavy, rusted-out laundry tub and climbed on top of it. His fingertips could just barely reach the package. He used the edge of the flashlight to work it loose, and finally, after several minutes, it fell down into his grasp.

"Give it to me."

Jack held out one hand, and Chase started toward him, but the gun lifted. "No, toss it to Allison." He shoved Allison forward, and she stumbled, then righted herself. Staring at Chase, she held out her arms. He carefully tossed the heavy package and she caught it in both hands.

Jack grinned and snatched it away from her. "Excellent.

You know, I'm thrilled to finally have these, but I swear, Allison, I would have enjoyed having you, too."

She shuddered in revulsion, then sneered at him. "I didn't want you, though, and that's all that matters."

He laughed. "Because your damned ghost said it had to be *passionate?*" He gave Chase a man-to-man look. "Can you believe that nonsense? When she first explained it to me, I went along. I mean, what the hell, she's pathetically naive, and I figured it'd be fun."

Chase turned his molten-hot gaze on Allison. "You actually planned to sleep with this bastard? You went so far as to explain to him why?"

Allison's face turned bright red. "I didn't think you would be . . ."

"Obviously. Hell, Allison, even Zane would be preferable to him."

She lowered her head, chagrined.

Chase inched closer. He didn't know quite what Jack had planned, but he didn't doubt for a minute that it wouldn't be pleasant.

Before he could take two steps, Jack snarled at him. "That's enough. Both of you, over in the corner."

Allison stared up at him. "What are you going to do?"

"I'm going to lock you both down here until I can get away, that's all."

But Chase knew he was lying. His brow furrowed as he realized exactly what Jack would do. Had Rose let him read another mind? "You're going to set the house on fire."

Jack looked abashed at first, then wary. "How did you know?"

"Rose told me."

Jack began backing carefully up the steps, keeping the gun on Chase the whole time. He tried for a sneer but wasn't overly successful. "I don't believe in ghosts."

The lightbulb flickered, almost going out, then blazing so brightly, Jack had to lift one hand to shield his eyes.

Chase smiled. "Neither did I, until I met two of them."

"It a trick! How the hell are you doing it?"

"I'm not. Rose and Burke are. And if you're smart, you'll put the gun away and give Allison back her jewels."

"Ha!" He had almost reached the top step. "So she can sell them?"

Allison gasped. "I would never do that!"

Jack stopped on the top step. A cold wind blew down the stairs with an eerie whistle. Jack's breath frosted as he shouted, "Stop it!" He lifted the gun. "I don't know how you're doing it, but—"

Suddenly he was pushed forward and his gun hand went up in the air, then resounded with a loud crack as Jack instinctively pulled the trigger. Allison covered her ears, while Chase covered her with his body. Jack lost his balance and tumbled head over heels down the hard stairs, squealing the whole way. He landed in a heap, the gun skidding a good three feet from him. Chase jumped up and grabbed it, then leaned over Jack. The man was unconscious but alive. Judging by the twist of his right leg, it was broken. He turned to Allison and held out his arms.

With a small gasp, she ran to him, and it felt so good to hold her, to know she was again safe, he knew for certain he'd never let her go.

Suddenly there was a flurry of footsteps from above. *"Chase!"*

Chase lifted his brows. "Cole? What the hell are you doing here?"

Not only Cole filled the open doorway at the top of the narrow stairs. Zane and Mack, both wide-eyed, joined him. "What the hell happened? We walked in, and here's this maniac, holding a gun and shouting."

"It's just Allison's old boyfriend," Chase explained, and though he was still holding her close with one arm, she managed to punch him in the side. He grinned and pulled her closer, then started up the stairs.

Zane peered down at him. "We were rushing over to help, but then . . ." He looked at Cole. "Did you, uh, push him down the stairs?"

Cole stiffened. "Me? I thought you did it somehow."

"Well, no." They both turned to Mack.

"Don't look at me!"

Chase chuckled as he joined his brothers upstairs. "It's a long story."

"Then you better make it quick. I, uh, called the police."

"Why the hell did you do that?"

Cole shook his head, then looked away. "Damned if I know. I was sleeping with my wife—which is usually enough distraction to block out the rest of world—and suddenly I just . . . knew you were in trouble." He shrugged. "It was the strangest damn thing. I called the cops, then Zane and Mack, and we all met outside."

The kitchen where they had all clustered suddenly glowed with warmth. The brothers looked around. Mack turned to Zane. "I think I'm ready to get the hell out of here."

Zane nodded. "I'm with you." They both turned to go. "If you need us for anything later on, just give a holler."

Mack snickered as they walked out. "First Cole, and now Chase. I can't wait to see what the hell you get into."

"Ha! I hope you're not holding your breath, because you'll be the next entertainment, not me."

"I'm still in school!"

"And I'm having way too much fun to start acting crazy over one particular woman."

Their voices faded as they went through the house to the front door. Cole, Chase, and Allison stared after them.

After shaking his head, Chase raised a brow at Cole. "What about you? You going to stick around?"

Cole sighed. "Well, I did leave a rather warm, willing female in my bed." Then he laughed. "But I suppose Sophie will wait. Hell, I'm anxious to see how you rationalize this to the cops."

It was several hours before the police left, content with the explanation that Jack was simply an insane intruder, the story neatly shored up by his loud claims of ghosts.

Allison and Chase were alone, back in the massive bed. It had taken Chase quite some time to get the dress off her, but the end result had been spectacular. Allison curled up at his side, then sighed.

Chase smoothed her hair. "What are you thinking, sweetheart?"

She froze, turning quickly to look up at him. "Don't you know?"

The expression on his face was comical. "Uh, no."

Her heart pounding madly, she asked, "You can't read my mind anymore?"

Chase frowned, then shook his head. "I don't have a single clue."

"Oh God. Does that mean Rose and Burke are really gone? Have they moved on?"

Chase touched the modest emerald and diamond necklace around Allison's throat. The jewels weren't ostentatious or enormously valuable, except maybe to a collector. But they were beautiful, and she'd cried as Chase hooked the latch at the back of the necklace and helped her to slip the pierced earrings in. The ring was a little big for her fingers, so it was now on Chase's pinkie.

He kissed her cheek. "The jewels are where they belong, sweetheart. It's only right that they find peace now."

"I'll miss them."

"But you still have me."

His small jest didn't make her feel much better. Would she have Chase? A thought occurred to her, and she asked, "Could you read my mind while we were, you know. Making love?"

Her face felt bright red, thinking of the way Chase had lingered over removing the dress, how he'd positioned her on the edge of the bed, how she'd eventually pleaded with him to take her.

He pulled her up over his chest and framed her face with his hands. "Come to think of it, no. But I didn't need to read your mind when your little moans told me everything I needed to know."

She swallowed hard. "Chase? Do you really like my old-fashioned dresses? I mean, there's trunks full of them, left over from one of the spinsters, and I like wearing them and—"

He placed a hand over her mouth. "Hell yes, I like them. They're the type that inspire fantasies, sweetheart. At least, they do when you're wearing them."

She pulled his hand away and asked, "Do you like my house? Because I don't ever want to leave here. I know it needs some work, but—"

Again, he covered her mouth, this time grinning. "I like your house. A lot. I think it'd be fun to do some repairs, without changing the looks of things."

With her words muffled against his palm, she asked boldly, "Do you like me?"

Very slowly he shook his head. "No. I don't *like* you." Her heart nearly punched out of her chest, and it was all she could do not to wail. The disappointment seemed like a live thing inside her. Then he lowered his hand and kissed her and he whispered, "I love you. All of you."

"You love me?"

"I've never known a woman like you, Allison. How the hell could I not fall in love with you? You casually converse with ghosts, defending them, fighting for them. Befriending them. You burn me up in bed, taking everything I have and giving it back tenfold. But you make the rest of the world think you're such a good little girl. You even turned down Zane, and that makes you unique as hell." He grinned, tangling his fingers in her hair. "You're smart and independent and brave, and best of all, you love me, too."

With tears threatening, she whispered, "Did you read my mind to know all that?"

He very slowly shook his head. "No. It's right there, in your pretty blue eyes for me to see. You do love me, don't you, sweetheart?"

"Yes. I have, almost from the first time I saw you."

"Will you continue to indulge me in the bedroom?"

She bobbed her head. "Oh yes."

This time he laughed out loud. "You sounded awfully eager when you said that."

She pressed her forehead to his rock-hard shoulder. "I'm so glad Rose tangled up my dreams and sent them to you."

"I'm so glad you had the good sense to dream about me in the first place."

They both grinned, and then Chase rolled her beneath him. They neither one noticed, but there was one last, happy flicker of a light—and then it was gone.

Tangled Images

Chapter One

Mack Winston was minding his own business, as usual. His thoughts were focused inward, mostly on career choices and disappointments, but he whistled carelessly, unwilling to let anyone witness his concern. The day was snowy and cold, getting colder by the moment, and his nose felt frozen. He was distracted enough not to care.

But the second he entered the family-owned bar he saw them, all three of his damned older brothers and his two sexy sisters-in-law, huddled together at a single tiny table. They looked . . . conniving.

They'd been working on him lately, trying to cheer him when he didn't want them to know he needed cheering. It irritated him. He liked being known as the carefree brother, the fun brother. It suited him.

Since it was early and the bar was not yet open, they

all glanced up at him when they heard the door close. Then they did a double take. The women suddenly smiled, and their smiles were enough to make the slowest man suspicious. And despite his brothers' ribbing, he wasn't slow.

Mack's whistling dwindled. He thought about making a strategic retreat, but then Zane, only three years his senior, called out, "Ha! A lamb for the slaughter! What perfect timing you have, Mack."

Cole, the oldest brother and the most protective, shook his head, looking somewhat chagrined that Mack had shown himself at this precise moment. Chase, the second oldest and the quietest, glanced at Mack and snorted. Both their wives looked as if an enormous problem had just been solved. Whatever the problem, Mack knew he didn't want to be the solution.

Zane grinned. "I tried to save you, honestly, but I'll be out of town."

Cole rolled his eyes. "You're too damn willing, Zane. It unnerves me."

Chase merely snorted again. His wife, Allison, patted his arm. "You were never even considered, honey, so relax. There's no way I want the female masses of Thomasville ogling your perfect body. You're a married man now, and that means I'm the only one allowed to ogle."

Mack backed up two steps.

Sophie, Cole's wife, now seven months pregnant, ran over to Mack and latched on to his arm. "You understand, I couldn't let Cole do it. Not that he would have, anyway.

You know how reserved he is. But my God, it would have started a riot! Can you just imagine how the women would react to Cole?"

Mack didn't know what she was rambling on about, but he almost smiled anyway. Sweet Sophie harbored this absurd notion that Cole was perfect, and that every female he met wanted him in the most lascivious manner imaginable.

Mack had to agree that in many ways, his oldest brother did border on perfection. Cole had pretty much raised him and Zane, with Chase's adolescent help, after their parents' deaths, and he'd done a great job of it. But Cole was so over the top in love with his wife that he no longer even noticed other women. They could riot all they wanted, and Cole wouldn't care.

Both Cole and Chase had only recently married, and Zane swore Mack would be next, that the Winstons had somehow been either cursed or blessed, the two remaining bachelors still uncertain which it was. Oh, their brothers felt blessed, and the sisters-in-law were wonderful. It was just that Zane didn't ever want to marry, and Mack didn't want to marry anytime soon.

He'd been very cautious around women ever since Chase had unexpectedly succumbed, proving the virus to be very real. Of course, Mack had been shunning the dating scene for other reasons as well. While he was in college, his studies had taken precedence over everything else. Well, everything except one very sexy, very enticing woman—who hadn't wanted a damn thing to do with him. There were still times when he dreamed of her, and someday he hoped to meet a woman like her, one that could turn him on with just a look. But until then . . .

Sophie's hand tightened on his arm, and Mack tried to step away. He didn't get very far. Though she looked small and delicate, Sophie had a grip like a junkyard dog hanging on to a prized bone.

Zane sauntered over, his eyes glinting with humor. "I still think I'd have been the best choice. But you know I'm going out of town for that convention, so that leaves you, little brother."

Mack swallowed, eyeing each relative in turn. "What exactly does that leave me to do?"

Sophie squeezed a little closer, and her tone became cajoling. "Why, just a little modeling."

His brows shot up. "Modeling?"

"Yes."

Chase snorted again.

"All right." Mack decided enough was enough. "Sophie, turn me loose, I promise not to bolt. Zane, I'm going to flatten you if you don't stop grinning. And no, Chase, there's no need to snort again. I already gather this isn't something I'm going to enjoy."

"Nonsense!" Allison, his other meddling sister-in-law, whom he adored to distraction, leapt to her feet to join Sophie. Mack felt sandwiched between their combined feminine resolve. He assessed their wide-eyed, innocent stares warily.

With a sigh Cole came to his feet too. "Sophie has some harebrained idea of offering a new line of male lingerie at her boutique."

Male lingerie! Mack stiffened and again tried to back up. The sisters-in-law weren't allowing it.

"It's not lingerie, Cole," Sophie insisted in a huff. Since her pregnancy had gotten under way, she huffed more often. "It's loungewear. And it's very popular."

Mack's head throbbed the tiniest bit. "Loungewear?"

"Yes, you know, like silk boxers and robes and—"

Zane leaned forward. "And thongs and lace-up leopard-print briefs and leather skivvies and—"

Allison slapped her hand over Zane's mouth. "Women appreciate those nice things on a man."

Zane, Mack, and Cole all stared at Chase, who immediately started to bluster, while frowning at his wife. "Oh, no. You can forget those thoughts right now! That's just an assumption on Allison's part. You wouldn't catch me dead in any of that goofy stuff."

Disappointed, they all returned their attention to Mack. He looked around at their expressions, which varied from amused to resigned to hopeful, and he shook his head. "Hell, no."

Sophie glared at him. "You don't even know what it is that I want yet."

"Honey, I don't need to know. If it involves this . . . this . . . *male loungewear,* I want no part of it."

Her eyes narrowed in a calculating way. "All I need you to do—"

"No."

"—is to let the photographer get a few pictures of you in the clothing to advertise it in a new catalogue."

"No!"

"Because there's no way I can afford to hire a real model, who would probably have to come all the way from New York or Chicago, and I have the feeling you'd look better anyway."

Well, that was a nice compliment, but . . . he shook his head. "No."

Zane pried Allison's hand away. "Not as good as *I'd* look, but as I said—"

Three voices yelled in unison, "Shut up, Zane!"

Zane only chuckled.

Sophie continued, her voice coercing, her eyes wide. "This is a great opportunity for me, Mack. The photographer is a friend of mine, willing to do this cheap for the exposure it'll bring the studio. I'm getting a special deal here. It'll only take two or three days—"

"No."

"—so it won't really interfere with your schedule or anything—"

"Damn it, Sophie—"

"—and Valentine's Day would be the perfect time to advertise the new line."

Mack groaned.

"So it's all set, then. And Mack, I *really* appreciate it." She gave him a sideways, very calculating glance. "You can consider this payback for all those study sessions with me for your college science classes."

He felt doomed. He could only mumble, "Unfair, Sophie."

She batted her pretty blue eyes at him and said, "You'd never have passed anatomy without me."

Cole's mouth fell open. "All those late nights she helped you study, it was for *anatomy*?"

Mack rolled his eyes. "Just female reproduction. That stuff's confusing."

Zane roared with laughter, and this time Chase and Allison joined him. Cole, still huffing, pulled his wife possessively to his side while Mack groped for a chair and fell into it.

"Well, hell." He looked to the heavens, but all he saw was the ceiling of the bar. He supposed there was no help for it at all.

He tilted his head toward Zane. "You'd actually have done this if you weren't going out of town?"

"Are you kidding? The women will love it. You'll have so many new dates, you won't have time to be in a funk."

"I'm not in a funk."

Chase snorted.

Rubbing his brow, Mack tried to ignore them all. He knew Zane probably would like to flaunt himself a little. He was a born exhibitionist and wallowed in the female attention heaped upon him. But Mack wasn't that way— at least, not as much so as Zane. There'd been only that one woman he'd ever wanted to wallow with.

He glared at Sophie and said, "I'm not wearing anything stupid."

She glared right back. "I wouldn't carry anything stupid at my boutique!" Then she softened. "But don't worry. There'll be a selection available, and you and the photographer can decide together which things to photograph.

Other than a few definites that have to be in the catalogue, you can pick and choose."

"Gee, thanks."

Sophie handed him a card that read "Wells Photography," and listed a downtown address. She gave him a huge hug and kissed his cheek. "Be there Friday at two o'clock, okay?"

At least that gave him two days to get used to the idea. Or rather, two days to dread it.

$\backsim$

*Mack parked in the small lot to the side of Wells Pho*tography, as directed by a hanging wooden sign. He'd checked his mail before leaving his apartment, but still no word from the board of education. He'd been a good teacher, damn it. The best. The kids had loved him, the parents respected him. His class had scored much higher than past averages, much higher than expected.

But the principal still hadn't recommended him.

His hands fisted in his coat pockets as he walked across the broken-concrete lot. He stared at his feet, ignoring the blustering wind, the beginning of wet, icy snow as it pelted the back of his neck. The sky was a dark gray, matching his mood. He'd never felt so helpless in his life, and he hated it. The principal's judgment of him, as well as her decision not to recommend, were beyond unfair, but there wasn't a damn thing he could do about it.

Finally, after Mack had crossed the nearly empty lot to the front of the building, he focused his thoughts enough to realize that the studio wasn't a studio at all but rather an older home. The redbrick two-story house was stately in a sort of worn-out way. It was hemmed in by the empty lot to the right and another older home advertising apartments for rent on the left.

Squinting against the freezing January wind, Mack bounded up the salted concrete steps to the front door and knocked briskly.

A thin, freckle-faced girl of about thirteen answered. She grinned, flashing a shiny set of braces. Mack grinned back. "Hello."

"Hi."

"Ah . . . I'm looking for the photographer?"

She nodded. "Are you here for the two o'clock shoot?"

"Yep. I'm Mack Winston."

The girl opened the door and let him in. "You can follow me. My mom is just finishing up another session, so you won't need to wait long. We had two cancellations because of the storm. Our receptionist is sick, so I'm sorta filling in."

She closed the door behind Mack, then started down a short hardwood-floored hall. To the right was an open set of curtained glass doors, revealing an office of sorts inside, though the outside wall was mostly used up by an enormous fireplace. To the left of the hall was a flight of stairs leading to a closed door that separated the upper story. Mack continued to look around. "You say your mother is the photographer?"

The girl tucked long brown hair behind her ear and nodded, while stealing quick peeks at Mack. "Yeah. She's real good."

They entered a room that had a utilitarian beige couch and a single chair in it, a table full of magazines, and a coffee machine. To Mack, it looked to be converted from a kitchen, judging by the placement of the window and a few exposed pipes.

The walls were decorated with dozens of incredible photographs, ranging from babies to brides to entire families. There were outdoor scenes with animals in them, indoor scenes around a Christmas tree. Babies in booties, men in suits, children in their Sunday best.

All of the photographs were beautiful, proof of very real talent.

Another set of glass double doors, these closed with opaque curtains, apparently separated the studio. Mack shrugged off his coat, hung it on the coat tree, and then chose the chair in the far corner.

The girl smiled shyly at him. "You want some coffee or something?"

"No, thanks." He returned her smile. "What did you do? Skip school today?"

"We had a half day for teacher in-service."

"Ah. Lucky for your mom, huh? I bet she really appreciates your help with the receptionist missing." He grinned his most engaging grin. The girl blushed and again tucked her hair behind her ear.

Before she could say anything, the phone rang, and she dashed off to answer it. Mack chuckled. He just adored kids, which was one reason why he was determined to get a teaching position.

Of course, at the moment, his teaching possibilities

looked grim. That thought had him scowling again, ready to sink into despair. God, he hated brooding—it didn't suit him at all.

Fortunately the photographer chose that moment to open the door. Mack heard two sets of feminine voices and his senses prickled. Something about one of those voices was familiar, sending a wave of heat up his spine. There'd been only one woman who had ever affected him that way, but it couldn't possibly be her. Still, he leaned forward to peer around the coffee machine.

A young woman holding a squirming baby faced him, while the photographer had her back to Mack, displaying a very long, very thick braid hanging all the way down to her bottom. *Oh, damn, he knew that braid!* He leaned a little more, feeling ridiculously anxious, holding his breath. Then she turned slightly, giving him her profile, and Mack felt like a mule had kicked him in the ribs.

Jessica Wells.

His heart slowed, then picked up speed. It was a reaction very familiar to him. Just like the last time he'd seen her, he felt his muscles tremble, his stomach knot, his body go simultaneously hard and hot.

He hadn't seen her since college, almost two years ago, and hadn't suffered such an extreme reaction to a woman since then. But Jessica had always been unaware of the turmoil she caused him regardless of how he'd tried his best to be friendly with her, to get her attention. She was maybe six, eight years older than he was, quiet and very serious. Even a little withdrawn. He'd always thought her adorable with her standoffish ways and reserved manner.

She had beautiful chocolate-brown eyes that made him think of soft, warm things—like the way a woman looked after making love. She had a narrow nose slightly tilted up on the end, high cheekbones, and a small, rounded chin.

She also had the most impressive breasts he'd ever laid eyes on. They made his mouth go dry and his palms sweat. Not that he was hung up on physical attributes . . . except that he'd dreamed about her at night, about getting her out of her conservative sweaters and her no doubt sturdy brassiere so he could see her naked, touch her lush flesh and taste her nipples . . .

He swallowed hard, still staring, taking advantage of the moment, since she remained unaware of him.

Mack had always felt intrigued by her. She'd been so different from the flighty girls who'd flirted with him continually. But the few times he'd tried to talk to her, she had turned her small nose up in utter disregard.

Well, she'd have to talk to him now. *Thank you, Sophie.*

Jessica spoke easily with the woman, who struggled to control the chubby baby boy dressed in a miniature suit. She smiled, and Mack felt the impact of it clear down in his gut. In the time they'd spent together in class, he didn't think she'd ever smiled, not even a glimmer of a smile. No, she was the epitome of seriousness, and it had made him nuts.

Mack was a natural smiler. He liked being happy, friendly, courteous to everyone. But trying to wheedle a smile out of Jessica had been like trying to get a fish to sing.

He still recalled the first day he'd seen her, when she'd walked into the same photo tech class, loaded down with books, looking conspicuous and nervous and uncomfortable. He'd been sitting in the front, and she'd sat as far in the back as she could get. He'd twisted all the way around to see her, but her gaze had met his only once, then skittered away.

He'd taken the photography class out of casual interest, thinking it might be a way to make some of the lessons more fun for his students. And it had. But obviously it had been much more for her.

While tickling the baby's chin, she said, "I'll call in about a week after I get the proofs together, and then we can set up an appointment for you to make your choices."

The woman sighed gratefully. "You're a saint, being so patient with him. I don't know why he was so fussy today."

Mack figured any guy stuffed into a suit had a reason to be fussy.

The baby kicked, prompting his mother to hurry along. After they'd gone, Jessica checked her watch, rubbed her brow, then headed for the coffee machine. That's when she noticed Mack.

Drawing up short, she stared, her dark eyes widening, but only for a single moment. Then, with a carefully blank expression, she stepped forward and extended her hand. "Mr. Winston?"

Mack resisted the urge to mimic Chase's snort. There was no way she didn't recognize him. *Was there?* Surely he'd made some sort of impression! But when her expression remained fixed, he started to wonder. Narrowing his eyes, he slowly stood and extended his hand. Here he was, indulging in erotic daydreams, and she didn't even remember him. "That's right," he said, keeping his voice moderate. "Actually, we met in college a few years ago."

She blinked lazily as his hand enclosed hers. He felt her tremble the tiniest bit as she summoned a look of polite confusion. "We did?"

Okay, so she'd always ignored him. She'd been as far from impressed by him as a woman could get. She'd still been aware of him, he was sure of it. And two years wasn't so long that she could have totally forgotten him.

He held her hand when she would have pulled away and tried for a cocky grin. "Yeah. We had a class together. Photo tech. Remember?"

Suddenly she smiled, a very phony smile that set his teeth on edge. "Ah, I remember now! Mack Winston. You were the class Romeo who kept all those silly coeds in a tizzy."

She tugged hard and he let her hand go. "Class Romeo? Hardly."

She waved his words away, as if he were only being modest. "Yes, yes, I remember now. All those foolish girls crowded around you. Half the time I couldn't hear the instructor for all their whispering and giggling. I think you probably dated every one of them. I was always rather amazed by your . . . stamina."

Every single word she said, though softly spoken, sounded like a veiled insult. It wasn't something Mack was used to. But of course, nothing with Jessica, including his feelings, was ever as he expected.

He rocked back on his heels and slowly looked her over, from the form-fitting jeans to the loose white sweater and braided brown hair. Physically, she hadn't changed at all. She still turned him on. Even now, he could feel his muscles tightening, the heat beneath his skin. He wanted her, and all she'd done so far was insult him.

Carefully gauging his words, he said, "I remember you being a recluse—and maybe just a little stuck up."

Her expression darkened, her brown eyes turning nearly black. "I was not stuck up! It was just that, compared to you . . . well, I was there to learn, not to socialize."

She sounded defensive, and he wondered about it. He also wondered what it would be like to kiss the mulish expression away from her lips. "This may surprise you, but I learned. I just had fun doing it."

"Now, *that* I can believe. The fun part, that is."

There was nothing distracted about Mack's brain at the moment. No, he felt razor-sharp, focused, full-witted and aroused. He prepared to coach her on his idea of fun, when the young girl suddenly raced into the room. When she saw her mother and Mack facing off, she skidded to a halt. "Uh, Mom, I don't mean to interrupt—"

With obvious relief, Jessica turned away, effectively dismissing Mack. "That's all right, honey. You're not interrupting anything . . . important."

Her choice of words made Mack feel relegated to the

back burner. He almost laughed because he recognized her efforts to distance herself. Yeah, she remembered him. She could deny it all she wanted, but he wasn't buying it.

"Well . . ." The young girl played with her hair, sneaking looks between her mother and Mack. "Since you don't have any more appointments today, I was thinking of going to Jenna's. Her dad will pick me up. She . . . uh, invited a few friends over."

"Friends, as in guy-type friends?"

The girl grimaced, then leaned forward and said in an excited stage whisper, "Brian's going to be there!"

Mack watched as Jessica fought with her smile—another genuine smile this time. "Oh, well, in that case, how could I possibly refuse?" Before Trista could work up a loud squeal, she added, "I assume Jenna's parents will be there the whole time?"

"Yeah."

"All right, then. Call when you're ready to come home and I'll come get you."

Trista ran forward and hugged her mother, then with the energy exclusive to the early teens, charged out of the room.

Mack chuckled. "She's really cute."

"Thank you." Jessica said it with pride, and for the first time Mack felt her defenses were down.

"I gather Brian is a guy she likes?"

Jessica almost laughed. "My daughter is suffering her first crush. And so far, the 'totally awesome' Brian hasn't even noticed her."

"It's a tough age for kids."

"You're telling me! She went from wanting Barbie dolls to pierced ears overnight. Shopping has become an all-day expedition. And she absolutely hates her braces."

She seemed so natural, so at ease discussing her daughter, that Mack felt encouraged. He stepped a little closer, appreciating the softness in her eyes, the slight smile playing over her lips. He wanted to touch her, but of course, that would be over the line. "I didn't realize you had a daughter. Especially not one that old."

Jessica immediately stiffened. "No reason you should know."

"Are you married?"

She ignored him. "Sophie told me she was sending a male model."

"She sent me." He held his arms out to the side.

"Are you a professional?"

"Not at modeling."

She didn't take the bait. "This might be a problem. Getting just the right pose isn't easy."

"I think I can manage—with a little direction."

She continued to eye him, then shook her head. "I've known Sophie for a while, knew that she married, but I never connected the last name."

Mack followed her as she started into the studio. Her jeans did interesting things for her bottom, and hazardous things to his libido. Jessica Wells was a lushly rounded woman. "Hmm. Why would you have? You didn't even remember me, right?"

She stalled and he almost bumped into her. His hands settled on her straight shoulders, but then she hurried away. "That's right. Now, we should get started." Again she checked her watch. "We've got a lot to get done today."

Mack folded his arms over his chest. "Sophie told me it might take a couple of shoots to get everything done."

"Oh, no. With any luck, I can finish up today." She sounded nearly desperate as she said it, then rushed over to a long, narrow table and picked up a folder. "I have the catalogue layout right here. We'll need about thirty pictures. Some of them just of your . . . uh . . ."

Her gaze skimmed his lap, then darted away. "Just of the garments. Others will need all of you in them."

She seemed nervous, flitting about, grabbing up various papers and carrying them from one table to another. Mack leaned against the wall to watch her. For the first time in a long while, he felt totally absorbed in something other than worries about his future teaching position.

The room was interesting. Props occupied every corner and filled several shelving units. One entire wall was empty except for large pull-down screen devices that held various backdrops. All of the camera equipment was centered at the far end of the room.

The studio was at the back of the house and had two windows each on three walls. Dark shades kept out any sunlight, and bright lights had been turned on instead. Finally Jessica seemed to get herself organized. She began hauling a large box toward the table. Mack stepped forward to help her.

Against her protests, he picked up the box and asked, "Where do you want it?"

Resigned, she motioned toward the table. "Set it on the floor there. We have to figure out which things you'll model. There's a pretty good sampling of the, uh, briefs inside, and on the rack there's other stuff."

She wouldn't quite meet his gaze. Suspicious, Mack opened the box and peeked in. He immediately slammed the cardboard lid down again, then stared at Jessica.

"What?" She leaned toward the box, but he pulled it out of her reach.

Damn. He cleared his throat. "Let's start with some other stuff."

She looked equal parts curious, hesitant, and determined. "Why? Sophie wants at least eighteen shots of briefs, to give a good sampling of what she'll be offering. We're supposed to do nine shots to a page."

Eighteen shots of him in tiny scraps of material? When he was already half hard? Ha! "Couldn't they just be shot on a mannequin or something?"

Her efforts at indifference weren't overly effective. Her cheeks had turned a dusky-rose color and she wouldn't quite meet his gaze. "Wouldn't matter to me. But Sophie might not like it. She said she wanted her customers to see a real man wearing this stuff, to prove real men look good in it."

Mack grinned. "A real man, huh?" The color in her face intensified, and Mack totally forgot his own hesitation. He shoved the box toward her. "All right. You pick."

"Me?"

"Sure. You have a trained eye, so you should probably be able to tell what'll look best on me." Feeling a little outrageous, he stood up to tower over her. He widened his stance, spread his arms out to his sides. "You might want to, ah, *study* my form first, right? I mean, so you have a good idea of what would look most complimentary on my particular physique." She'd know he was aroused, but so what? He wanted her to know how she affected him.

He watched as stubbornness surfaced in her expression. She stared back at him, hard, her gaze never leaving his face. Then without looking away from him, she reached into the box. She felt around and finally tugged out a teeny-tiny pair of paisley-print thong briefs. She thrust them toward him like a challenge.

Mack almost laughed. With his baby finger, he accepted the briefs, which had no apparent backside and were so sheer that they weighed about as much as a hankie. Trying to sound earnest, he asked, "Do they, perhaps, come in a larger size?"

Pretending to take him seriously, Jessica searched through her papers. "Nope. One size fits all."

Mack gave the outrageous briefs a dubious inspection. "Hmmm. I must be unique, then, because there's no way these puppies are gonna fit me."

She lifted one slim brown brow. "Oh? They're too . . . big?"

Mack choked, but quickly recovered. He liked it that she now felt comfortable enough to tease. "Jessica, I don't think you actually looked at me when I told you to."

She shrugged. "I did, but then I guess my mind wandered."

"Ah. Got you thinking of *other things,* did it?"

"Actually, I forgot my glasses so I couldn't really see the insignificant things . . ."

This time Mack did laugh. She hadn't looked at his body, only his face, or she'd have seen some *very* significant things. "You're very damaging to a man's ego, you know that?"

She made a rude sound and shook her head. "As if your ego needed any help."

Just that easily, she went from playful to insulting again. He squatted down in front of her and leaned over the box to make certain he had her attention. "Why do I get the feeling you've made some assumptions about me, and none of them are particularly favorable?"

With him so close, she looked startled and breathless. She jerked way back—and toppled onto her bottom. Amused by her telltale response, Mack stood up and pulled her to her feet. She quickly shook him off, as if his touch bothered her more than it should, then took two hasty steps back.

"This is ridiculous," she protested. "I don't have all day to banter with you."

She was suddenly so flustered, he knew damn well she couldn't have been as indifferent to him as she'd claimed. Only a woman aware of a man could be so affected by a simple touch. Why did she continue to deny it?

He didn't understand her. They'd been joking like old friends, having fun, and then suddenly she'd seemed to realize it and retreated back into herself. He crossed his arms and gave her a curious stare. "If you're pressed for time, then we should probably get this cleared up right now."

She turned away and stalked to the clothes rack. She yanked down a hanger that held a black silk kimono robe with red piping and matching pull-on pajama pants. She thrust them toward him. "I have a better idea. Let's just get some photos taken, like we're supposed to."

Mack refused to take the garments. "Since you claim to barely remember me, and I know damn good and well I never did anything to make you dislike me, your animosity seems pretty strange."

"Look, Mr. Winston—"

He barely choked back his laugh of disbelief. "Mr. Winston? Get real, Jessica. At least admit you remember my damn name."

There was a second of vibrating silence, then she seemed to explode. She tossed the clothing aside and thrust her chin toward him. "Well, with the girls all talking about you all the time, I suppose it'd be hard to forget!"

Her sudden anger inflamed him. Her dark eyes were impossibly bright, her chin firmed, her cheeks flushed. Her lush breasts rose and fell in her agitation, and she had her fists propped on her rounded hips.

He wanted to kiss her silly.

He wanted to watch all that anger and frustration turn into passion. Just the thought made him catch his breath. He wanted to howl, because she made him hotter than a sultan's harem, but she refused to let him close.

Never in his life had a woman reacted to Mack the way

this woman did. She seemed more comfortable ignoring, antagonizing, or insulting him than she did just getting along with him. It didn't make sense—and for some insane reason, he felt more intrigued than ever.

Marshaling his limited control, Mack shook his head and managed a relatively calm reply. "I'm definitely missing something here, and it's not your hostility, because that's pretty damn clear. So why don't you just spell it out, Jessica? What's the problem?"

She struggled in silence, her nostrils flaring, and then, after a deep, calming breath, she nodded. "All right."

She looked so serious, Mack held his breath.

After licking her lips nervously, she said, "I resented you. Back then. Not now. As I said, I barely remember you."

Her breasts were still doing that distracting rise-and-fall thing that was making him nuts. He tried to pay attention to her words, but it wasn't easy. "Uh-huh. So why did you resent me?"

"Because I worked my behind off in college. It wasn't easy going back, being so much older than everyone else and having so many more responsibilities. And I was raising Trista alone, and half the time the class was interrupted by the instructor fawning over you, or one of the girls asking me to pass you a note, or you making eyes at the girls—"

Mack blinked at her, pleased by her admission. "If you'd been paying attention to the instructor, instead of me, you wouldn't have noticed me making eyes, now, would you?" He watched her face heat again, the color climbing from her throat all the way up to her hairline. She had very delicate skin, not overly pale, just smooth and silky-looking.

He wondered if she would flush like that during a climax.

Her eyes, clean of any makeup, almost exactly matched the golden-brown shade of her hair. And that hair . . . he'd always noticed it in college. She kept it long, but he'd never seen it out of the braid. It was so thick, the braid so heavy, he could only imagine what it'd be like loose. He used to wait to take a seat until she had, so he could occasionally sit behind her. Without her knowing it, he'd touched her braid, felt how warm and silky it was.

At least, he'd thought she didn't know—until she started sitting in the middle of a cluster of students, ensuring he couldn't get close.

He watched her now as she gathered her thoughts. Little wisps of hair escaped her braid to float around her face, teasing him. He wanted to reach out and smooth them down, to reassure her, but judging from her expression, she'd probably sock him if he tried it.

"Jessica?"

She worried her bottom lip for a moment, then finally sighed. "You're right, of course. And I did try to ignore you. But you were a terrible distraction and I suppose I resented that more than anything."

Cautiously, drawn by an inexplicable mix of emotions he'd never dealt with before, Mack stepped closer. "Why?"

She laughed. "You'll think this is nuts, but you remind me of my husband."

That wasn't at all what he'd been expecting. He stilled. She'd said that she'd raised her daughter alone, so he assumed she wasn't married. He *hoped* like hell she wasn't married. *She'd better not be* . . . "Are you widowed?"

She shook her head hard, causing her braid to fall over one shoulder and curl along her left breast. Mack gulped, forcing his gaze resolutely to her face.

"No, divorced. For quite some time now. But just as you seemed to be the life of the party, so was he. Nothing mattered to him but having a good time. Even when Trista was born, he refused to grow up and settle down, to be a husband or a father. And he was about your age when I stupidly married him."

"I see." But he didn't, not really. He wasn't a husband or a father, but he knew in his heart he'd take those responsibilities very seriously.

She smiled, and again shook her head. "I'm sorry. It's none of my business if you choose to make life fun and games. That's certainly your choice, and I had no right to sit in judgment of you. Whew. I feel better now."

She felt better? Mack clenched his jaw, he was so annoyed. He wasn't irresponsible or immature. He knew what his priorities were, and he kept them straight. No one had worked harder in college or taken his lessons more seriously than he. Yet she automatically labeled him because he'd managed to make school fun. Enjoyment was the standard he'd set for his students, his teaching method for making information stick. It was also one of the reasons the principal hadn't recommended him for the available teaching position. She and Jessica evidently had a few things in common. They were both self-righteous and far too somber.

Only the principal didn't turn him on, but Jessica most certainly did. She always had.

Mack kept his expression impassive. "So now your conscience is clear?"

"Exactly. Imagine, a woman my age reacting to a two-year-old resentment, especially toward someone so young."

"I'm twenty-four."

She nodded, as if that confirmed her suspicions. "It's ludicrous. Why, obviously your outlook would be different from my own."

"Because you're so . . . old?"

"Well, if thirty is old, which I suppose to someone your age, it is." She smiled again. "So, can you forgive my surly attitude? Do you think we can start over and go ahead with the shoot?"

He didn't want to; he wanted to keep talking to her, to get to know her better. But he had promised Sophie. And he had no doubt Zane would ride him forever if he let his reactions to this one woman keep him from getting the job done. He could console himself with the fact that she'd noticed him, she just didn't like noticing him.

When he hesitated, she sighed again. "I don't blame you, I guess. But really, I'm not one of those bitter divorcées who can't talk about anything else. I promise not to even mention it again. And to tell you the truth, I was really looking forward to this shoot. It'll be a nice opportunity for me, more than I've ever done before, since my work usually only includes portraits."

"So you want this job?"

"Yes, of course."

Mack nodded. Now he had something to work with. "I'll stay."

He saw the subtle relaxing of her shoulders, the relief she tried hard to hide. "Good."

"We only have one problem."

"Oh? And what's that?"

"You promised not to mention your husband or your divorce again."

"That's right."

Mack smiled, and he knew damn good and well his eyes were gleaming with intent. Good. Let her know he wouldn't be brushed off. "I want to know about your husband. And your divorce. I want lots of little details. Since I remind you of the guy, it only seems fair. Don't you think?"

Chapter Two

*Jessica stared at Mack Winston, caught between want-*ing to laugh and wanting to smack him. She was used to that particular reaction—and other, more sexual reactions as well, if she was honest with herself.

He was so incredibly gorgeous, so young and hand-some and sexy. He'd whizzed through college, not caring about his grades, always joking, always having a good time, while she'd been forced to struggle to make mediocre B's.

His carefree attitude and abundant charm did remind her of her ex-husband, and that's why her attraction to him scared her so much. Why couldn't she be drawn to a staid, mature man, one that would be steady and responsible? She'd tried dating a few times a year after her divorce was finalized, but the men she wanted to be interested in didn't stir a single speck of interest in her.

And the one who did, the one who made her feel young and alive again, was exactly the type of man she knew she should stay away from.

When she'd graduated, she'd thought to never see him again. It had been both a relief, because he was a terrible temptation, and a crushing pain, because she still thought of him often, still awakened in the night after dreaming of him. And now, here he was, in the flesh, and if anything, two years had added to his appeal. *Darn Sophie Winston, anyway.*

Drawing a deep breath and dredging up another nonchalant smile, she asked, "What exactly would you like to know?" She had no intention of letting him see how uncomfortable he, and the conversation, made her feel.

Mack picked up the sexy pajamas with a smile. "How about I change while we talk? That way I won't hold you up."

He'd gotten his way, so now he'd be accommodating? She swallowed her huff of annoyance. "That's fine. You can change behind that curtain."

He gave her a smile that she was certain had melted many a female heart. When Mack Winston smiled, you saw it not only on his sexy mouth, but in his dark eyes that always glittered with humor, in the dimple in his lean cheek, in the warmth that seemed to radiate from him. She expected that nearly every female in Thomasville, Kentucky, had fantasized over him at least once.

But fantasizing was all she would ever do.

While he was occupied, Jessica rummaged through the cardboard box, looking in vain for items that wouldn't expose his body overly.

"Tell me why you divorced him."

She glanced up and saw Mack's flannel shirt get slung over the curtain rod. She gulped as a sharp twinge of excitement raced down her spine. A white T-shirt and belt quickly followed, making her imagination go wild.

"Jessica?"

"I, ah . . . I told you. He wouldn't settle down. He kept losing jobs, running through our money. Trista was not quite seven when I filed for divorce, eight before everything was finalized. I decided to go back to college so I could bone up on the newest photography techniques. It was something I'd always wanted to do, but I'd worked to get Dave through college, and then Trista was born, and, well . . . I just never got around to it. After the divorce, I needed a way to support us both—"

"Is he still around?"

His worn, faded jeans landed on top of the flannel, and her tongue stuck to the roof of her mouth. *Mack was naked behind the curtain.* "Who?"

"Your ex."

"Oh. Uh, no. Well, sometimes. He lives in Florida, and every so often he remembers Trista and sends her a card or a gift." She looked down at the pile of so-called briefs and quickly tried to decide which ones would conceal the most.

"He doesn't pay child support?"

"Ha!"

"You could sue him for it, you know."

Everything she picked up was far too scanty, too revealing, to actually suggest that he wear it. She was a thirty-year-old woman who'd been celibate for too many years to count. Her heart wouldn't take the strain. "But then I'd have to suffer his presence. This way, he's almost completely out of my life, and he's not messing with Trista's emotions."

"What have you told her about him?"

She stared at the damn briefs, imagined them filled out by his masculine flesh, and felt flustered. "Only that we didn't get along, but it had nothing to do with her. When she asks me why he doesn't come around more, I tell her that he does love her, it's just that some people have a hard time settling into domestic roles."

"That's pretty wise of you, you know. So many times, parents are bitter and they force their kids into the middle of things without even meaning to. And the only ones who get hurt by it are the kids."

"I would never tell Trista what a jerk her father is. Hopefully, by the time she gets old enough to figure things out on her own, he'll have gotten his act together."

She glanced up as Mack stepped around the curtain— and froze. He adjusted the waistband, leaving the sheer pants to hang low on his lean hips. The robe was draped over his arm. He was barefoot, his hair appealing mussed, his hairy chest wide and sexy and hard. His abdomen was sculpted with muscle, and a line of silky hair led from his navel downward. She wanted to look away, but she couldn't quite manage it. Her heart beat so hard it hurt, and her stomach did strange little jumps that felt both sweetly tantalizing and very disturbing.

Oh, Lord, it had been so long since she'd seen a mostly naked man.

And she'd *never* seen a man like Mack Winston.

He paused in the center of the floor, then simply stood there, hands on his hips, and let her look. His eyes narrowed, direct and hot and probing, and his smile tilted in a sensual, teasing way.

Finally, when it dawned on her how long they'd both been silent, she jumped to her feet. An impressive array of colorful, silky underwear fluttered off her lap and onto the floor, like a platoon of male butterflies folding ranks. She looked down, realized she'd been practically buried in the damn things, and almost groaned. She swallowed, staring at the heap on the floor. "I was . . . was looking for which ones you should pose in."

She felt more than heard him move closer. "It's not going to be an easy job."

Didn't she know it! "We'll figure out something." She cleared her throat roughly. "Now, would you like to put on the robe?" She contrived a polite smile, managed to raise her gaze to his face without lingering too long on all the exquisite male flesh in between, and then wished she hadn't bothered. He was just so handsome, he took her breath away.

"The robe is a little tight in the shoulders. I'll put it on when you're ready to take the picture."

She nodded dumbly, stared some more, then shook herself. She was not, and never had been, a giddy coed.

She was a mother and an independent businesswoman. "Right. Uh, just let me get a few things ready."

It took her only seconds to arrange the set as she wanted it. She pulled down a background that looked like a kitchen, set a tall stool and a coffee mug nearby, then motioned him over. "You're going to pretend you're just out of bed, okay?"

"I'm supposed to have slept in this stuff?"

"Is that a problem?"

"I sleep naked."

Jessica faltered, verbally stumbled over a few gasps, then glared at him. "It doesn't matter what your normal sleeping habits really are. This is just to show the clothing to advantage."

"Jessica, no man in his right mind would try to sleep in this stuff. Have you felt it?" He offered his thigh for her to test the material. She backed up, feeling foolish, yet utterly appalled at the thought of actually touching that thick, hard thigh.

Mack blinked lazily at her, his look so knowing she felt another blush. "It's slippery. And there's no give to it. No man would sleep in it—"

"Then pretend you just pulled it on after you got out of bed!"

"When I'm alone? Why would I do that?"

She closed her eyes and counted to ten, doing her best not to imagine Mack traipsing around his home impressively naked. She failed. The image flashed into her mind and refused to budge.

It felt like a Bunsen burner had been turned on inside

her, especially low in her belly, where the heat seemed to pulse. "Mack." She said his name through her teeth. "Just sit on the damn bar stool and sip your coffee, okay?"

He shrugged. "If you say so, but it's a dumb pose."

She gave up. "Okay, how do you suggest we set it?"

"Maybe in the evening, in front a fire." His gaze met hers. "With company."

"Company?"

He stepped closer, and the lamplight shone on his hard shoulders, heating his skin. "Sure. This stuff is supposed to appeal to women, right? So wouldn't a guy only wear it for a woman?"

She hated to admit it, but he had a point. "All right. Let's try this." She replaced the kitchen backdrop screen with one that featured a glowing stone fireplace. With Mack's help, a plush easy chair replaced the stool. Jessica used the stool to situate a female mannequin's arm, holding a wineglass, just to the side of the chair. The arm would be visible from the elbow down, as if a woman were offering the glass to Mack.

He approved.

They got several nice shots of him lounging at his ease, smiling in the direction of the phony woman. The robe was open to show his hard belly, his sculpted pecs.

She probably took more shots than she needed, but he was such a natural, she could almost feel jealous of the damned plastic arm.

After that, they took two sets of photos of Mack in drapey silk boxers. He admitted to liking them, and she admitted, only to herself, that he'd definitely draw in the female customers, just as Sophie had expected.

Though the snow continued to fall and the temperature continued to drop, Jessica felt much too warm. She realized she was turned on just from photographing him, and prayed he'd never know.

"What now?"

"Reading the morning paper on the terrace—and no, don't tell me you wouldn't go outside in your underwear."

"Sure I would."

She almost laughed, he was so incorrigible. They arranged the set together, using a small bistro table and chair, a pot of silk flowers, and a screen showing morning sunshine and blue sky.

"Now we need to pick the underwear."

Mack glanced doubtfully at the pile she'd left on the floor. "I don't know . . ."

She hesitated as well. She didn't *want* to see him in nothing more than a strip of silk or mesh or vinyl. Her pulse raced just at the thought. The damn boxers had been difficult enough, though at least they weren't so blatantly suggestive. They hung over his masculine endowments, rather than hugging them. But the skimpy briefs . . .

She really had no choice.

And, she thought, if it was any man other than Mack Winston, it wouldn't even be an issue.

She glanced at her watch, dismayed to see that they hadn't gotten nearly enough done, then struggled to achieve a level of professionalism in her voice. "After this shot, we'll just take some of the various briefs. The photos will show only your navel to your upper thighs."

Mack blinked at her, and no wonder. Her voice had sounded like a frog being ruthlessly strangled.

She forged onward. "Would you like to choose the briefs or should I?"

Mack waved at the pile. "Be my guest."

Bound and determined to get it over with, she grabbed the pair closest to the top. "Here."

Mack frowned. "What's wrong with them? They're kind of bunched up."

She looked at the thin blue underwear carefully, then wanted to kick herself. Lifting her chin, she explained, "They have a seam down the back."

"Why?"

"It's . . . it's a . . . well, here. I'll just read the description to you." She rushed over to the table and picked up her file. After flipping through a few pages, she found the item number. "It says, 'cheek-enhancing feature with rear seam to shape comfortably—'"

"You can damn well forget that pair!"

There was no way she could look at him. "Mack . . ."

"My backside doesn't need enhancing, thank you very much."

She couldn't have agreed more. "Ah, fine. You pick. You're the one who has to wear them. But keep in mind, if you choose a thong, you'll probably have to shave."

"Why? I thought the shots were only from my navel down."

It felt like her heart lodged in her throat. "Yes, and that's where you'd have to shave. Too much body hair—"

"You can forget the damn thongs, too!"

Relief made her chatty. "All right. Good. I mean, fine. We can maybe take a shot of you hanging them on a clothesline—"

He grunted, as if that idea didn't appeal to him at all either, but he'd accept it rather than the alternative.

"Are you almost ready?" The longer he took, the edgier she got.

"I'm looking. But I can tell you right now, no thongs, no animal prints, and no vinyl."

She peeked out of the corner of her eye, pretending to rearrange her papers, while Mack held up pair after pair, finally choosing the one with the most fabric.

"I'll be right back." He stomped off behind the curtain, and Jessica held her breath until her lungs hurt.

Ridiculous, she told herself. She was thirty years old. She'd been married and divorced. She was an independent woman. She'd more than learned her lesson about run-around, frivolous men who . . .

Mack stepped out.

Her wits scattered, every logical argument vanishing in an instant. *Impressive.* She no sooner thought it than she squeezed her eyes shut. Good grief. She was not a sex-starved woman who went about measuring men's endowments. But—well, he looked incredible. Better than incredible. Perfect. A very impressive male specimen.

He cleared his throat impatiently, and she opened her eyes again. It was an effort, but she essayed a look of outward indifference, when inside her body was dealing with numerous responses to his appeal.

Then he stepped into the harsh lamplight, and she saw that the material miraculously turned transparent. *Oh, my God.*

"Jessica, you're staring."

The black briefs now looked like a mere shadow on him, and she'd never seen anything so enticing.

"If you continue to stare, I won't be responsible for what happens."

She swallowed hard and tried to get her gaze to move, but the effort proved more than she could manage. The man was all but naked. Surely no sane woman would look away.

"It's a perfectly natural response, you understand, when a sexy woman stares at a man like she wants him."

That got her attention. Her gaze shot to his face. "Sexy woman?"

He didn't move, except to frown slightly. "You."

"I'm not—"

"Yes, you are." He sounded very positive and his eyes glowed hotly. "Very sexy. Just about as sexy as a woman can possibly get." When she gave him a blank stare, his expression turned tender. "You didn't know?"

"But . . . that's ridiculous."

"Afraid not."

"You never paid a bit of attention to me," she said in near desperation.

He started forward, prompting her to back up. But at least he was moving away from the light, and his briefs

were once again opaque. The relief afforded her a mod-
icum of sensibility.

"Mack, we were in the same class for two semesters.
Other than a few smiles tossed my way, you ignored me."

"That's not the way I remember it. And I bet if you
think real hard, it's not even the way you remember it."
He kept moving forward until he stood a mere foot in
front of her. Her searched her face, his gaze lingering on
her lips. "Jessica, you always fascinated me. I tried my
damnedest to get your attention, but all you ever did was
turn your nose up at me."

She'd backed up so far, her bottom was pressed to the
edge of the table. She reached back and gripped the table
for support. "You had about a million girlfriends. All
young and silly and—"

"They were *friends,* honey. That's all."

She snorted as rudely as Chase ever had. "You expect
me to believe that?" Before he could answer, she added,
"Not that it matters, anyway! You could have slept with
the instructor and I wouldn't care."

"I think you do care."

"Well, you're wrong."

"Jessica, I have a lot of friends, a lot of female friends.
That doesn't mean I'm sleeping with them all. And that
doesn't mean I react to them all the way I'm reacting to
you, the way I've always reacted to you."

Her heart rapped up against her breastbone and she
trembled. "I don't know what you're talking about."

One side of his mouth kicked up in a very boyish grin.

"I have an erection, honey. In these stupid flesh-hugging briefs, it's not really something I can hide."

Of course she looked, just as he knew she would.

He chuckled softly. "Your staring is what caused that in the first place. If you hope to take any more pictures today, I think we need to cool things down a bit."

He wanted her? The truth of that hit her like a thunderclap. Her hands shook, and she curled them into fists. Her breathing became shallow, her skin too warm. She drew in a slow, uneven breath, but it didn't help.

"Then again," he said, his voice a low, rough rasp, as he watched the signs of arousal blooming in her features. "maybe not."

She felt the heat pouring off him, felt his sexual tension. She looked up, and it was her undoing. His eyes had darkened, narrowed intently. His cheekbones were flushed. He touched her chin with the edge of his hand, raising her face more. Then slowly, giving her a chance to pull away, he leaned down.

She didn't want to pull away. It had been so long since she'd been with a man, long before the divorce became final. Though she did her best to deny it, there were times when her body ached with need. But never so much as it did right now. Mack affected her in a way she hadn't even known was possible; every nerve ending felt acutely alive and needy.

His mouth barely touched hers, moved away, came back. The kiss was tentative, exploring. He skimmed her lips, teasing, moving over her jaw, the tip of her nose, her chin. She panted, following his mouth, hungry for it. She went on tiptoe to bring his mouth closer.

He only touched her with that one hand, holding her face up, keeping her expectant. Rational thought was nonexistent. She stepped away from the table to get closer to him.

Their bodies brushed together, and he groaned. "Damn, I've dreamed about this."

"Mack . . ."

He settled his mouth against hers, and she felt drowned in the moist heat, the delicious taste of him. His hand opened, his calloused fingertips sliding over her jaw and into her hair. His hand curled around her head, tilting it slightly. His mouth moved, urging her lips to part for his tongue.

Her hands were still fisted at her sides, and she realized he wouldn't come closer until she invited him to do so. In a near daze, mindless with heat and lust and desperation, she raised her arms. His shoulders were hard, his flesh incredibly hot and smooth under her palms, and she felt him, greedy for more. She stepped closer still, pressing her breasts into the hard wall of his chest. The low, harsh sound he made sent goose bumps dancing up her spine. She clutched at him, and he wrapped one muscled arm around her waist, practically lifting her off her feet.

His erection throbbed against her belly.

"Mack . . ." She pulled her mouth away, gasping.

In between kissing her throat, her shoulder, he whispered, "I love hearing you say my name." He pressed his forehead to hers and sighed. "Am I moving too fast, Jessica?"

She could only groan, which he evidently took as encouragement. Kissing her again, he slid one hand down her back to her bottom, then urged her closer, moved her against him. She felt his fingers caressing, cuddling, squeezing. His hand was so large, and she could feel the heat of his palm even through her jeans. He lightly bit her bottom lip. "God, I'm about a hair away from losing control. You feel so good, so sexy and soft."

No man had ever told her such things. Her husband had wanted her in the early part of their marriage, but he hadn't indulged in much pillow talk. And not long after they were married, he'd gotten bored and started to roam.

Remembering caused her to stiffen. Mack immediately noticed the change. Even as he continued to nuzzle her, he cradled her face in both large palms. After one more light kiss, he looked at her intently. "What is it, babe? What's wrong?"

It was so difficult to get the words out. He appeared to be consumed with tenderness, with desire. He was on the ragged edge of desire—she could feel his muscles quivering—but he was also concerned. And the dual assault of a man wanting her and caring about her made her vulnerable. She looked away from him so she could gather her wits. She absolutely could not do this. Not again. "This is insane," she whispered.

His thumb brushed her temple, and he turned her back to meet his gaze. His smile was gentle. "It doesn't feel insane to me." He searched her face. "It just feels right."

"Mack." She caught his wrists and lowered his hands, then stepped away. Her legs didn't seem too steady, so she kept one hand braced on the table. "How can it possibly be right when we barely know each other?"

"Jessica . . ."

"No! You've only been here a few hours, and we're carrying on like . . . like animals."

He gently tugged on her braid, and she knew without looking that he was smiling. "You say that like it's a bad thing."

Here she was on fire, and he found the wit to tease. It was just like him, just like the man she knew him to be, and it reinforced her impression of him. Swallowing hard, she said, "You're just out for a little fun, aren't you?"

He gave a short, incredulous laugh. "Well, hell. If it wouldn't be fun, why do it?"

She groaned and covered her face.

"Jessica?" His tone dropped, became more intimate. "You *would* have fun, sweetheart. I'd make sure of it."

Shaking her head furiously, more to convince herself than him, she said, "Is that all you think about? Having fun?"

His fingers touched her hair, trailed down the length of her braid next to her breast. "I think about you. I've always wanted you."

She wouldn't look at him, not when all he wore was a heated look and what amounted to mere decoration. She knew her own limits, and she didn't want to tempt herself. After a deep, steadying breath, she whispered, "I'm a little embarrassed, if you want the truth. You might be used to women throwing themselves at you, but I swear I'm not usually like this."

"Which only goes to show that we're both very aware of each other, because despite what you think, I'm not usually this way either."

Oh, he was good. Not that she would buy it. He was just so experienced that he knew exactly what to say and when to say it. She bit her lip, then forged onward, searching for a credible explanation, something to defuse the situation.

Nothing, not even the truth, seemed overly redeeming. "It's . . . it's just that it's been a . . . a long time for me, and I guess that's why—"

"How long, honey?" He continued to play with her hair, and it was maddening.

She wanted to step away but couldn't quite get her feet to move. That overwhelming hot need still pulsed inside her. "Since before the divorce."

He stared, leaning down to see her face. He looked shocked, but also fascinated. "You're saying . . . *years?*"

She turned her back on him. If he laughed at her, she'd . . .

He stepped closer, and she could almost feel him touching her back. All her nerve endings seemed to scream, and she wasn't sure if it was an alarm, or a plea.

"Not that you'll believe me, but it's been a damn long time for me too. Not as long as you, but . . . well, long enough. I didn't expect this any more than you did. No one in his right mind has indiscriminate sex these days." She nearly choked over that little truism, prompting him to give her a squeeze. "I know you don't think much of my morals, but I'm not an idiot."

"I never said . . . !"

"You called me the class clown, a goof-off, remember?"

She could feel her bottom lip starting to tremble, but she would have died before she'd cry in front of him. "I didn't mean to insult you."

"Well, now, I think you did. And you know why? Because we're having a little fun together, and that scares you."

"No."

"And because you want me." She could feel his breath on her nape, the touch of his warmth. "You were as aware of me two years ago as I was of you. And you didn't like it any more then than you do now."

She turned without thinking. "That's not true!"

His expression softened. He looked at her face, down the length of her body and up again. Her breasts tingled when his gaze lingered there, and she knew her nipples were stiff, pushing against the sweater. His smile seemed ruthless, when she'd never thought of Mack that way.

"You want me still," he growled. "Why don't you admit it and let's see what happens?"

She felt cornered with him standing there so tall, so strong, his body all but bare. She'd forgotten all the wonderful differences men afforded, the incredible scents, the heat. Or maybe no other man had been like this. Though she'd tried to deny it, there had always been a chemistry between them, a sexual awareness that had taken her by surprise and stormed her senses. When they'd shared the class, she'd been painfully aware of every small move he made. And he was right—that awareness frightened her.

"I think we're done for the day."

He sighed. "I'll go. But promise me you'll think about what I've said, okay?"

"There's nothing to think about."

"There's this." He bent and kissed her again, a short, quick kiss that curled her toes and made her heart leap. Then he turned and walked away, unconcerned with his near nudity, with the tempting display he made as muscles and sinew shifted under his smooth flesh.

Jessica stepped out of the studio. The room, changed over from a master bedroom and bath, had always seemed immense to her. But with Mack inside, it was almost crowded, and at the moment she needed some space.

She waited by the window in the outer room, watching the ice and sleet fall, hearing it tap against the window-panes. Confusion swamped her, but also shame, because despite what she knew was right, she didn't want him to go.

She heard his footsteps come up behind her. As he was pulling on his coat, he asked, "When do you want me again?" She stiffened, then heard his soft laugh. "To fin-ish the shoot, I mean."

God, she didn't know. She needed as much as wanted the job. Even with giving Sophie a deal, she'd stand to make a lot of money off this. And adding the catalogue to her portfolio would bring in other commissions, would expand her possibilities. She shook her head, unable to sort through all the ramifications. And then the phone rang.

She felt so tense and edgy, she nearly jumped out of her skin. Mack watched her as she stepped around him and hurried down the hall to the phone. He silently followed.

"Hello?"

"Mom, can you . . . can you come pick me up?"

She frowned at the strained tone of her daughter's voice. "Trista? What's wrong, honey?"

"I just wanna come home now."

"All right. Hang on, sweetie. I'll be right there."

"Thanks, Mom."

Mack looked at her as she laid the receiver back in the cradle. "What is it?"

"Trista." She headed out of the room to get her coat and keys, and Mack again followed. "Something's wrong. She sounded about ready to cry. I . . . I have to go pick her up."

Mack nodded. He didn't question her decision to walk out with things still unresolved. He just kept up with her hurried pace, even helping her to slip on her coat. "Do you think it's anything serious?"

"No." He opened the door for her and she stepped out into the biting wind. "Jenna's parents are nice people. It's probably just an argument with a friend, but . . ."

"You have to go. I understand."

"I know we have . . . unfinished business, but . . ."

"Jessica." He squeezed her shoulder. "She's your daughter. If she needs you, of course you have to go."

He sounded so sincere, she blinked up at him. "You mean that, don't you? You don't think it's silly for me to rush out to get her?"

He gave her that endearing crooked smile again. "If you say she sounded upset, then I'm sure you're right. If I had a daughter, I'd do the same thing."

And he would. Though it amazed her, she could tell he did understand, and a small knot of regret settled in her belly. Maybe she had judged him too quickly. "My husband used to say I spoiled her."

As soon as the words left her mouth, she gasped. Good grief, she hadn't meant to share that.

Mack touched her cheek. He kept touching her, as if he couldn't help himself. "You can't spoil a child with too much love."

They had circled to the side lot, and as she neared her car she looked up at him. "Thank you."

Mack stared at her car with a frown. "Don't thank me yet. I have a feeling you're going to need my help."

Confused, she followed his gaze and saw her car was literally frozen beneath a layer of ice. The old house didn't have a garage, so her car was at the mercy of the elements. And since she hadn't driven it in a couple of days, she knew it would take a while to get it ready to go.

Mack held out his arms like a sacrifice. "Behold, your white knight. Or maybe I should say your chauffeur."

She didn't want to prolong her time with him, but she was already shivering, and it didn't make sense to stand out in the cold arguing about it. Especially not when she knew Trista was upset and waiting for her.

Mack stood there, determined to come to her assistance despite what had happened between them. Unlike most men, who would have stormed away mad over being rebuffed, he wanted to play the gallant. Frost collected on his dark hair and his cheeks turned ruddy. He looked young and strong and capable; she'd almost forgotten what it was like to have a man share her burdens. She'd wanted to forget, to prove herself independent, capable of handling anything alone.

Right now she was simply relieved to have a good excuse to keep him close.

Knowing that her own nose had to be cherry-red, she lifted it anyway and said, "Fine. Let's go."

Chapter Three

Since he'd been expecting more stubbornness, Mack was nearly bowled over by her compliance. But only for a moment. He took her arm and quickly ushered her toward his truck. He held her close and said, "Be careful. The pavement's slick."

There was a coating of ice on his truck as well, but he easily forced the doors open. Once inside, Jessica huddled into a corner. Her long braid was tucked beneath her coat, and she shivered uncontrollably. He wanted to pull her close, to share his warmth, but she'd already made it clear what she thought of that idea.

It was his own fault for going too fast. Not that he could have helped himself. He'd simply wanted her for too long, dreamed about her too many times, to pass up such an opportunity. She'd looked at him with her soft doe eyes filled with lust, and he'd damn near exploded.

She'd tasted better than he'd expected, felt better than he'd imagined. All the fantasies he'd stored up hadn't prepared him for the reality. Damn, but she packed one hell of a carnal punch.

Yet for some reason she'd apparently sworn off men. He wouldn't give up on her. He wanted her too much for that.

Her breath frosted the air between them as she watched him fasten his seat belt, start the truck, and ease out onto the road. She was silent, but he could almost feel her thinking. He glanced her way as she gave him directions, and noticed how cute she looked with a red nose and rosy cheeks.

It was already dark, and the streets were in terrible shape, but they made the few blocks to where Trista was waiting in less than five minutes.

Mack sat in the truck, relieved that the thermostat was finally warming up, while Jessica climbed out to get her daughter. Trista saw her from the doorway and met her on the sidewalk, looking curiously at the truck. Mack gave her a smile of encouragement as she slid into the seat between him and Jessica.

"Can you get the seat belt okay?"

She nodded, and kept sneaking glances at him. She looked utterly morose, and Mack smiled, remembering how life-altering everything felt when you were a teenager. "You're wondering why I'm here, right?"

Her answer was a cautious look toward her mother.

"Hey, I like your mom, and she was all in a dither to get to you, and her car was completely frozen over, so I offered to drive. I hope you don't mind. Just pretend I'm not here."

Both Jessica and Trista stared at him. He chose to take it as an encouraging sign.

The silence was heavy, so he asked, "It's got to do with that Brian guy, right?"

Trista tucked in her chin, watching him warily.

"I could be a big help, you know. I mean, who better to understand the warped-guy psyche than a guy? Think of all the insight I can give you." He leaned closer and whispered, "I was thirteen once myself."

Jessica cleared her throat. "Uh, Mack . . ."

He interrupted her with a wave of his hand. "We could discuss it over hot chocolate. What do you think?"

He'd rushed the physical side of things earlier. Now that he wasn't holding Jessica, now that he was fully dressed and his body was back under control—thanks mostly to the frigid February weather—he could think more clearly. Or at least, he could think without salacious intent clouding his judgment.

He wanted her. He wanted to make love to her, to explore her body, especially those incredible breasts of hers. He wanted to taste every inch of her and listen to her moan his name. More than anything, he wanted to see her beautiful dark eyes as she climaxed with him.

But he also wanted to talk to her, to tease her and listen to her huff and watch her face when she blushed. He wanted her to share her sharp wit, the love she felt for her daughter. He wanted to know more about her work, her divorce, how she felt about things, and what her life had been like.

Despite their moment of intimacy, she was determined to push him away, hesitant to get involved on any level. But it wasn't because of lack of mutual appeal, that much was certain. He could still feel the burning touch of her stiff little nipples against his chest when she'd rubbed against him, the way her fingers had dug into his shoulders, how hot she'd tasted on his tongue. He shuddered with the memory.

All he needed to do was keep his cool, ignore her occasional insults, and figure out why she had such an aversion to men in general and him in particular. She'd said he reminded her of her ex, but it had to be more than that; he felt sure of it. She was an incredibly sensual woman, yet she'd been years without a man. The very thought boggled his mind.

Patience, that's what he needed.

Patience, and a lot of determination.

Trista tucked her hands between her knees and said to the windshield, "I don't care what Brian does. He's a jerk."

Pretending offense, Mack said, "Well, give me some credit! I already figured that out."

"You did?"

"Of course I did. You left with a smile, but came back with a frown. Only a jerk could cause that."

Trista gave him a half smile before remembering she was piqued. "He called me a dummy."

"He's a jerk. I rest my case."

"I don't do too good in science, and we're going to have a big project coming up. I thought he'd be my partner, but he asked Jenna today instead."

Jessica reached over and squeezed Trista's hand. "Let me guess. Jenna said yes?"

"She only likes him because I do."

Mack pulled into the lot behind the house, parking as close to the brick structure as he could in hopes that some of the icy wind would be deflected. "You know, I had a lot of trouble with science, too. My sister-in-law used to help me study. Sometimes all you need is a little help."

Jessica patted Trista's leg with a smile. "I can't claim to be a whiz at seventh-grade science, but I'm sure we can study up together."

Mack cleared his throat in an imperious way, and though it was sneaky, he spoke directly to Trista. "Well, now, considering I'm a bona fide teacher, and I've finally mastered science, I *can* claim to be a whiz. So whatdya say I tutor you a little? Not so you can prove anything to Brian, because what he thinks doesn't really matter, right?"

Trista grinned. "Right."

"But this way, you'll know he's wrong if he ever says anything so obnoxious again."

Trista immediately turned to her mother. "Could I?"

Mack knew he had her. He added, just for good measure, "I need to be here a couple more times anyway to get the magazine photos all taken care of. We could work on that while Trista is in school, then I could stay after and do some studying. What do you say?"

She looked like she wanted to smack him, but since Trista sat between them she held back. "If you're a teacher, won't you need to be at school?"

That stumped him. He hated to admit he hadn't landed a permanent job yet, but he really didn't see any way around it. He hedged just a bit instead. "I'm still waiting for my final placement. The school board has to go through several interviews, and until that's done, my days are free. Unless, of course, someone calls for a substitute, but that doesn't happen that often."

Trista looked excited. "Are you going to teach at my school?"

"Nope, sorry, kiddo. I've sort of specialized in inner city. That's where good teachers are needed most because the kids have so few advantages. I'm hoping for a permanent placement at Mordmont." He glanced at Jessica. "And I'm a very good teacher. That's where I did my student teaching, and I'm kinda close to the kids now, so I'd like to go back there."

"Bummer. It'd be cool to brag that we had a model for a teacher."

He could just imagine how that info would go over with the school board. Not that it would really matter to them. They'd tried using his family connection to a bar as a reason to get rid of him, but that didn't carry any weight, considering the backgrounds of some of the other teachers. Most of them were questionable old relics who wouldn't know a modern method if it bit them in the butt, and that's why they hadn't wanted him. He challenged their outdated methods, refused to conform, and any non-conformity scared them shitless, even when they could see the advantages to the students.

If worse came to worst, he'd have to go out of the area. But that would be a last resort, because in the inner city he'd felt he made a real difference, and that's what teaching was all about for him.

The truck had gotten toasty warm, but they couldn't keep sitting in it forever. He looked at Jessica and said, "About that hot chocolate . . ."

She stared him straight in the eye. "Not tonight, Mack. I'm sorry, but it's been a long day. I started early this morning and I spent all day in the studio. I still have tons of household chores to get done. And my weekend, as well as a good part of next week, is already booked. I was going to see if Thursday morning would work for you to do our next shoot. That'll still give us plenty of time to get everything together for the catalogue."

And it would give her plenty of time to forget about him. He needed to make a diplomatic withdrawal, before she could refuse him everything, but no way would he withdraw enough to let her rebuild all her defenses.

He smiled at her. "No problem. I wouldn't want to get in your way." She looked slightly dazed at his easy acceptance, and he added, "But Trista and I don't need you to help us study, anyway. Saturday I'm busy, but I could come Sunday and the rest of the week until you're ready for me."

Her eyes narrowed, and he could just imagine what she

thought he'd be doing on Saturday. He had no doubt her thoughts included sexual indulgence and wouldn't be overly flattering. If only she knew what a recluse he'd become. Working at the family bar on Saturday had been the highlight of his social life lately.

Trista filled in the gap of silence. "I'll bring home the instructions for my science project on Monday. Maybe you can give me a few good ideas?"

"I'd be glad to." He turned off the motor and walked around to open Jessica's door. "Come on, ladies. I'll see you inside."

Trista giggled, but he thought he heard Jessica growl, "We don't need you to—"

Mack looped an arm through each of theirs and proceeded onward, ignoring Jessica's protest while practically gliding her across the icy ground. "Hang on tight. The walk is pretty slick."

She huffed, but had no choice except to hold on or fall. "I gather you think you're steadier than we are?"

"Sure. I've got bigger feet, don't I?" Jessica wasn't amused, but Trista chuckled.

When they reached the door, Jessica fumbled with the key while Mack turned to Trista. "I don't suppose you have your science book at home, do you? It'd help if I could see where you are in it."

"I don't have my book, but I have all my papers from last week."

"How about I take them home with me and look them over? Then we can get started right away on Sunday afternoon."

"I'll go get 'em!" She dashed inside and Jessica, still with her back to him, started to do the same.

Mack caught her arm. "Whoa. Can we talk just a second?"

Reluctantly, she turned to face him. She didn't look pleased, and the second she spoke, he knew why. "I don't like being manipulated, Mack."

Though he knew he'd do it again in a heartbeat, he did feel bad about cornering her. He wasn't in the habit of forcing his company on women. "I'm sorry."

She gaped at him. "You're not even going to deny it?"

"Why should I? I want to see you and this seemed like my only chance. You didn't really think I'd give up that easily, did you?"

She looked astounded and chagrined and, if he was reading her right, a little complimented.

"This is ridiculous—"

"You keep saying that, but damned if I see what's so ridiculous about it."

"I'm too old for you."

He laughed.

"Will you be serious!"

His smile disappeared, but she could still see the slight amusement in his eyes. "Okay, how's this for serious? If I kissed you right now, would you think about me tonight?" She drew a deep breath and he added, "Try being honest with me for once, okay?"

Her chin lifted. "All right. Yes."

"Yes, you'd think about me?" He was so pleased with her he wanted to lift her in his arms, swing her in a circle.

He wanted to kiss her silly, to touch her all over. He wanted to devour her, actually, and not even the damn cold could temper his lust.

"Yes, I probably would. But you're not going to kiss me, Mack, so it's a moot admission."

There was no way he could contain his grin. "I bet you'll think about me even if I don't kiss you."

She made a disgusted sound. "Oh, for pity's sake."

"Won't you?" He ducked his head, trying to see her averted face. "Jessica? Tell me you'll think about me, because I'll damn sure be thinking about you."

"No."

"No, you won't tell me or no, you won't think about me?"

She laughed, covering her face with her gloved hands. "You're impossible!"

He pulled her hands down and kissed the end of her icy-cold nose. "I'm infatuated." She started to back up and he let her, pretending it didn't bother him. "I really will enjoy working with Trista. Don't think I'm not serious about that, because I am. Even though I used it as an excuse to spend more time around you, I do think I can help her out. I'm a good teacher." Modesty kept him from total honesty. In truth, he was an *exceptional* teacher.

"It's hard for me to imagine you at the head of a classroom."

He looked away. "Yeah, well, the principal has the same problem."

Tipping her head back to look at him, she asked, "What does that mean?"

He was saved from any morbid confessions by Trista's return. She looked embarrassed as she handed him a stack of papers. "Some of the grades on those aren't too good."

He'd seen the same uncertainty on dozens of different adolescent faces, and it always filled him with compassion. School, in his opinion, shouldn't be about failures so much as accomplishments. He neatly folded the papers in half and stuck them in his pocket. "Did you do your best?"

"Yeah."

"Good girl. No one can ask for more than that, regardless of how you scored on the paper. Let's forget about these grades and concentrate on the next ones, okay?"

"You really think I'll do better?"

"We'll both give it our best shot."

When she smiled, the streetlamp reflected off her braces. He loved making kids smile. Sticking out his hand, he said, "Trista, it was a distinct pleasure."

She shook his hand, giggling, then said a proper good night. With a quick, calculating look at her mother, she ducked back inside and pulled the door shut. She even turned off the porch light. Jessica groaned.

Without conscious thought, Mack moved closer to her, sharing his warmth. Their breath mingled. "Your daughter likes me."

"My daughter doesn't really know you."

He bridged both hands against the brick wall on either side of her head. He felt her nervousness, her excitement. "This may surprise you, but you don't really know me either."

She lifted her chin. "I know what I saw in college. There's not only a big age difference between us—"

"A few piddling years."

"—but we also have very different outlooks."

"Because I want to have fun and you don't?" He'd leaned down so close, his nose brushed her soft, cold cheek. She smelled sweet and fresh and like the brisk outdoors. He nuzzled against her, drinking in the wonderful scent.

"Mack."

It was a weak protest, and they both knew it. But he was a gentleman and he didn't want to push her. He wanted her to want him, to admit she felt the same incredible things he felt. He rested his forehead against her crown for just a moment, relishing the simple enjoyment of holding her. "If you change your mind over the weekend, call me."

"I won't change my mind."

She sounded less than certain about that, and he smiled. "Sophie has my number."

"I won't change my mind."

He leaned back to look at her. "Tonight, when you're in bed alone, think about me." Her brown eyes were huge in the darkness, and she stared at him without answering. He opened the door and gave her a small nudge in the right direction. "Sleep well, honey."

Just before she pulled the door shut, she whispered, "Mack? Be careful driving home." Stunned, Mack stood there a moment until he heard her turn the lock. Then, slowly, he started to smile. He even laughed out loud, but the sound seemed more ominous than not in the cold, quiet night.

Damn, he felt good.

And then he remembered the Winston curse.

☙

Sophie was ringing up a customer when Mack walked in. The little bell over the door jingled, and she looked up with a smile of welcome. Three other women looked up as well, then proceeded to stare rudely, as if he'd invaded their private territory. Mack merely grinned, sauntered over to some lacy bras, and began browsing.

Allison came out of the back room and spotted him. "Hey, Mack. How did the photo shoot go?"

Why did Allison look so suspicious when she asked that? He narrowed his gaze at her, then shrugged. Maybe she was waiting for the curse to hit him. She couldn't know that he'd already resigned himself to his fate. Hell, he was half anticipating it.

"It went okay. Though some of that stuff isn't coming anywhere near my body."

"Spoilsport."

Sophie joined them, looking indignant. "Which stuff?"

"G-strings? Those filmy briefs with the see-through front? And what about those clear vinyl thingies—"

Laughing, Sophie put a finger to his lips. "Hush. Every lady in here is eavesdropping."

Allison looked at him over the rim of her round glasses. "See-through vinyl?"

"Yeah. You should get Chase a pair." He tried to hide

his amusement, but it was impossible when Allison seemed to be seriously considering the idea.

Sophie took his arm and dragged him to the other side of the room, where there were fewer ears to listen in. "Some of those things are just for fun. They're not meant to be taken seriously."

"Well, I'm seriously not modeling them."

"Is that why you're here? You're not going to back out on me just because a few of the items are a bit . . . risqué, are you?"

"No, I'm not backing out."

She suddenly stiffened, then grabbed both his hands. "Oh, wait! Did you hear from the school board? Did you get the position?"

"No, I didn't hear anything yet." He almost wished she hadn't reminded him. His preoccupation with Jessica had driven away much of his frustration. Which was just as well, because he absolutely hated to sit around fretting like an old schoolmarm.

Sophie looked ready to embrace him, and he quickly sidestepped her. She had this mothering tendency that sometimes made him uncomfortable. It had been especially noticeable since she'd gotten pregnant. "I'm fine, Sophie, really. It's not a big deal."

"Baloney. I know how hard you've worked to be a great teacher."

"Yeah, well. A lot of good it's done me."

"Oh, my God. I just thought of something. What if the school board sees you in the catalogue?"

"That's not an issue. Nothing I wore is that revealing,

and I seriously doubt they'd ever see it, anyway, since they're two districts away. No offense, hon, but it's not like your boutique is well known across the state."

She sniffed. "No, it's a quaint local shop."

"Very local. And the school board can't touch me on morals charges. Not when one of the teachers moonlights at a strip club and another has been picked up twice for brawling. Their big gripe is that I don't follow their procedure, even though I've proven my procedure to be more effective."

Sophie gave him a sad smile. "This matters a lot to you, doesn't it?"

Damn. How had he let the subject get so sidetracked? "It matters," he admitted, "but that's not why I'm here." He suddenly felt a little self-conscious and reached out to touch a satiny-soft camisole hanging on a rack. "I, uh, I wanted some advice."

Allison crept back over to them. "Oh, good. I love giving advice."

Mack ran a hand through his hair. "The thing is, I know Jessica."

"No!" Sophie put a hand to her chest.

Allison nudged her, then cleared her throat. She gave Mack her undivided attention. "You know her? From where?"

Something wasn't right, but damned if Mack could figure out what. He'd never understand his sisters-in-law, and he'd given up trying. "I knew her in college. We took a class together. I always liked her, but she—well, she's not too fond of me for some reason."

Sophie raised her brows in theatrical surprise. "Wait a minute! Jessica isn't the woman you always talked about when I helped you to study, is she?"

"One and the same."

Allison leaned back against a display table of panties. "Fascinating coincidence."

Frustrated, Mack paced away, then back again. "Yeah, I know. I didn't think I'd ever see her again. But now that I have seen her again, I want her."

Allison straightened at that. "Maybe I'm too young to hear this."

Sophie smothered a laugh. "I'm not. Go ahead, Mack."

He stared at both of the women, then blurted out, "Which of those goofy lingerie things do you think she'd like the most?"

They looked at each other before Sophie asked, "You want us to tell you which things will be likely to . . . uh . . ."

The women were staring at him so wide-eyed, he felt his ears turn red. He wanted to get this over with so he could get back to his planning. "To turn her on. Yeah. So what do you think?"

Sophie choked, but Allison gave it serious thought. "I like the soft cotton stuff. Cotton feels so good on men and it hugs all those sexy muscles. Chase looks just adorable in cotton boxers, especially the snug-fitting kind." She turned to Sophie. "Weren't there a few of those in the box?"

Sophie tried unsuccessfully to get rid of her grin. "Um,

yes. They have little"—she gestured toward Mack's fly—"silver snaps up the front."

Allison patted his arm. "With your dark coloring, try the black ones. Or the forest green."

Sophie shook her head. "I rather like the silky ones. In white."

"So you think if I wear those for Jessica, I mean for the shoot, she'll . . . ah, enjoy the sight?"

"Most definitely."

"Absolutely."

Mack shook his head, grinning. "Why do I get the feeling you two are up to no good?"

Sophie shrugged. "You obviously have a suspicious nature."

She looked too innocent, and he didn't like it. "Where exactly did you meet Jessica?" He didn't think he had ever shared her name with Sophie, though he had described her on numerous occasions. Hell, for a while there she was all he could think of, until he'd resigned himself to never seeing her again.

"She shops here."

Mack felt like someone had doused him in fire. He looked around at all the sexy stuff on mannequins, hanging in displays, stacked softly on tables, and his heart thumped. He pictured her stretched out on a bed, *his bed*, her lush body barely covered in black satin or white lace. "She really wears this stuff?"

Allison gave him a pitying look. "What did you think she wore? Burlap?"

"No, but . . . which stuff?"

"Ah, now that would be telling, and I can't do that."

"Sophie?"

Sophie crossed her arms and lifted her chin. "Allison's right, Mack. If you want to know what kind of lingerie Jessica wears, you'll just have to find out on your own."

He damn well intended to.

A few minutes later Mack walked out the front door, thinking what lucky dogs his brothers were. He glanced back once and saw Allison and Sophie collapsed against each other, laughing hysterically. He smiled. He didn't mind their ribbing at all since they'd been totally honest with him. Poor Jessica. She didn't stand a chance.

Chapter Four

Jessica felt so confused, she didn't know what to think, or precisely how to handle her new decision.

Mack had been hanging around all week, working with Trista, laughing and joking, making his presence unmistakably known. When he was around, Jessica felt it in every pore of her body. She'd catch herself listening for his laugh, or looking to catch a glimpse of him in between appointments. He and Trista mostly worked in the office, but after the first day Trista had asked if Mack could go upstairs with her to help make lunch. The upstairs was where they lived, and Jessica didn't want him invading her home as well as her office, but she couldn't find a reasonable excuse to deny him. And after that, they often went upstairs, getting drinks or looking for books, or using the computer. Trista adored him, and already she had new confidence in her abilities at school.

Often, when Jessica's workday was over and Mack had gone home, she'd find signs of him upstairs still. Notes he'd scrawled for Trista, a hat he'd left behind, even his scent lingered. Sleeping was difficult, because no matter how she tried, she couldn't stop thinking of him and how he'd made her feel. He'd only kissed her and barely touched her, yet she'd been more aroused than she could ever remember. She wanted him, and the wanting wasn't going to go away.

He hadn't been especially familiar with her since that first day. He was, in fact, a perfect gentleman, talking politely, minding his manners, respecting her wishes to be left alone.

Though it shamed her to admit it, she hated it that he'd given up so easily. Or had he?

She hoped not, because she'd already decided she wanted, needed, to know what it was like to be with him. He looked at her and it affected her more than a physical touch. She hadn't felt like her old self since he'd first kissed her, and she saw no reason she shouldn't indulge herself for once. But just once.

Today he'd be back for the shoot, and she didn't quite know what to expect or how to make her declaration. Since that first day Trista had been close by to act as a buffer, and she supposed that could possibly account for part of Mack's restraint. When he was studying with her, his attention was undivided. But now Trista would be in school, and she and Mack would have quite a few hours alone and uninterrupted.

And Mack would be wearing those damned seductive undergarments again.

Just the thought of it made her palms sweat, her heart jumpy. She looked around the studio, making sure everything was in place. With any luck, they could finish up early and then, if Mack was still willing, use the rest of the afternoon to make love.

The doorbell rang and she jerked around, feeling guilty about her thoughts even though no one would know. She hurried out of the room, but at the door she stopped to compose herself, feeling like a foolish coed yet unable to help herself. She pasted on a smile and pulled the door open.

Mack leaned on the door frame, arms crossed over his chest, his breath frosting in front of him. At the sight of her he smiled lazily. "Hey."

Just that small smile, and her insides fluttered in anticipation. "Hello. Right on time." She opened the door wider and he came in. Only he didn't step to the side of her. He came right up to her. He cupped her face in his gloved hands and, casual as you please, he kissed her.

"I missed you," he whispered against her mouth.

Flustered, she stammered, "You've seen me all week!"

"Hmmm. Seen you, but not been able to touch you." He kissed her again, a light, barely there kiss, making her want more. "Did you miss me too?"

"Mack. This is—"

"Ridiculous?" He touched the tip of her nose and

stepped around her, then peered into the empty office. "Where's the receptionist?"

Swallowing nervously, Jessica tried to remind herself that she was thirty years old, an experienced woman, a divorcée who knew how to handle herself in any situation, never mind that she hadn't been in this situation in too many years to count, and never with a man like Mack.

She laced her fingers together to keep her hands from shaking. "You're the only appointment I have today, so there was no need for her to come in. She helps out mostly with appointments to view proofs or to pick up packages."

Mack looked at her intently, one brow raised. "Then we're here all alone?"

Now he would probably kiss her again. She licked her lips, anticipating his unique taste, the heat of his mouth. "Yes."

He nodded, still looking at her. "I suppose we should get started?"

Disappointment filled her, but she hoped it didn't show. "Yes, of course." She didn't understand him at all. He seemed to still want her, but if he did, then why was he waiting? She started down the hall and for the first time questioned her choice of clothes. The scoop-neck, cream-colored sweater was soft, and her plaid skirt almost reached her ankles. True, she often wore long skirts to work in because they were so comfortable, but today it had been a deliberate choice; she'd wanted to look more feminine for Mack. That decision now seemed beyond pathetic, and she had the irrational fear that he'd know it.

She cleared her throat once they were in the studio.

"Sophie called and mentioned a few other things she wants you to wear."

His brow shot up a good inch. "She did?"

"Yes. There's some snap-front boxers and matching ribbed undershirts she definitely wants in the catalogue."

Mack grinned, and an unholy light entered his eyes. "I see."

Jessica handed him the first change of clothes, and Mack went behind the curtain. While he was there, she readied her camera and set up some scrims to filter the light, making the scene softer, more intimate. This particular scrim, or mesh filter, had denser spots, which provided a dappled look, like sunlight through leaves. She placed an old-fashioned quilt on the floor over artificial grass, then added some props to give it an outdoor look. She used a birdbath, a small bush, some flowers.

Mack stepped around the curtain just as she smoothed the quilt one last time. She smiled at him, barely managing to still her sigh of appreciation. The snug boxers and ribbed undershirt showed his big muscled body to perfection.

"For this shot," she said, her voice just a little husky, "it's going to look like you're resting outside, enjoying the sunshine, totally at your ease. It's to sort of show how comfortable the clothes are."

"I can buy that." He rubbed one large hand over his abdomen. "They do feel nice."

She swallowed hard, wondering how it would feel to her hand—not just the fabric but his body beneath it. With a sigh, she looked him over from his tousled dark head, his intent eyes and stubborn, clean-shaven jaw, to his broad shoulders, lean hips, and long legs, all the way down to his big feet. She couldn't imagine a man who looked more perfect or more sensually enticing, than Mack Winston.

Her heart beat a little too fast, and she had trouble drawing an even breath. Mack watched her face, and after a moment, he said softly, "I like it when you look at me like that. You know, I memorized your features back in college. You'd sit there, refusing to look at me, staring at the instructor as if she spoke gospel, and I'd study you. Every little angle, the tilt of your nose, the slant of your jaw, how your lashes left shadows on your cheeks. I'd go nuts looking at the profile of your breasts."

Jessica knew that was always the first thing men noticed about her, and it annoyed her. From the time she'd hit puberty, she'd worn a C cup. It had always been more of a nuisance than anything else. "All women have breasts."

"All women aren't you." He came closer, then dropped to his knees directly in front of her. With only one hand, he touched her jaw, smoothed her hair back to her braid, then trailed his fingers down her neck to where it met her shoulder. He lifted his other hand and cradled her head, using his thumbs to stroke her jaw. Jessica felt herself trembling in anticipation, and knew he felt it too.

After a moment of heavy silence, he tilted his head to the side. "What is it about you, Jessica, that makes me feel this way?"

She stared at his collarbone, at where the low neck of

the undershirt showed just a bit of hair on his chest. This close, she could smell him, the musky smell of aroused male. She swallowed hard and asked in a whisper, "What way?"

"Like I have to have you." His hands drifted down to her shoulders, then inward, his fingers spreading wide over her upper chest. "*Have* to, just like I have to breathe, or eat. It was pure torture in college, trying to concentrate when I had a hard-on all the time. And all you wanted to do was snub me."

She shook her head, unwilling to be pulled in with lies. "How could you have been thinking of me when all those skinny girls kept throwing themselves at you?"

He was looking at her breasts, and his hands skimmed over her sides to her waist. "I didn't—"

Jessica scrambled back, wrinkling the quilt. "You did. You flirted and played around, and all the girls adored you."

Mack dropped back to sit on his heels, studying her closely. "I also got straight A's. Which I earned."

"That's impossible!"

"Ah, surprised you with that one, didn't I? I guess you figured I coasted through with the lowest passable grades possible? Did you think that's why I was interested in teaching inner-city kids? Because no influential school district would have me?"

She shook her head. "I don't know." But of course she had thought it.

"You're confusing me with him," he said gently. "I'm not the one who hurt you, not the one who used you." He lifted one shoulder, and his look was sad. "Honey, having fun doesn't make you a bad person. It doesn't make you irresponsible or frivolous. It's okay to enjoy everything you do—your schoolwork, your friends, your job. Life."

It hurt her to admit he might be right, that she might have been the one with the wrong outlook. "I guess that's easier for some people than others."

"Why? Why can't you have a little fun?"

Despite herself, she smiled. "Fun, as in fooling around with you?"

"No fooling to it. Sometimes you need to take your fun very seriously."

She had no idea what to make of that. His look was direct, hot, and very sensual. She shivered, then admitted, "I . . . I want to."

His eyes gleamed, and though he didn't quite smile, she saw the dimple in his cheek. "But?"

"It's not easy to explain."

"Well, now. I can be a pretty good listener when you give me a chance."

No doubt Mack would be good at anything he did. But talking about her inhibitions, the problems that had nearly suffocated her just a few years ago, wasn't easy. Talking about them with Mack was doubly hard, because she suddenly cared what he thought. He scooted closer, crossed his legs Indian style, and gave her a look of encouragement.

He looked young and sexy and caring and considerate. His body was hard and beautiful, his smile gentle. He was a female's fantasy come to life, the epitome of temptation and magnetism. And he sat before her, waiting.

With a sigh, she gave in. "My husband and I met when I was a high school senior and he was in his second year of college. I'd always been sort of mousy, real quiet, and he was the first really popular guy to pay attention to me."

Mack picked at a loose thread in the quilt. "It's tough for me to imagine you as mousy." He glanced up and caught her gaze. "You're so damn sexy now."

She blushed. "Mack . . ."

"Go on."

He flustered her so with his compliments, it was hard for her to gather her thoughts. "He was so much . . . *fun*. I was completely overwhelmed by him, and like a dummy, I wasn't as careful as I should have been. I got pregnant."

Mack snorted. "He was older, and no doubt more experienced?"

She shrugged, a little embarrassed to have to admit it, but she did. "I was a virgin."

"So why the hell wasn't he being careful? Any man who cares about a woman protects her as well as himself. My brother pounded that into my head when I was about fifteen, long before I ever got around to even trying anything with a girl." He grinned slightly. "I guess after Zane, who's more wild than not, he wasn't going to take any chances."

"Your brother is older than you?"

"Yeah, by about fifteen years. My mom and dad died when I was young, so Cole pretty much raised the rest of us."

"Oh, Mack." Her heart swelled. She was still so close to her parents, she couldn't imagine losing them. "I'm so sorry."

He gave her that adorable boyish grin. "It's okay. It was a long time ago, and Cole made certain we had everything we needed. He was a mom and dad and big brother all in one."

Fascinated, she asked, "How many brothers do you have?"

"I'm the baby." He grinned shamelessly at that admission. "Then there's Zane, who's a complete and total hedonist, but we forgive him because he's a damn good brother too. And Chase, who's pretty quiet, except maybe not so much now that he's married to Allison. And then Cole. He's married to Sophie."

"You're all pretty close, aren't you?" At his nod, she said, "I was an only child. My folks are great, but I know they were a little disappointed when I got pregnant. They wanted to help out, for me to stay at home and go to college, but I really thought I loved Dave and that we'd have a good marriage."

"Didn't work out that way, huh?"

"No. Dave was never very responsible. Oh, he married me, but then I couldn't go to college because we needed me to work to pay his tuition. He said his studies took up too much time for him to hold down a job. Only his grades were never very good, and then he flunked out the first semester of his third year. I hated to admit how badly I'd screwed up in marrying him, so I made excuses for him and told everyone what a great job he'd gotten. But then he lost that for missing too much work."

Mack's eyes had narrowed, but his tone remained calm. "He sounds like a real winner."

"That's just it. Everyone thought so. He was the life of the party, a real charming guy. People met him and they naturally liked him. Especially the women. I always came across as a terrible nag. His relatives complained about how I had dragged him down, because he was saddled with a wife and a kid, and they said that was why he'd failed college, because he had too many responsibilities."

Mack touched her cheek. "I can only imagine how that made you feel."

"It wasn't *fun*, I can tell you that."

"Not for you, but it sounds like he did all right."

Jessica pulled her knees up, making sure her long skirt covered her legs. She crossed her arms over them and rested the side of her face there. She didn't want to look at Mack. She didn't want to see his pity at the stupid girl she'd been. "He did better than all right. He ended up with a nothing part-time job that left him plenty of free time to run around. I worked full time at a restaurant, and my parents watched Trista for me. Dave had a lot of friends, and they all thought I was a bitch if I suggested he should skip hanging out. Then one day Trista got sick and I needed him to get medicine. I called the house where he was supposed to be playing cards with his buddies, but when a woman answered, I could tell it was a huge party. I went to get the medicine myself, and on the way home I stopped by there."

Mack scooted around to sit behind her. He pulled her back to his chest, closed his arms tightly around her, and kissed her temple. "He was cheating on you."

It wasn't a question, so she didn't bother to answer. "Here I was, still wearing my stained, wrinkled waitress uniform, Trista beside me. I looked horrible from working all day, and Trista had a runny nose and red eyes. But Dave looked great. He was laughing and having a good time. When the woman on his lap looked up, I didn't want to admit to being his wife. They all stared at me, and I could tell they felt sorry for Dave. They thought he'd gotten a bum deal with me. I just turned around and walked out."

She could feel the tension coming off Mack, only this time it was anger. She twisted around to see him, but the minute she was turned, he kissed her. His mouth opened on hers, and his tongue stroked her lips, making her gasp. He seemed almost desperate, his hands in her hair, holding her close, devouring her. His urgency alarmed her a bit, overwhelming her. His hands stroked everywhere, down her back to her bottom, over her stomach and up to her breast, and then his fingers found her stiffened nipple, making her shudder and gasp. A thick, low groan erupted from his throat and she felt him tremble.

All her reservations vanished. She wanted him, and there would never be a better time than now.

⤳ ⟶⟞

Mack cursed roughly when Jessica suddenly relaxed, her arms wrapping around his neck, her breast pressing into his palm. "Jesus. I feel like I'm going to explode."

"Mack . . ." Her small, cool hand touched his jaw, bringing his mouth back to hers. He couldn't think of anything he'd ever wanted as much as he wanted her right now. He understood her so much better after all she'd told him, and he wanted—needed—to prove to her that he was different. He wanted to stake a claim. He kissed her, long and deep.

Then he pulled away, struggling for control. "Sweetheart, we need to slow down. I'm sorry. It's just that . . . damn, I'm jealous."

Her slumberous eyes opened to stare at him. Her pupils were dilated, making her eyes look nearly black. She looked dazed and aroused and beautiful, so damn beautiful.

"I don't understand."

How could he tell her everything he felt? Her ex was an idiot, but Mack was glad, because if he hadn't screwed up, Jessica might still be married, when Mack knew in his bones she belonged with him. Even now she clung to him, her breath hot, her body quivering with need. And he'd barely touched her. The thought made him frantic with lust.

Easing her down slowly, he laid her on the quilt. Her chest rose and fell, and she opened her arms to him.

"Shhh. Let's get these clothes off you. I'm all but naked, and you're bundled up from head to toe."

He reached for her sweater, and she turned her head away. Mack stilled. "Jessica?"

Her eyes squeezed tightly closed. He wanted her so bad, his body burned, but damned if he would do anything to make her uncomfortable. "Tell me what's wrong, honey."

He saw her slender white throat tense as she swallowed, saw her hands fist. "You're used to beautiful women."

He stroked her shoulder, keeping the touch feather light. "And you think you're not?"

"I'm . . . I'm thirty years old, not twenty with long legs and no hips. I've had a baby and . . ."

"And because you're a mother, you can't be sexy anymore?"

"That's not what I'm saying and you know it!"

He stroked her cheek, smoothed back her hair. "I'm sorry, babe, but you're being silly. I think you're the sexiest woman I've ever known. Do you think I walk around with an erection for every woman on the street?"

She made a sound that was a cross between a groan and a laugh. "I wouldn't put it past you."

"Well, you'd be wrong." He reached for the hem of her skirt and slowly began dragging it up her legs. She stiffened, but she didn't say anything. Mack stared at her shapely legs and tried not to be affected. He wanted his tone to remain calm, not rough with lust. But it wasn't easy. She wore some kind of elastic-topped nylons that ended just above her knees and left her pale thighs bare. The elastic was decorated with small cream-colored roses. His breath rasped unevenly as he touched her knee, urging her legs to part just a bit. "Did you buy these stockings from Sophie?"

Her eyes popped open. "What?"

"She told me you shop in her boutique, that that's where she met you. Did you get them there?"

"Yes."

Things were starting to come together, the goofy way Sophie and Allison had acted. The reason *he'd* been picked to model. It was a setup—and he owed them both more than he'd realized.

The bright photography lights were still aimed at them, illuminating the square of quilt and the two people stretched out atop it. Mack smiled. "I can see you, all of you, very well. I like this."

His fingers trailed above the stockings, moving the skirt higher and higher, until the pale sheen of her silky beige panties reflected the light. The material looked damp between her legs, and he groaned. Without even thinking of her reaction, he bent and pressed a heated kiss there.

She nearly leapt off the floor. "Mack!"

He nuzzled closer. "Damn, you smell good." In a rush, he sat up and unbuttoned the skirt, then tugged it down her legs. "I think I'll leave the stockings. They turn me on."

She panted, staring at him in mingled embarrassment and need. He laid a hand over her belly. It wasn't concave, sinking between her hipbones, but it was soft and silky and . . . "How could you think this isn't sexy? Do you have any idea how you feel to me?" He closed his eyes, stroking her, relishing the touch of her warm, satiny skin, then slid his fingers into her panties and tangled them in her feminine curls. Her hips lifted, and he pulled away.

Straddling her upper thighs, he cupped her face and

smiled. "I feel like a teenager again, having to pace myself so I can last long enough to get inside you. God, woman, you affect me. Forget any other man you've known. Right now there's just me. Okay?"

She looked him over, then whispered, "Will you take off your shirt so I can see you again?"

"Hell, yes. And then yours." He pulled the undershirt over his head and tossed it aside. Her hands were immediately there, caressing his shoulders, touching his small nipples to make him shudder. He gave her time to look, to touch him, and when he couldn't take it anymore, he jerked her sweater up. He was awkward and trembling and laughed even as he cursed. Jessica lifted her arms so he could pull it free, then rested back on the floor. She watched him anxiously, her soft brown eyes wide and uncertain, her breath held.

The bra she wore was incredible, beige satin to match the panties, but with a lace overlay, looking sexy as sin and making his heart race. He could just see the dark shadows of her erect nipples beneath the sheer fabric. He locked his jaw, fighting for control, and with one finger he circled a nipple and watched her shiver. He looked up and met her eyes. "I want to take you in my mouth. I want to lick you and suck on you."

Her body arched as she moaned.

"Can we take off the rest of our clothes now, babe?" His voice was a rasp, a bare echo of sound.

For an answer, she sat up so he could reach the back closure on the bra. His hands shook as he expertly slipped the bra open, then slowly slid the straps off her shoulders.

Her breasts were so full and white, resting softly against her body. He'd never considered himself a breast man, at least not in any sort of preference and not when he loved everything about women's bodies, but with Jessica . . . The sight of her made his insides twist with need.

He cupped both breasts in his palms, closed his eyes as he felt her, and whispered, "You thought you didn't compare to other women?"

"I . . . I breast-fed. And it shows. I'm not as firm as I used to be. Dave used to tell me—"

"Forget Dave." He looked and saw a few faint lines on her breasts and imagined her swollen with milk, mothering her child. *"God."*

He smoothed the lines with his thumbs, then bent and took one nipple into the heat of his mouth. Jessica moaned, and her fingers tangled in his hair. He switched to the other nipple, sucking strongly, making her cry out. She tried to pull away, but he held her securely, greedy, lifting her breast high, continuing to lick and suck until he knew he had to stop or he'd come.

She collapsed back against the quilt, panting, her body warm and rosy, her nipples drawn tight, wet from his mouth.

She gasped at the look in his eyes, then blurted out, "Dave never wanted me much after Trista was born. I had picked up weight, and my body looked different. He said that's why he started going to other women . . ."

"What a goddamn fool." Heat clouded the edges of his vision and he knew he was near the end. "I'm not him, sweetheart. I didn't break your heart, and I never will.

You're beautiful, all of you, in so many ways. I can't imagine ever not wanting you."

"Oh, Mack."

He could see the small quivers in her body, the way her lush breasts shimmered with each ragged breath. "Be right back."

Never taking his eyes from her, he stood and then back-stepped to the curtain where he'd left his jeans, blindly reached for them, and came back to her. With the jeans bunched in his fist, he pressed her legs apart and knelt between them. She looked almost pagan lying on the quilt with the bright lights flooding down on her. Her skin appeared translucent, her breasts swollen and rosy, her thighs open. He hadn't known for certain what love was, but now he knew this had to be it, because seeing her total acceptance of him meant more than he'd ever known was possible.

His heart slowed with the realization that despite all her efforts to fend him off, despite her resistance, he'd fallen head over heels, and he liked it. The Winston curse be damned. He felt blessed. After locating a condom in his wallet, he tossed the jeans aside. He laid the condom nearby, knowing he was near the edge of his control.

He touched her chin, down her chest to circle both breasts, pushing them together, gently rasping his beard-rough cheeks against her. He tickled his fingertips down her belly and watched her squirm, then stopped at the edge of her panties.

"I'm sorry, Jessica," he said, forcing the words out

around the constriction in his heart, "but I can't wait much longer. Usually I'm pretty good at this, but now . . ."

She choked on a laugh. "Pretty good at what?"

"Waiting. Making the anticipation build. But you make me burn." He dropped the jeans and hooked both hands in the waistband of her panties, then bent to kiss her belly as he slowly tugged them to her knees. Her laughter turned to a ragged moan. "Lift your hips."

She did, but rather than just removing her panties, he slipped both hands beneath her buttocks, raising her, and tasted her again, this time without the barrier of cloth. Jessica twisted on the quilt, making incoherent sounds of pleasure. Her fingers tangled in his hair, tugged.

"Easy," he whispered, then kissed her again, using his tongue to stroke deep. "Damn, you're so wet. You want me, don't you, Jessica?"

Her body bowed, her head thrown back. He could feel the fine quivers running through her, but he wanted to hear her say it, wanted her to admit that what was happening was special. He blew softly against her heated flesh, ruffled the curls with his fingertips. Slowly, watching her face, he worked one long finger into her. Her thighs tensed and her buttocks flexed.

"Tell me, honey. Tell me you want me."

"Mack. *Yes.*"

His finger pressed deeper, and he was shocked at how tight she felt, proof of her long abstinence. She sobbed, straining toward him. He kissed her sweet female flesh, drowning in her scent, and demanded, "Tell me this is special for you too, babe."

"Yes, Mack, please . . ."

He broke. He couldn't wait another minute, and for the first time in his life, he resented the time it took to use the condom. Jessica shook beneath him, squirming, needing him. As he came over her, she gripped his shoulders so tightly her nails stung, then she strained up against him, trying to hurry him along. Mack entered her with one long, even stroke. They both groaned, but Jessica didn't give him a chance to wait any longer, locking her thighs around him and holding him tight. He began moving into her with a hard rhythm, loving the feel of her lush breasts against his chest, her hot breath fanning his throat. She accepted him, wanted him, and the knowledge drove him over the edge. As he gave a stifled groan of release, he felt her internal muscles clamp tight around his erection, intensifying his pleasure and assuring him she'd found her own climax.

He sank into her, sated, awash in burgeoning emotions, and then he heard her soft sob.

⟡

Jessica tried to cover her face, but Mack wouldn't let her. She'd barely made a sound, and she'd assumed he'd be too far into his own pleasure to hear her anyway. But now he was over her, his expression alert, his hands holding hers so he could search her face.

His brows drawn in concern, he asked, "What's wrong? Why are you crying?"

"Mack, I want you to go now." He had to leave before she totally fell apart. God, she'd been so stupid. She'd thought she could make love with him, enjoy him for a time, then get back to her staid, responsible existence. She knew now that that was impossible, and she felt the sharp bite of panic. How could she ever go back to her old ways after having been with him, after knowing what it could be like?

She'd felt so alive while he loved her, so mindless with pleasure, she knew she'd been existing in a void. All she'd managed to do was show herself what she'd missed.

Mack's frown grew ferocious. "Like hell! I'm not going anywhere until you tell me what's wrong."

But she couldn't tell him. That would be like the final indignity, proof of how desperately pathetic she'd become. She shook her head and pleaded, "Please. You need to leave now. Trista will be home soon—"

"Not for at least another two hours. And we haven't finished the shoot." He smoothed her hair in that gentle way he had, making her heart ache. "Did I hurt you?"

Appalled that he could even think such a thing, she shook her head. Her voice was choked, strained, but she said, "It was wonderful. You were wonderful."

With a slight smile, he pulled her braid loose from behind her and played with it. "I love how you feel, the warm silk of your hair, the texture of your skin." His big hand cupped her breast, stroking it possessively. His gaze locked on hers, too intent, too compelling. "Everything about you excites me. You smell too good to describe, and you taste even better."

She blushed slightly, remembering the places where he'd tasted her. Mack smiled. "I love you, Jessica."

Her eyes widened. "Don't be—"

"Ridiculous?" Slowly, he pulled the tie from her hair and dragged his fingers over it, untwining her braid. "I know what you're going to say. That we don't know each other well enough. That nonsense about you being older than me." He laughed. "Do you realize how much influence your ex had on you? He convinced you somehow that you're old and worn out, but when men look at you, they see a young, very sexy woman. Not a housewife. Not a mother. A woman."

"How would you know what other men think?"

"I'm male." He drew a deep breath. "I dreamed about you even after we were out of college. It was like I knew something very important had slipped through my fingers. We hadn't talked a lot, but I'd studied you every chance I got. I knew you were serious and withdrawn and shy and a little wounded. I knew you were so sexy you made my teeth ache, and I saw how all the other guys looked at you. It made me nuts. I knew even then you were the woman I wanted."

Tears gathered in her eyes despite her resolve. She didn't know what to say, except to be honest. "I did the same."

"Yeah?" He looked pleased, then leaned closer to whisper, "Did you ever touch yourself . . . you know, while you were thinking of me?"

Her face went hot, her breath catching. "What kind of question is that?"

He shrugged, looking mischievous. "I did, thinking about you. I wanted you so damn bad, no other woman even interested me. I won't lie to you and tell you I stayed celibate, as you did, but my sexual encounters were few and far between. And I haven't been with anyone for almost six months. I was so disgusted over this teaching business that I haven't been able to think of much else. I guess that's why my meddling family set us up."

She was still embarrassed—and intrigued—over his very private admission, but managed to clear her mind enough to ask, "What are you talking about?"

His hand slipped down her body, stroking her, petting her. "Sophie used to help me study, and I told her all about you. Not your name, but everything else, like about your incredible breasts, your sexy braid, your beautiful brown eyes. She sympathized with me, in between badgering me enough so I'd learn that damned science that I hated so much."

He lifted her hand and kissed her fingers. "Did you ever tell her which college you went to?"

Jessica thought about it, then reluctantly nodded. "And what years, and that there was this annoying, utterly distracting young stud who kept interrupting my concentration. But she was Sophie Sheridan then, not Winston, and after she married I just never put the names together."

Mack barked a sharp laugh and bit her finger. "A stud, huh? Well, I think Sophie put two and two together, with some help from Allison, my other meddling, very adorable sister-in-law, and the result was this cooked-up catalogue of goofy men's lingerie."

Jessica licked her lips, then admitted, "I don't think it's

goofy at all. I think you look downright scrumptious in this stuff."

"Is that right?"

She nodded.

"Scrumptious enough to give me a chance? To give us a chance? Because I really do love you, you know. At first I thought it was just an obsession, that eventually I'd get over you. But I didn't. And now, after being inside you, feeling you squeeze me tight, watching you come, I know it's more. I know I don't want to do that with anyone else but you, because it could never be as good."

She bit her lips to keep them from trembling. Could it be true? Could he really love her? He kept touching her and looking at her body, and she could feel him, hard again against her thigh.

He sounded just a tad uncertain as he continued. "I don't have the teaching position nailed down yet, but I'll figure that out one way or another. In the meantime, I work with my brothers at the bar. Cole bought it long ago so he could support us all, give us jobs as we got older. I worked there to pay my way through college, as did Zane. Now that we're getting other jobs, Cole and Chase have expanded and hired a few outside people. You'll love the place. It's incredibly popular, especially with the women, but it also has a nice family atmosphere."

Talking was impossible. Even swallowing was too hard to manage. Jessica launched herself against him, squeezing him tight. "Mack, I'm so sorry. I've been so wrong about you."

He rolled onto his back and held her close. "Ah, babe, don't cry. Please."

"You're the most amazing man and I don't deserve you."

"Now there's where you're wrong. Tell me you won't boot me out, honey. I'm in an agony of suspense here."

She kissed his face, his ear, his throat. Mack moaned, so she continued, and then she moaned too because he tasted so good she wanted to kiss him all over.

"Is this a yes, Jessica?" His voice shook and his hand held her head as she kissed his belly. "Does this mean we can have an honest-to-goodness relationship? You'll quit expecting me to be some kind of bum you can't depend on?"

Her hand wrapped around his throbbing erection and she kissed his navel. "Yes," she whispered. And in the next instant, Mack had her beneath him, kissing her, exciting her. *Loving her.*

Epilogue

Mack barely got in the door before Trista leaped up, waving her report card in front of his face. "I got three A's," she yelled, and Mack, so proud he thought he'd burst, lifted her up for a massive hug. When he set her back down, she stayed glued to his side and walked with him down the hallway as he perused her report card.

"Three A's and three B's." He put an arm around her and smiled. "I sure hope you're proud of yourself, especially since one of those A's is in science."

Her braces shone brightly when she grinned and confided, "I got the highest score on my science project. Higher than Brian's!"

He couldn't help but laugh. Then Jessica was there, her hair loose down her back, swishing around her hips, distracting him. Just the way she knew he liked it.

"Hey, babe." He leaned forward for a kiss, which she freely gave. God, he loved being greeted this way. "You don't have a shoot right now?"

"Nope. I took the rest of the afternoon off."

His brows lifted. "Oh ho. Any special reason?"

"Yes, but first, how did your day go?"

He realized she was anxious, worried about him on his first day back, and his love doubled. He tossed a few papers on the coffee table in the waiting room and dropped into a chair. "It was great—except for the principal poking her nose in every hour to check up on me."

Jessica perched on his lap, affronted on his behalf. "She didn't!"

"She did. Seems that even though she gave in to the parents' demands to have me back, she's still not happy about it. But I also got a visit from the head of the school board, and he told me they're behind me one hundred percent, so I'm not going to let the principal get me down. Especially now that I know the parents won't hesitate to lobby in my defense." He grinned shamefully, still amazed that the parents had taken on the school board to get him back.

Trista leaned forward and in a low tone meant to mimic his own, said, "Well, I hope you're proud of yourself."

"Come here," he growled, and pulled her onto the arm of the chair, close to his side. In the past few weeks, he'd grown to love Trista like she was his own. And she treated him as naturally as if he'd been around forever.

Mack couldn't imagine being any happier than he was now. Since he had been with Jessica, time had gone by like a dream. The parents of his students had organized and appealed to the school board, which had gotten him hired in the position he wanted, despite the principal's continued opposition. Sophie's catalogue, delivered in time for the Valentine's Day sale, had proved a huge hit. The women swamped her boutique every day now, and the main topic was the model. But with Jessica's insistence, all the photos had been cropped, so only Mack's body was visible. She'd gotten very huffy over the idea of other women knowing it was him in the racy loungewear, once she'd staked a claim.

Zane found the whole situation beyond hilarious.

"So what's your good news?" He toyed with a long lock of Jessica's hair, knowing that she'd left it loose for him.

"I'm going to be shooting another catalogue—this one for kids' clothing."

She looked so pleased with herself he kissed her again, making Trista giggle.

She pulled away with a sigh. "I also heard from the church today. Our wedding date is set. June sixth."

"It's official?" He had to hide his excitement. His damn nosy sisters-in-law had been insistent that Jessica deserved a big wedding this time around. He didn't mind that, because he would do anything to make her happy. But every time they'd come up with a date, they'd run into a glitch. He was beginning to think the Winston curse would fail him.

She looped her arms around his neck and said, "*Everything* is official for June sixth—the hall, the flowers, the dress, the guests, everything. Sophie will have the baby around the end of March, and Allison isn't due until November. The only problem, and it's only a tiny one, is Zane."

"What the hell has Zane got to do with this?"

"Well, your brother keeps complaining about a Winston curse, and he says if he comes to the wedding, it's liable to get him. But I know you want him there . . ."

Mack laughed and hugged her close. "Don't worry about my damn brother. He'll be there, probably with bells on. And I have no doubt he's up to tackling any curse there is."

Trista tilted her head at him and leaned close, fascinated by the talk of curses. "Did you tackle the curse, Mack?"

He touched the end of her nose and grinned. "No, honey. I welcomed it with open arms."

Stay tuned for a sneak peek at
Zane Winston's story,

Wild

Available now from Jove Books!

"I want you."

The suggestive, husky whisper stroked over Zane Winston with the effect of a soft, warm kiss to his spine. It devastated his senses.

He froze, then clenched hard in reaction, his muscles tightening, his pulse speeding up. He nearly fell off his stepladder.

The motherboards balanced precariously in his arms started to fall, but Zane managed to juggle them safely at the last second.

He didn't want to look, didn't want to acknowledge that soft whisper. He knew without looking who had spoken to him. Still, as was generally the case where *she* was concerned, he couldn't *not* look.

His gaze sought her out, and he found her standing a

mere two feet away, her eyes downcast, her waist-length, witchy black hair partially hiding her face like a thick ebony curtain.

People shuffled through the small computer store, taking advantage of the sale prices he'd advertised, grabbing at clearance items, storing up on disks. Yet no one bumped into her, no one touched her. Alone in the crowd, she stood there to the side of his ladder, and Zane could feel her intense awareness of him. It sparked his own awareness until his breathing deepened, his skin warmed.

Damn it, but it always happened that way around her—which was one reason why he tried to avoid her.

Since she didn't say anything else, didn't even bother to look at him, Zane went back to restocking the shelf. Perhaps he'd misunderstood. Perhaps he'd even imagined it all. He hadn't been sleeping well lately, or rather, he'd been sleeping too hard, dead to the world and caught up in erotic, lifelike dreams that left him drained throughout the day. He felt like a walking zombie—a *horny* walking zombie, because the dreams were based on scorching carnal activities.

They were based on *her.*

Zane's computer business had done remarkably well the past year, and it required a lot of his attention. The location in the small strip mall was ideal. But her antiquated two-story building stood right next door, only a narrow alley away, and the scent of her sultry incense often drifted in through his open door. Worse than that, her tantalizing, pulse-thrumming music could be heard everywhere, and it made his heart beat too fast. With her distracting him, concentrating on software and modems wasn't always easy no matter his level of resolve. And now with the damn dreams plaguing him, his iron control was fractured.

His brothers had taken to heckling him, tauntingly accusing him of too much carousing. Zane didn't bother to correct them. No way would he tell any of his brothers the truth behind his recent distraction—that his carousing had only been in his dreams, and his distraction was a little gypsy who he didn't even find appealing.

Especially since he was determined to deny any such distraction.

The last thing he needed was a personal face-to-face visit with her.

Though he wasn't looking at her, Zane felt her inch closer; he was aware of her all along his length, in his every pore, even in the air he breathed. The ladder had him several feet above her, which placed her face—her mouth—parallel with his lap. *Damn damn damn.* He tensed, waiting, and more images drifted into his mind.

"*I want you,*" she repeated, a little louder but still low enough that no one seemed to notice.

He hadn't imagined it!

Anger erupting, Zane glared down at her, this time catching and holding her mystical dark gaze. Her long, coal-black lashes fluttered, but she didn't look away from him. Staring into her eyes, he felt her, her thoughts and emotions invading his mind. Her nervousness touched him bone deep, the way she forced herself to remain still. And that, too, affected him.

How the hell did she manage to toy with him so easily? It outraged him, left him edgy and hot and resentful. Despite what some of his female associations might think, he was always the pursuer, not the pursued. He subtly controlled every intimate relationship, took only what he needed, gave only as much as he wanted, and no more.

Zane realized he was breathing too hard, reacting to her on an innate level, and deliberately he jammed the boxes of motherboards onto the shelf before climbing down the ladder.

Facing her, his arms folded over his chest, he did his best to intimidate her while at the same time hiding his discomfort. He needed her to leave. He needed to stop thinking about her.

He was nearly certain his needs didn't matter to her in the least.

"What do you want?" He sounded rude to his own ears, obnoxious and curt. But this was a battle for the upper hand, and he intended to do his best to win.

Her full lips, painted a shiny dark red, were treated to a soft, sensual lick of uncertainty. Filled with tenacity, her gaze wavered, then returned to his. Her chin lifted. "As I said, I want . . . you."

God, she'd said it again! This time straight out, to his face! Zane braced himself against the lure of her brazenness and her bold request. She looked like walking sex, like a male fantasy—*his fantasy*—come to life. He would *not* let her suck him in with obvious ploys.

"For what?" There, he thought, deal with that Miss Gypsy. And she was a gypsy, no doubt about it. He almost believed the signs painted in the front window of her shop, claiming she could read palms and predict the future. The signs, backlit by the eerie glow of a red lamp and dozens of flickering candles, also said she could cast spells and enlighten your life.

It was the spell-casting part that made Zane most uncertain. After all, he was familiar with curses firsthand. And he didn't like them worth a damn. At least, not when applied to himself. For his brothers it had worked out just fine. Better than fine—*for his brothers*.

Agitated, she shifted her feet and the tinkling of tiny bells rose above the din of the crowd. Zane found himself staring at her small feet beneath the long gauze skirt of bold colors and geometric designs. The skirt was thin and would be transparent if she stood in the right light.

Luckily for his peace of mind, they were more in the shadows than not. But that didn't stop him from imagining what he couldn't see. And it pissed him off that he visualized her, that he could guess at just how she'd look.

Twin ankle bracelets of miniature silver bells, worn above the skinny straps of her sandals, had caused the music when she moved. More silver circled her painted toes in dainty rings with intricate designs.

Zane looked at her hands, each finger adorned with a silver, pewter, or gold ring. A multitude of bracelets with inlaid colored stones hung on her slender wrists and jingled when she clasped her hands together.

Around her neck and disappearing into the neckline of her loose midnight blue peasant blouse, were several strands of small beads, some jet black, some bright amber, some ruby red.

He noticed the necklaces, then immediately noticed, too, that she wasn't wearing a bra. Her breasts lay soft and full beneath her blouse.

An invisible fist squeezed Zane's lungs, stealing the oxygen from his body, making him lightheaded. For God's sake, they were only breasts, and not all *that* impressive. But he could see the faint outline of her nipples beneath the dark, thin material and it set him on fire.

He wanted to curse, but that would give too much away, so he refrained.

When he took a deep breath, trying to relieve some of his tension, that musky, earthy scent of incense filled his head. He stared at her hard, intent on keeping his gaze on her face. "I'm waiting."

She glanced at the surrounding crowd. Her large eyes were heavily lined, looking mysterious and sensual. No one paid any attention to them, and she said low, "I want you for sex."

Her gaze melted into his, touching his soul, dredging up those hot, taunting dreams that had plagued him nightly. In his sleep, he'd already taken her every way known to man. Now she offered to let the dream become reality.

Breathing was too damn difficult, and he nearly panted.

"I want you," she boldly continued, fanning the flames, "to share your body with me, and let me give you mine."

Slowly, hypnotically, she lowered her lashes and added with a small shrug, "That's all."

That's all? *That's all!* Urgency throbbed through his veins, as if he'd spent hours on leisurely, detailed foreplay, and Zane wanted to smack her.

Even more than that, he wanted to drag her into the backroom and lift her long flirty skirt and take the body she so willingly offered. He wanted to inhale her scent, wanted to taste her in all her hottest, sweetest places. And he wanted to bury himself deep inside her.

Damn it all, he had a hard on to end all hard ons, and here he stood in the middle of his shop with hoards of people ready to spend money and purchase his wares.

Nostrils flared, and with as much disdain as he could muster given his acute state of arousal, Zane growled, "Thanks, but no thanks."

Her gaze clashed with his, startled, upset. Her lips drew in, got caught by her teeth, and color scalded her cheeks. She took two slow breaths, then asked in a wavering voice, "You're certain you're not interested?"

He was so damn interested it wouldn't have taken much more than a few touches to make him insane. Zane locked his knees, clenched his fists and hardened his resolve. "Positive."

Her long silky hair hung past her lap as she bowed her head. For a suspended moment, Zane feared she might actually cry—or cast a hideous spell on him. He wasn't entirely sure which would be worse. Not that he normally believed in such things as spells and incantations. But there was the Winston curse. He believed in it, had seen its effects on his brothers as one by one they'd been caught and married off. Happily, in fact.

One curse per family was more than enough. Little Gypsy could just take her mesmerizing voice and her intrusive sexuality and leave him the hell alone. He liked his life just as it was, just as he'd made it.

Without looking at him again, she turned and left. Her departure struck him like a punch in the gut. She hadn't been crying, he thought with concern, but she'd been so silent. . . .

Oh hell, she was always silent, he reminded himself. She used it as part of her mystique. He refused to be drawn in by her and her feminine cunning and what amounted to no more than theatrics to shore up her ruse as a gypsy.

The gentle, enticing sway of her skirts as she slowly retreated held his attention. She might be leaving, but her scent remained, circling around him, filling his head and his heart. Her effect remained, too, keeping him hot and tight and far too aware of his physical needs. And that last look on her face remained, making him curse himself for being such a bastard.

He was good with women, damn it. *Great* with women, in fact. He always treated them gently, whether he was interested or not. So why the hell had he been so rude to her? Why had he felt compelled to grind her under with his rejection? He'd been out to prove . . . what? That she didn't affect him after all?

Zane snorted at that. The tent in his pants proved otherwise, no matter his behavior toward her.

Now that she was gone, only the essence of her remaining without the threat of her appeal, he was ashamed of himself.

A customer touched his arm, causing him to jump. Forcibly, Zane brought his mind back to the job at hand. Even with two employees in to help, they were swamped. The line at the register was long and continuous. People had questions, and the shelves had to be constantly restocked. He couldn't afford to be distracted with his witchy neighbor. He would run the register—where he could hide his arousal behind the counter—and do his job.

But for the rest of the day, she lingered in his mind, an unwelcome invasion that kept him jittery and taut, the same way he felt when he'd gone too long without sex.

He hated what he knew he would have to do.

But since he was resigned to doing it, he'd damn well put himself in charge. No more letting her toy with him, no more letting her overwhelm his senses. It was Thursday, the weekend fast approaching. He'd have time to spend with her, and on her. And if anyone would be overwhelmed, it'd be her.

That thought finally had Zane smiling.

In anticipation.